Hob Osterlund

BRIAN DOYLE is the editor of *Portland Magazine* at the University of Portland and the author of many books of essays, fiction, poems, and nonfiction, among them the novels *Mink River*, *The Plover*, and *Martin Marten*. Honors for his work include the American Academy of Arts & Letters Award in Literature and the Oregon Book Award. He lives in Portland, Oregon.

ALSO BY BRIAN DOYLE

Novels
Martin Marten
The Plover
Mink River
Cat's Foot

Short Stories
Bin Laden's Bald Spot & Other Stories

Poems
How the Light Gets In
A Shimmer of Something
Thirsty for the Joy: Australian & American Voices
Epiphanies & Elegies

Nonfiction
The Grail: A Year Ambling & Shambling
Through an Oregon Vineyard in Pursuit of the Best Pinot Noir
in the Whole Wild World

The Wet Engine: Exploring the Mad Wild Miracle of the Heart

Essay Collections
So Very Much the Best of Us
Reading in Bed
A Book of Uncommon Prayer
Children & Other Wild Animals
The Thorny Grace of It
Grace Notes
Leaping: Revelations & Epiphanies
Spirited Men
Credo
Saints Passionate & Peculiar
Two Voices (with Jim Doyle)

Additional Praise for *Chicago*

"As its title suggests, *Chicago*'s foremost subject is the city itself, and the book is very much a paean to Chicago."
—*Paste Magazine*

"Doyle's charming tale of a young man's brief residency in this 'rough and burly city in the middle of America.'"
—*Chicago Reader*

"A lyrical coming-of-age story . . . While Doyle's reputation as a gentle storyteller precedes him—I've encountered his essays online—I wasn't prepared for the sheer musicality of his prose, which is positively Fitzgeraldian."
—*Arkansas Democrat-Gazette*

Praise for Brian Doyle

"Doyle is a born storyteller."
—*The Seattle Times*

"Brian Doyle writes with Melville's humor, Whitman's ecstasy, and Faulkner's run-on sentences."
—Anthony Doerr, author of
All the Light We Cannot See

"Brian Doyle's writing is driven by his passion for the mystery of all else."
—Mary Oliver,
Pulitzer Prize–winning author

"Brian Doyle has a fine, quick mind alert for anomaly and quirk—none of them beyond his agile pen."
—Peter Matthiessen, National Book
Award–winning author of *Shadow Country*

"Doyle's sleights of hand, word, and reality burr up off the page the way bits of heather burr out of a handmade Irish sweater yet the same sweater is stained indigenous orange by a thousand Netarts Bay salmonberries."
—David James Duncan, author of
The Brothers K and *The River Why*

CHICAGO

BRIAN DOYLE

PICADOR

A THOMAS DUNNE BOOK
ST. MARTIN'S PRESS
NEW YORK

CHICAGO. Copyright © 2016 by Brian Doyle. All rights reserved. Printed in the United States of America. For information, address Picador, 175 Fifth Avenue, New York, N.Y. 10010.

picadorusa.com • picadorbookroom.tumblr.com
twitter.com/picadorusa • facebook.com/picadorusa

Picador® is a U.S. registered trademark and is used by Macmillan Publishing Group, LLC, under license from Pan Books Limited.

For book club information, please visit facebook.com/picadorbookclub or e-mail marketing@picadorusa.com.

The Library of Congress has cataloged the Thomas Dunne Books edition as follows:

Names: Doyle, Brian, 1956– author.
Title: Chicago : a novel / Brian Doyle.
Description: First edition. | New York : Thomas Dunne Books/St. Martin's Press, 2016.
Identifiers: LCCN 2015043223| ISBN 9781250061997 (hardcover) | ISBN 9781466868076 (e-book)
Subjects: LCSH: Young men—Illinois—Chicago—Fiction. | Chicago (Ill.)—Fiction. | BISAC: FICTION / Literary. | FICTION / Coming of Age. | GSAFD: Bildungsromans.
Classification: LCC PS3604.O9547 C49 2016 | DDC 813/.6—dc23
LC record available at http://lccn.loc.gov/2015043223

Picador Paperback ISBN 978-1-250-11812-7

Our books may be purchased in bulk for promotional, educational, or business use. Please contact your local bookseller or the Macmillan Corporate and Premium Sales Department at 1-800-221-7945, extension 5442, or by e-mail at MacmillanSpecialMarkets@macmillan.com.

First published by Thomas Dunne Books, an imprint of St. Martin's Press

First Picador Edition: March 2017

10 9 8 7 6 5 4 3 2 1

For Mary

We struck the home trail now, and in a few hours were in that astonishing Chicago—a city where they are always rubbing a lamp, and fetching up the genii, and contriving and achieving new impossibilities. It is hopeless for the occasional visitor to try to keep up with Chicago—she outgrows her prophecies faster than she can make them. She is always a novelty; for she is never the Chicago you saw when you passed through the last time.

—MARK TWAIN

I have struck a city—a real city—and they call it Chicago. . . . I urgently desire never to see it again. It is inhabited by savages.

—RUDYARD KIPLING

And then when I went to Chicago, that's when I had these outer space experiences and went to the other planets.

—SUN RA

1.

ON THE LAST DAY OF SUMMER, in the year I graduated from college, I moved to Chicago, that rough and burly city in the middle of America, that middle knuckle in our national fist, and rented a small apartment on the north side of the city, on the lake. I wanted to be as near the lake as possible, for Lake Michigan is no lake at all but a tremendous inland sea, and something about its vast blue sheen, and tumultuous weathers, and the faraway moan of huge invisible tankers and barges, and its occasional startling surf after storms, appealed to me greatly; also then I was young and supple and restless, and I wanted to run for miles along the beaches and seawalls, trying to dream myself into being a man, a remote frontier for me then and now; maturity turns out to be a question you can never answer with confidence, despite advanced age and wage.

The building in which I lived was three storeys high, on a brief street of old apartments and brownstones, with a Jewish temple at the lake end and a gay bar at the other, and there I lived for five seasons, leaving my street only to play basketball at a playground a couple of blocks away, or to run the lake, or to run the lake dribbling my worn shining basketball, or to take the bus downtown and back for work every day. Occasionally I would walk west to Lincoln Avenue, to sip whiskey in blues bars and wander happily in used book stores; and occasionally I would catch a train to the South Side of the city, to hear jazz, or savor the motley chaotic beery muddle of the White Sox and their exuberantly shaggy and inebriated fans, who were much more fun than the staid stuffy museum-goers at Cubs games. But otherwise I stayed not only on my brief street but in my modest and undramatic apartment building, and it is that building, and the men and women and other beings who lived in it then and perhaps even now, that this book is about.

★

Almost all the people and animals I lived with were kind and generous; some were remarkable in ways I have never forgotten, and never will; and three in particular were so riveting in their own mysterious and astonishing ways that I want to account them, as best I can, before no one is left to tell you about Edward, and Mr Pawlowsky, and Miss Elminides, who was the owner of the building, though she was quite young, and regrettably, as she said with her gentle smile, *bereft of skills in the maintenance and repair of substantial things,* which is why she deferred such matters to Mr Pawlowsky, who was aided in his work, and in many other things, by his companion Edward, a dog.

But to say of Edward merely that he was a dog, and

leave the description at that, would be a grave disservice not only to him but to you, for he was one of the most subtle and gracious beings I ever met, and the litany of his adventures alone would fill a shelf of books, before even getting to his influence on other beings, for example, which was both considerable and renowned, so much so that creatures of various species would come to Edward for consultation and counsel, from birds to people of all manners and modes of life.

But I am ahead of myself already. Let's pause here, and stand in front of the apartment building for a moment—it's a lovely September afternoon, crisp and redolent, and we can smell roasting lamb from the Greek restaurant around the corner, and the first fallen leaves from the oaks and maples along the lake—and begin as I did, by walking up the three stone steps, carrying my worn shiny basketball and crammed duffel bag, to meet Mr Pawlowsky.

*

Usually when you recount your first meeting with someone, you start with their physical appearance, but what Mr Pawlowsky looked like was the least of his subtle virtues, so I will note only his military bearing, his thinning hair, his glinting spectacles, his battered United States Navy jacket, and his immediate open friendliness, which had nothing of false bonhomie about it, but was both accessible and dignified at once; a sort of reserved invitation, so to speak. You had the instant sense that he was quite willing to be helpful and even friendly if you were open to that, but that he also had plenty to do and no pressing need for your attention.

As de facto manager of the building Mr Pawlowsky was fully aware that I was the new resident, and with a smile he showed me my mailbox, and its key, and the alleyway where the garbage bins hunched like sleeping rhinoceri, and then he led me upstairs and showed me my apartment, from which you could just see a corner of the lake, steel-blue and restless, rippling like a flag. He ran through the utilities and their billing cycles, pointed out truculent idiosyncrasies in the stove and the heating system, forked over two more keys (one for the apartment and one for the building), reminded me that while pets were welcome, immense pets like emus and rhinoceri were not, asked me if I needed help with any other luggage, grinned with pleasure when I said my basketball and my duffel bag were the sum and total of my possessions at the moment, told me the nuns in the dwindling convent around the corner would be happy to sell me a bed and a table and a chair if I could carry these out myself, briefly outlined the bus schedules both on Broadway to the west and Lake Shore Drive to the east, shook my hand, welcomed me to the building, and told me to stop in any time at his apartment on the fourth floor if I needed help in any way.

"This is an apartment building, not a house or a hotel, and we are each on our own, with no maids and concierges and chefs," he said, smiling. "Yet there is a friendly feeling to the place, and most of the residents are decent souls. The owner is Miss Elminides, whom you will meet soon enough, and you can discuss rental details with her. Mail comes every afternoon. Our mailman is not much for packages and you will have to claim them from his truck. He will leave you a note to that effect. A wonderful man who studies dragonflies. I believe he knows more about dragonflies than anyone in America. Occasionally we have meetings for all residents but those are rare and usually happen because someone is roasting goats in the alley or shooting seagulls from the roof. Edward refers to these as our Come to Jesus Meetings. Occasionally we have social events for all residents but that is even more rare. I believe we had a picnic once some years ago but you would have to check with Edward about that. We do not have disputes and conflicts and fisticuffs here and Miss Elminides is proud that the police have never set foot in the building. If disputes arise, see Edward. If you lose your keys, see me. Dragonfly questions, see the mailman. His name is John. You may paint and decorate your apartment in any way you like, but be aware that you will be expected to restore it to the condition in which you found it when you leave. You may leave at any time with a month's notice to Miss Elminides, but it is my hope, and surely hers, that you enjoy your residence here, and stay as long as you like. Some of our residents have been here for many years. You will meet most of us in the course of the social ramble, but there are some who are quite private, and I would ask that you await their invitation, if it comes, rather than seek to meet them. We get a great deal of snow in the winter. If you procure a car, put a red rubber ball on the tip of the radio antenna before the snow begins, so you can find your car when it is buried. The street is usually plowed within two days of heavy snowfall, but not always. There are places of worship for every conceivable religion and faith tradition within ten blocks of the building in any direction. The grocery store one block over is excellent and reasonably priced. There is no moral clause in your lease but we do expect that residents will in the main observe common laws and standards of civil behavior. Did I mention no emus are allowed in the building? Ask Edward about *that* story. We also do not have any cats in the building. I do not think we have ever had a cat in the building, come to think of it. Edward is not much for cats. For all other matters, I suspect that seeing Edward is probably the most useful counsel I can offer. Would you like some coffee after you get settled? Wander up when you like. Our door is unlocked, and if I am not present Edward will show you the ropes."

★

I had a job, of course, or I would not have had the means to pay my rent; and while I much enjoyed my job, with a Catholic magazine under the elevated train tracks on Madison Street, I was not much for beer after work, or the usual romantic mania of the urban young, so I spent a lot of time in and around the apartment building, and I came to know its corners and crannies almost as well as Edward, who knew it best. Within a few days of my arrival he and I were steady companions, if not yet close friends, and he showed me around with pleasure; I think the thorough review of the building was refreshing to him, as Mr Pawlowsky no longer rambled the building as freely with Edward as he once had.

First Edward and I explored the basement, which was officially the first floor, and which was mostly storage space for the residents. It was astonishing what was stored there, in some cases since perhaps the War Between the States. There was a huge stuffed horse, I remember that, with a coat of the most startling bronze color, and faded green-glass eyes. There were skis and sleds galore, though the nearest mountains were hundreds of miles away. There was the chassis of what was surely an old Hudson or Packard car; I asked Edward about this, but all he knew was that it belonged to an Armenian librettist on the third floor. There was the usual jumble of lamps and couches and chairs and tables and boxes and trunks, two or three of the latter classic old steamer trunks from the great days of ocean travel. Each resident had an assigned space walled off by wooden partitions for his or her possessions, and while some of the stalls were crammed to the ceiling, and some stood stark and empty, some had been turned into tiny workshops, and one looked and smelled like a miniature bakery; this belonged to Mrs Manfredi, who baked the most extraordinary perfect magic savory empanadas, and sold them to the local cafes, although you could, I learned from Edward, buy them direct from her on Saturday mornings, if you caught her early enough, before she made her rounds of restaurants and grocery stores.

I was then only a couple of years removed from my teenage years, and so quite used to sleeping late on the weekends, but after sleeping in late on my first Saturday in Chicago, and waking at noon to the scent of those extraordinary pastries filling the whole building, and rushing downstairs to find her stall still redolent but long empty, I never again missed a chance to get on line, sleepy and rumpled, outside Mrs Manfredi's storage stall, and for one dollar buy three warm glowing holy amazing empanadas, which she served in a tiny brown paper bag. On average I would guess that easily half the empanadas made in the basement were eaten on the spot, and most of the rest were gone minutes after Mrs Manfredi sold them to shops along Broadway, where customers waited for her to trundle in, smelling of garlic and spinach; and more than once, according to Edward, a resident or customer also quietly ate the tiny brown paper bag, to get the very last drop of Mrs Manfredi's genius. This sounds hard to believe, but in all the time I lived in that building I never knew Edward to stretch a fact; not even in service to what I soon discovered to be a wry and capricious sense of humor.

2.

EDWARD AND MR PAWLOWSKY lived in 4B, the windows of which faced west "for the last sad fading light of afternoon," said Mr Pawlowsky; 4B was also closest to the narrow staircase that led to the roof, and it was up on the roof that I saw him most in the beginning, before the snows arrived in December. He was a serious student of astronomy and of the guitarist Wes Montgomery, and he and Edward would go up on the roof on clear nights and gaze at the stars while playing Wes Montgomery quietly on an ancient record player that actually had, no kidding, a crank-handle. One of the first amazing things I saw in Chicago was Edward diligently cranking the record player; when I remarked on this to Mr Pawlowsky, however, he smiled and said it would be a significantly cooler feat for Edward to select and play the records, which Edward did not like to do because he worried his claws would score the grooves.

"A legitimate worry on his part," said Mr Pawlowsky, "and not one I can easily dispel, not having claws myself, but it leaves the choice of music entirely to me, which means it is poor old Wes all the time. I sometimes wonder if Edward loves poor old Wes as much as I do, but he is not much for complaint. Although who could complain about poor old Wes? You never heard such lovely music in all your life. Worked all day making radios in a factory and then played the guitar at night, which is maybe why he died young. We play his music at night because Wes played at night. He was not even fifty when he died, poor old Wes. A man of the middle of America, born and lived in Indianapolis most of his life, and died there too. He had seven children. Imagine your dad coming home from the radio factory and sitting to dinner and smiling and listening to each child explain his or her day and then getting them all started on their chores and homework and kissing his wife Serene with the deepest affection and reverence and then he carries his miraculous guitar to the club for a show and then to another club for some jamming after hours with other men who are absorbed by the magic of the music. Edward believes you can hear the weary grace and courage of the man in his music, and something of the thrum of his children at the table, and the gentle tumult of his life, in his unusual harmonics. I am not so sure about this but Edward knows more about music than I do. He is for example a serious student of the music of the great guitarist Django Reinhardt, who of course influenced Wes Montgomery, but we do not play Django up here at night, partly because when we did so once Edward got excited and started dancing and nearly fell off the roof, and partly because someone who used to live in 3E complained bitterly about the *noise,* as he said. He moved very soon thereafter, and his name has never been mentioned since in the building. Can you imagine someone calling the music of Django Reinhardt *noise*? And yet that actually happened, as Edward can attest."

★

This was how Mr Pawlowsky talked, gently and thoroughly, ranging freely from past to present to past, often on the roof, that burnished autumn, but also in his apartment, which I visited occasionally, initially because of imbroglios with keys and window putty and plumbing fixtures, but later just because I enjoyed his company, and Edward's.

I remember the first time I went up to 4B that it was Edward who opened the door when I knocked, and I found Mr Pawlowsky huddled in a chair by the window, under several faded blue blankets adorned with the fouled-anchor logo of the United States Navy. He was smiling but clearly worn and weary, and that day it was Edward who dealt with my small problem; I discovered later from Edward that Mr Pawlowsky was subject to fits of illness or weariness that sometimes lasted two or three days, and left him huddled in his chair reading the letters and speeches of Abraham Lincoln while shivering under his Navy blankets. Because of these spells of illness, Edward gave me to understand, Mr Pawlowsky patched together a living from several part-time jobs as a jack-of-all-trades (plumbing, electricity, carpentry, general repair, and some custodial labor) for the temple on

11

the corner, for the local grocery store, for a grade school three blocks north, and for several shops of various kinds on Broadway, including the gyro shop with the greatest lamb gyros in the history of the world, on Broadway near Roscoe Street. I believe his labor and Edward's also paid the rent in our apartment building, but I never asked the details.

Their apartment, I noticed that day, was what you would call spare, or spartan: there were two beds, two reading chairs, a small wooden table with two spindly wooden chairs, a record player that seemed to be made completely of brass, and very little else except a whole wall of books and records and maps and maritime instruments and implements—"the ephemera of the sea, the detritus of mother ocean, the poor bits and pieces by which we try to navigate the oldest and largest wilderness," as Mr Pawlowsky once said, in a lyrical mood. Their tiny kitchen was as sparse and neat as the rest of the apartment, with two pots and two pans and a few utensils hanging in rows along the wall, arranged exactly like a ship's galley. Over the sink was the only artwork I noticed in the apartment, other than the maps: a small photograph of Abraham Lincoln, positioned so that the person washing dishes would be looking directly into the president's eyes.

"A certain communion with Mr Lincoln, I find, restores the spirit of endurance when courage quivers and quails," said Mr Pawlowsky from under his blankets, when I asked about the photograph, "and his effect is even more pronounced on Edward; when he is dim and weary I bring the photograph down to where he can contemplate it at length, and it seems to cheer him up wonderfully."

*

While Edward and Mr Pawlowsky lived on the fourth floor west, Miss Elminides lived on the third floor east, in a sort of alcove or bay in the building; it took me a couple of weeks to notice that the building was asymmetrical, and there was no equivalent bay on the west side. Mr Pawlowsky was of the opinion that the original owner of the building, Miss Elminides' grandfather, whom no living resident had ever met, had presciently designed the building for his granddaughter's residence, though it must have been designed and built long before Miss Elminides was born. No one could remember anyone other than Miss Elminides ever living in the bay room, and even Mr Pawlowsky, who knew everything about the building and the neighborhood, could not remember exactly when Miss Elminides had arrived—six years ago, ten, twelve? Edward was sure it was ten, and that she had looked exactly the same as she looked now, and that her arrival had something to do with a change in her family fortunes at about that time. The grandfather had given or deeded the building to Miss Elminides, and she had taken up residence in the bay room, and there she had lived ever since, elegant and gracious. Neither Edward nor Mr Pawlowsky had the slightest idea how old she was, or if she was a Chicago native, or what she did during the day when she was away from the building; Edward was of the opinion that she was a teacher, based on her weekday attire and warm personality, but Mr Pawlowsky said he knew nothing whatsoever of her career other than that she took the Broadway bus, and had a seat of her own, right behind the driver; one time when she had been bedridden with pneumonia the bus driver and several of his passengers had actually come to the building to check on her—which, as Mr Pawlowsky said, tells you a great deal about the esteem with which she is rightly held by anyone who knows her at all in the least.

★

While no one had ever met Miss Elminides' grandfather, he was, in a sense, very well known in the building, for Miss Elminides loved to tell stories about him: how he had a mustache as big as a large bird, and how he could play any instrument at all within minutes of cradling it reverently in his hands, and how he was a wonderful swimmer, and had once swum the Hellespont in Turkey, which is the body of water that separates Europe from Asia, and which was a mile wide where he chose to cross. The Hellespont, said her grandfather, had two competing currents, one flowing north and the other south; an apt and suitable metaphor for the sad history there, as he said. Even more amazing than once swimming across the Hellespont, said Miss Elminides, was the fact that her grandfather had swum right *back* across it, because he had left his pants in Asia, and did not wish to wander around pantless, like Lord Byron. Pants, said her grandfather, are *important,* and we take them for granted, and they do not get the respect and adulation they deserve. You never see a statue of the man who invented pants, for example, whereas there are endless statues of men brandishing swords and rifles and pistols, as if brandishing implements by which we steal the life from fellow holy beings is an admirable thing, more laudable than the genius of pants. By rights there ought to be a statue in every self-respecting sensible city of a man brandishing pants, or a frying pan, or a beer mug, to celebrate inventions that clearly and inarguably made life better. But no—civic statuary bristles with lions where there were never lions, rotund mountebanks who were once mayors, admirals who never sailed anywhere within a thousand miles of the city, senators and other thieves, and even *writers,* God help us all, as if scribbling with a pen was an act so admirable that we must devote civic funds and honest stone to its adulation. You would be better devoting a series of statues to dogs than to poets and playwrights and such; which is the more useful class of being, I ask you that? Which one could lead you out of a snowstorm, and which would be more likely to intelligently deal with you slipping and falling and snapping your ankle in the park? The one would write a sonnet; the other would go and get a policeman.

★

Indeed there were no statues of dogs in Chicago, that Edward knew about, although there were, to the city's credit, *four* statues of Abraham Lincoln—the Young Lincoln, sitting on a tree stump reading, at the Chicago Public Library; the Standing Lincoln at Lincoln Park, by Augustus Saint-Gaudens, who had actually seen the president alive, and later mourned bitterly as Lincoln's casket trundled past him in the street; another seated Lincoln, also by Saint-Gaudens, in Grant Park; and the famous Rail-Splitter in Garfield Park, which depicted the young man Lincoln holding an ax. There were also all sorts of the usual motley historical, hagiographic, comical, and religious statues and sculptural representations in the city, as Mr Pawlowsky observed, most notably the famous Picasso Something or Other, between Dearborn and Clark streets.

"Edward and I stop by that thing every time we are downtown on the social ramble," said Mr Pawlowsky, "and it is either the sculptor's genius or idiocy that you cannot tell exactly what it is supposed to represent or invoke, and to his eternal credit he never explained it. I believe it is a sort of a horse, and if you study the work of the sculptor you notice that he was obsessed by horses and women. You also notice that he was an unbelievable ass, a bully and a satyr of epic proportions, a self-absorbed little wizened pickle of a man, but this is another entire discussion, how great art can be made by unbelievable idiots, if indeed his statue downtown is great art. I believe it actually *is* great art, in part because it seems to mean something different every time you contemplate it, plus it has an airy angled soaring wit I rather enjoy.

Edward believes it is about dogness, and on snowy days I can see what he is getting at there, but on sunny days I believe it to be a comment on the angular faces and heroic noses of horses, myself. But you will have to go see for yourself and come to your own conclusions. Some people think it is a large joke, and others think it is the sculptor thumbing his satyrical nose at the very people who paid him handsomely for his steel idea, and others think it is an immense grasshopper, and still others are absolutely sure it is a woman, or a wry comment on femininity, and I am sure there are people who get off the bus on Dearborn Street every blessed day and have never even noticed what appears to be a fifty-foot cricket a few feet away. It would be easy to sigh over the blinkered existence of such people, but as Edward has reminded me, the very fact that they have *not* noticed means that the possibility always exists that they *will* notice; and isn't that a cheerful thought, that today or tomorrow might be the morning when one blessed sleepy soul steps off the bus, and something about the angle of the light makes her look up for once, and she *sees* the statue for the first time, as if it had been dropped from the starry heavens onto the square that very morning?"

THAT AUTUMN WAS THE LOVELIEST crispest brightest clearest bracingest autumn I ever saw, and I used
every brilliant minute I could find to explore my new
neighborhood. I ran up and down the lakefront for miles
in either direction, dribbling my shining old basketball
with either hand, spinning around startled passersby and
infuriating their dogs. I walked up and down Broadway
for miles, poking into shops and stores and alleys to get
a sense of the smells and sights and flavors and old brick
music of the city. I walked west as far as I could, so far that
I had to take buses home, so far that sometimes I would
walk through Estonian and Lithuanian and Greek and
Irish and Italian and Polish and Guatemalan neighborhoods one after another, changing languages and scents
and music by crossing the street. I made a concerted
effort to meet our neighborhood cop, on the theory that
familiarity might breed an eventually necessary break. I
wandered into the temple on the corner at the lake end
of the street, and registered to vote as a Chicago resident, claiming to be six feet six inches tall when the rude
woman registering new voters never bothered to look

up from her mounds of paper. I did visit the fading convent a block south, and bought a bed and table and chair for fifty dollars all told, and wrestled them back to my building and up the stairs, with Edward's assistance. I found a pitted basketball court three blocks north, in a school playground which turned out to be exactly on the borderline between the territories of the Latin Kings and the Latin Eagles, the dominant street gangs on the north side of the city; because the border was clear and established, and because schools and playgrounds were apparently neutral ground for gangs, visitors like me were tolerated, after it became clear that I was a resident of the neighborhood.

I tried to play there every afternoon, if I could, before the sun went down, if I could get home from work on time, and because it never rained that fall I got in hundreds of games with the Kings and Eagles, many of whom fancied themselves terrific ballplayers, and some of whom were. There was a young man called Monster, who was a silent efficient muscular rebounding machine, the kind of teammate you love for his work ethic and lack of running commentary. There was a quiet slip of a boy called Bucket with tattoos and earrings who was as quick as water and could slide through the lane and score any time he wanted to, although he much preferred to pass, and had to be coaxed to score in tense situations. There was a young man called Nemo, and another large youth called Bus, and a tall boy with an electric blue mohawk haircut and so many necklaces they jingled cheerfully when he ran; he could jump to the moon, that boy, and I learned to listen for him jingling behind me on fast breaks, and just flip the ball up over my shoulder for him to catch and dunk.

There was also memorably an Eagle called Not My Fault, so named because whenever he made a mistake, which he did quite often, he would interrupt his usual burble of self-aggrandizing trash talk to shout *"not my fault!"* when it most certainly and inarguably was his fault. Not My Fault, despite being short and round, dearly loved to fly down the middle of the court with the ball, try a wild ridiculous shot in dense traffic, fail to make the slightest effort to claim the inevitable rebound, and then either claim he was making a visionary creative pass, or denigrate a teammate for not being in position to receive the supposed miracle pass. He never claimed he was fouled, though—the usual excuse for a silly shot—which I found fascinating. I suppose he didn't want to put himself in a position where he would be laughed at. He had a most amazing concept of his skills and athletic ability, did Not My Fault, and even all these years later I am not sure if his overweening confidence was theatrical persona of sorts, or a confidence of such inviolable strength that it did not need reality as a foundation. Either way it seems to me that he was an early teacher of the art of fiction for me; he was so completely absorbed and convinced of his version of the world that his tart lectures to teammates who should have *known* he would be throwing a glorious *pass* that sure looked like a terrible selfish shot were believable, almost.

★

The roar and grumble and seethe of the city buses; the lash of the wind off the lake late in the afternoon when the wind changed compass points; the incredible shining silvery mounds of alewives washing against the beach in their millions, when the fish run was on; the crash of surf every once in a while, product of an unseen storm far out over the lake; the gulls drifting in from the beach and ghosting down Halsted Street and Addison Street; the eternal scent of roast lamb and garlic and olives from the Greek restaurant around the corner; the skulk and slink of cats who for some reason were frightened of our street, and were always looking over their shoulders for trouble; the occasional small brave smiling nun on her way to the fading convent in the next block, which could be accessed through the alley next to our apartment building; the occasional newspaper or umbrella or bus ticket or advertising flyer tumbling headlong down the street from the lake, and one time a tumbling headlong small boy in a yellow rain slicker far too large for him, so that it acted like a jib or topsail, and sent him careening from the bus stop all the way to our building. By happy chance Edward was just coming down the steps for his daily amble and he caught the boy without effort, escorting the child back to the bus stop and waiting there until he was safely aboard. The bus driver, I noticed, said something witty to Edward, who came back to our building amused. Mr Pawlowsky told me later that Edward and the bus driver had known each other for years, and that when Edward wanted to go downtown he generally rode that particular bus, which went along the lake rather than down Broadway through the city; this sort of subtle preference on his part, said Mr Pawlowsky, may well indicate a rural upbringing for Edward, or perhaps early years by water, as for example a river; but no man alive today knows anything about Edward's earliest years, and he himself is not forthcoming about it. And believe me, I have asked.

*

Along about October I was stargazing on the roof one night with Mr Pawlowsky, while Edward was off on the social ramble, and I asked him how he and Edward had met.

"He followed me home from work one day, and we became roommates without further ado or even much discussion," said Mr Pawlowsky. "That was when I was working at Navy Pier, down where the Chicago River enters the lake. I was in the Navy, although my service against savage empires to the east and west was to be a clerk in Chicago. That does not sound very dramatic but you would be surprised how much paper and storage and shipping and training and logistics and transportation and things like that matter in times of war. We had ten thousand Navy men on the Pier during the war, and the ships *Sable* and *Wolverine*. That was a busy time. I was young and strong then and often I would walk all the way home if the evening was clear. It is exactly four miles from the river to here, a little longer if you go along the lake. One summer night, I remember, I walked home along the lake, taking my time and enjoying the way the fading sun shimmered on the water, when Edward fell in alongside me and accompanied me home. I was immediately taken with his calm personality. Other dogs would say rude and vulgar things in passing and Edward did not deign to answer. He seemed above any sort of tart or curt reply. The only timed he veered off from our perambulation was to investigate fish. He is very fond of fish. When the alewife run is in full cry he is gone for days and comes back smelling to high heaven and appears to have something of a silvery sheen about his fur. I have sometimes wondered if this predilection for fish reflects something of his past; was he raised on the shore of the lake, or by a river, or by the sea? Was he perhaps raised by a fishmonger family, or the owners of a fish shop? But this business of trying to piece out clues to his past is chancy. Consider these things about Edward, and you tell me if there is a discernible pattern. He is adamantly opposed to violence on television and will leave the room and sulk if a war movie or a cowboy movie or a gangster movie comes on. He really likes coming up here to look at stars, as you know, and he will come up here on his own sometimes, returning to tell me if something interesting is going on. He loves Django Reinhardt's jazz guitar. He does not howl or bark or whimper, although he does sometimes issue a dark mutter which sounds just like grumbling. Also he makes a sound curiously like quiet laughter when he sees a hockey game or even hears the word 'hockey,' but if you accuse him directly of being a sports snob, or disrespecting our estimable neighbors to the north, he adopts a look of utter innocence. He adores Abraham Lincoln and loves to have Lincoln's speeches and letters read aloud to him and there are times I suspect he may read Lincoln himself when I am not home; I have found the volumes out of order occasionally, or bookmarks moved from where I was quite sure I had left them last. Also more than once I have found Lincoln's speeches and *The Personal Memoirs of Ulysses S. Grant* open on the floor and I am quite sure I did not leave them there. Also Edward has several times done what you would call heroic things as regards lost children, and pretty much every species of being respects him except cats, who are afraid of him. He likes riding the bus but dislikes cars and trains, and I do not believe he has ever been in a boat, although he likes water and will sometimes swim in the lake, usually chasing fish. He likes stamps, especially pink ones and stamps having to do with Abraham Lincoln, and keeps a large collection in a box near his bed. I believe he once owned a rosary. He has been inebriated once that I know about, although that was not by his own volition. He has the highest esteem and affection for Miss Elminides, and has twice risen roaring to her defense when she was accosted by ruffians.

"So what lessons can we draw from all this? I do not see that we can do much more than speculate. And while speculation can be enjoyable, as a form of fiction, it is also finally frustrating, for there is no end to the arc of the narrative, no end to the book, in a manner of speaking. You know what I mean, as a journalist. In a sense the contemplation of Edward's past is something of a detective story, and piecing out clues and patterns, and trying to draw from them some semblance of narrative, of cause and effect, is an interesting pastime, even riveting; but I find that it must be an occasional pleasure, for there can be no final answers; Edward is not forthcoming that way, and there is no documentation available of his journeys and voyages. Even his particular canine heritage and ancestry is a mystery. When people ask what kind of dog Edward is, meaning his breed, all I can say with confidence is that he is the kind of dog who contemplates the larger issues."

4.

IT WASN'T ALL BEACHES AND DREAM, of course, those first few months in Chicago. I paid attention, in my ambling and wandering and jaunting, and I saw a lot of broken and sad and ragged and dark. There were rats in the alleys, some of them as big as cats and arrogant as aldermen. There was a beggar with no arms or legs on the corner of Addison and Halsted; one shop owner nearby sneeringly called him Second Base, although he also quietly sent him a blanket on cold mornings. There were prostitutes at night on every other block along Broadway from Belmont to Addison, on alternate sides of the street, and sometimes I could see how their faces were sad and weary until a car slowed down and then they donned a smile like a mask and walked briskly out of the shadows; sometimes they even ran awkwardly to the cars, their high heels clacking like castanets.

Twice I saw blood on the street, and once a crime scene, cordoned off with yellow plastic tape and a police cruiser; once I saw a woman mugged, on a Sunday morning, on Broadway, although I also saw that thief get totally clocked, a block away, by an old man who stuck his arm out just as the sprinting thief had turned his head to see who was following him. Once I found jagged shards of human teeth in an alley; once I saw a man slap a boy of ten so hard the boy's eyeglasses flew off into the grass along the lakefront walkway. The man stalked off but the boy knelt down in the grass and felt around, sobbing, for his glasses. I ran to help, knowing all too well the feeling of thrashing around desperately for your lost eyeglasses, but by the time I got there another man walking by had picked them up and handed them to the boy, who put them on and ran away without a word. By then I was close enough to see that his eyeglasses were held together in the center by a gob of duct tape as big as a knuckle, and that the left lens was chipped, and I wondered how many times they had flown off his face.

Even the nuns in the fading convent nearby, sweet and gentle and generous as they were, were infinitesimally shabby around the edges, and maybe even taut with hunger, it seemed to me; the three times I was in their convent that autumn, twice to haul furniture out and once to haul it in (someone had donated six plush reading chairs, and Edward and I went to help), their kitchen was bare of food except for an apple by the toaster; and it seemed like the same apple the third time as the first, as if it was there for show, or as a talisman of some sort.

Most of all, worst of all, were the rattled kids I saw. It took me a while to notice them, but once I knew where to look I saw far too many. I'd see them on buses, especially, or waiting for buses: kids without socks on the coldest days, kids with mismatched shoes, kids with ragged coats that clearly had been donated to churches and shelters, little kids scrounging for bus fare and then not getting on the bus. I started noticing the kids who checked public telephones for forgotten change, and searched alleys behind restaurants for good garbage, and slipped thin packets of meat and cheese into their pants at the grocery store. Everyone sees the kids who do dramatic things like purse-snatching but I grew absorbed by the kids you hardly notice at all at the edges and fringes of stores and bus stops; it was like they were not altogether there, and just drifted around in their battered green parkas and old sneakers, scattering like sparrows as soon as someone stopped to look closely at their strained faces.

*

By November, when it began to get seriously cold, I had thoroughly explored the ten blocks or so in every direction from our building, ranging all the way west to Lincoln Avenue, north past Addison, south past Belmont, and for miles up and down the lakefront, and I began to make voyages farther afield, taking buses and even trains; and curiously it was in this expeditionary phase that I got to know Miss Elminides better, for she knew the city thoroughly, and dearly loved the many secrets of the South Side.

It was Miss Elminides who taught me how to take the train to Chicago White Sox games, and who whispered the name of an usher who would let me hop the turnstile and get in free after the first half of the first inning. It was

Miss Elminides who drew me a secret map of two tiny dark shadowy extraordinary half-lit smoky obscure astounding jazz clubs on the South Side, one of them in a dilapidated garage behind a seedy automobile chop-shop. It was Miss Elminides who wrote a note in Greek and told me to deliver it to a man named Panagiotakis, who would then take me to the greatest Greek cook in the world, who lived on the second floor of a building that supposedly was a hotel but was really a sort of hermitage for Greek mystics, several of whom were unbelievable chefs and cooks.

And it was Miss Elminides who one day asked Edward and me to deliver a message to a *friend of a friend,* as she said, deep on the South Side—a slightly awkward message, she said, which is why she thought Edward should accompany me, in case of misunderstanding. I said I would be happy to do so but with total respect Edward did not seem exactly physically prepossessing, and if a hint of intimidating burl was part of the package maybe I should bring my friend Tommy who had played football for Notre Dame; but Miss Elminides smiled and told me about the two times she had been accosted by ruffians and Edward had appeared out of nowhere to forcibly dissuade them, and the time a huge wolfhound a block away had gone rabid and Edward took care of things, and the time Edward had pursued and downed a purse-snatcher along the lake, and the time a representative of a northside gang called the Gaylords offered what he called a reasonably priced fire insurance policy to Mr Pawlowsky and Edward removed the top half of the man's left pinky finger so swiftly and deftly that there was hardly any blood, as the responding policeman observed, impressed with Edward's skill.

So it was that Edward and I traveled together in the city for the first time—first by bus along the lake, and then on foot through the wilderness of the South Side, along streets I did not know but Edward apparently did, and quite well too, it seemed, for he was brisk and sure, and twice led me through alleys that seemed dead-ends to me but turned out to save us several blocks of walking. Only once did he stop to get his bearings, at what seemed to be a shop selling baseball paraphernalia; he scratched at the window, the proprietor came out, they conferred quietly, the proprietor handed me a baseball card (White Sox pitcher Billy Pierce, 1959, the year he won fourteen games and lost fifteen), and then Edward led me through another alley to a church. Again Edward scratched at the door, and to my surprise a lovely young woman came out, wearing a beautiful blue cloak. I gaped for a moment, until Edward nudged me to show her the card, which I did.

All these years later I can still see the look that came over her face, and the way she knelt down to stare Edward in the eye. When she stood up again I handed her Miss Elminides' message, which instantly vanished inside her cloak as if by sleight of hand, and a moment later she too vanished, back into the church, with a swirl of her cloak; but she must have conveyed some silent warning to Edward, for we did not retrace our steps back

through the alleys and streets, but instead hustled directly
east to the lake, and then home by another bus, on which
we huddled in the two rearmost seats, on the lake side,
away from the street. On the bus he seemed distracted,
but by the time we were back in our building he was
himself again, bemused and attentive, and when we reported our progress to Miss Elminides, in the lobby, he
was as wry and engaged as usual. In some manner I could
not see he delivered a message to Miss Elminides, who
sighed and said it could not be helped, and expressed her
most sincere thanks for our assistance in a delicate personal matter.

★

Of course there were many other residents in our apartment building: the units went from A through F on each
of the three upper floors, for a total of eighteen apartments, in which lived something like fifty people, all
told, and during my time there I met nearly all of them,
although there were a couple of legendary hermits, and
I had to trust Edward that they actually did reside in
the building, in apartments 3C and 3D, respectively; according to Edward they were brothers who hardly ever
emerged, and had not spoken to each other in thirty
years, despite being separated only by a thin wooden
wall, through which they must have heard each other
conducting a life of eerie similarity. I once said to Edward that this seemed sad to me, such proximity without intimacy, and his response was something like as far
as he could tell there was an awful lot of exactly this sort

of thing among human beings, more than any other kind of being; a sad thing to have to admit is true.

I did meet the other residents, at least casually, mostly while we were getting our mail in the lobby, or in transit on the stairs, or waiting sleepily on line in the basement for Mrs Manfredi's empanadas on Saturday mornings, and after a few weeks I was able to put stories to some of them, with Mr Pawlowsky's quiet assistance. The Armenian librettist on the third floor, for example, was a man intent on succeeding in opera, despite the fact that his father and uncles were barons of industry, specializing particularly in classic cars, which perhaps explained the Hudson or Packard chassis in the basement. On the second floor was a tiny vibrant woman who must have been past eighty years old but had the most brilliant sizzling orange hair I had ever seen; in some way she was associated with the tremendous stuffed bronze horse in the storage area. Edward thought she had been a propmaster or animal-wrangler for a movie studio, while Mr Pawlowsky thought she had actually been an actress in old Westerns; there had been a film company shooting Westerns in Chicago in the old days, he said, over to the west side, on Argyle Street, and he was almost sure she had been an actress in the old Broncho Billy films; didn't she look awfully like the girl who was always Billy's wife or daughter or love interest or being rescued at the last second from a hurtling train?

There was a man who had been a sailor, though not in the Navy, said Mr Pawlowsky; there were four quiet thin dapper businessmen, who lived two by two on the second floor, and sometimes left for work in the morning all at the same time, all dressed beautifully; there were two young women from rural Arkansas, fresh out of college and just beginning advertising careers in the city, one in perfumes and the other in shoes and boots; there was a tailor of Scottish extraction, a department-store detective, a man who had once raised cheetahs, the inventor of children's propeller hats, and a tall man who had been a cricket star in Trinidad but who now taught remedial mathematics at a high school twenty blocks west; Edward showed me one morning how this man deftly carried a cricket bat in his overcoat, in a special pocket designed to accommodate it, in case of untoward incidents.

One time I said to Mr Pawlowsky that you could say of the building's residents that we were motley, by which I meant from all walks of life, but he said politely that he himself might choose another word, given the chance: " 'Motley' having the intimation of incongruous, or mismatched," he noted, "whereas I would say that we are utterly normal in our variety; such is the American way, that everyone is welcome, generally, if civil and reasonably behaved and able to foot their bills, or have them footed by someone else. The one thing we really miss here, I think, is children; we have only the three, and one of those a teenager, who doesn't count as a child, but as the larval stage of the uneasy adult, especially in his case; he is an *uncomfortable* young man, although Edward is of the opinion that he will end well, and Edward is usually right about such things." This was a boy named Ovious, who despite his orotund name was amazingly thin, and who conducted himself in public with a series of sighs and grunts, the former for his parents and the latter for everyone else; supposedly he attended the technical high school nearby, apprenticing to be an electrician, but since he used the back alley for his peregrinations I hardly saw him; even when I did spot him, furtively slipping through the alley, he seemed obscure around the edges, as if he wasn't fully formed yet, or had not been completely transported to this world from another one, where people were incredibly thin and didn't speak much.

5.

THE FIRST TIME I set foot in Miss Elminides' apartment
was that month—she had been on a sea-voyage, as she
said, and I had been absorbed in grappling with the opening weeks of my job at the magazine downtown, where
it seemed to me I was utterly useless to begin with, and
then slowly grew slightly less useless by the week—and
it was mid-November before I found myself in her bay
apartment, accompanied by Mr Pawlowsky and Edward.
The proximate event was a contretemps with keys; I had
misplaced mine, Mr Pawlowsky was sure he had left the
master keys with Miss Elminides, and Edward came
along to convey his regards to Miss Elminides, whom
he much admired.

We did not knock, when we arrived at her door—it
wasn't necessary, Mr Pawlowsky said, she knows when
visitors are imminent—and indeed just as we arrived the
door swung open and we stepped into her apartment,
which was flooded with light and seemed immense,
though I learned later it was only slightly bigger than the
other apartments. It was furnished with austere grace:
lean wooden tables and chairs, a modest marble fireplace,

and large arches through which I could see a small kitchen to one side and a sort of studio to the other, with tables stacked with books and papers, and a wall hung with maps and musical instruments, among which I thought I saw the gleam of a flügelhorn. There was no hint of a bedroom or necessary room, and given the dimensions of the building I couldn't imagine where such spaces would be in Miss Elminides' apartment; when I asked Edward about this later he had to confess that this had always been a puzzle to him as well, and that he had wondered if she slept in her studio, or in a daybed under her bay windows, or perhaps did not sleep at all; she certainly had the translucent complexion of someone who regularly bathed in moonlight.

She was tall, but not gangly; slender, but not weightless like poor Ovious; and she seemed to be that wonderfully indeterminate age that some women achieve after thirty or so, anywhere between thirty and sixty. Her hair was black and long; her eyes and eyebrows and earrings were also black; and her voice was murmurous as she stepped forward to say hello. I cannot remember to this day what she wore, and it afterward proved that I never could remember what she wore; oddly Mr Pawlowsky said the same thing, although Edward maintained that she was one of the few people he knew who could wear loose clothes like robes and shawls and never appear to be lost or hiding inside them.

The matter of the keys was quickly addressed, and our discussion of rent and terms and deposits, long dreaded by me because of my pitiful bank account, was also quickly settled, slightly to my advantage, and a moment later we were out in the hallway again. Mr Pawlowsky bustled off to fix a broken window upstairs, but Edward and I lingered in the hallway, trying to identify what we had smelled in Miss Elminides' apartment: honey, nutmeg, and what Edward thought was indisputably crushed or diced olives. He also thought that he could smell owls and books printed in Aramaic, but there he lost me. I was willing to believe him on the olives, until he claimed that he could smell the difference between crushed and diced olives, which seemed fanciful to me; but later Mr Pawlowsky said that Edward could indeed make such distinctions, and there were many stories to be told of his exquisite sense of smell.

"Some things," said Mr Pawlowsky, "you can easily imagine he is able to smell from either vast distance or from the faintest evidence, like fish runs in the lake or forest fires in the deep northern woods, but the other things are startling. He can actually smell a rising tide in the lake, for example. How can he possibly do that? Yet he does. He can tell which of the two standard morning lake-run buses are in operation, without even leaving the room; all he needs is the window to be cracked open an inch. He can smell imminent asteroid showers. He can indeed smell owls, although you would not think that was possible. He can smell snow a day and sometimes two before it happens. Both of the times Miss Elminides was confronted by ruffians he smelled trouble and was out and away faster than you can blink your eyes. He is a lot quicker than he seems to be when he needs to be. The one time that his superb sense of smell deserts him is during the alewife run in the lake, when they wash up by the uncountable thousands and Edward disappears for days at a time and comes back sleek and redolent and moaning gently with surfeit. You never saw a dog who liked fish more than Edward. At those times his nose is useless for a couple of days and I also have to give him a bath. He is not much for bathing, although he does like swimming in the lake, but if I didn't give him a bath then we would smell the alewife run for the rest of the year. I have the greatest respect for alewives but I do not want to live with their aura every day. I think he not only eats them but rolls in them for reasons that elude me. There is a lot to be said for the alewife, but the smell gets to be a little much. You'll see, come spring. Edward believes the run will be early this year, probably late April, and if he thinks it's so, it's so. You'll see."

*

My job with the magazine downtown, I should say, grew more entertaining by the week, or perhaps it was me becoming less obtuse by the week, for by Thanksgiving I was enjoying it so much that I happily volunteered to fill in for several colleagues who wished to be off in various directions for various tribal feasts and ritual slayings of native fowl with gun and bow. In general my duties were so various that I did not have time to be bored, and in the course of business I got to meet reporters, editors, printers, deliverymen, truck drivers, priests, nuns, monks, post-men, writers, teachers, photographers, painters, type-setters, a sculptor, a woman who painted holy icons, and a man who had spent his career running a linotype machine, who in turn introduced me to a man who had spent his career setting hot-lead type for small-town newspapers; suffice it to say that in my time with that magazine in Chicago I may well have met every riveting unfamous person in the city, including water mystics, street preachers, a quiet woman who fed a thousand people a day, beggars, all sorts of men and women in law enforcement, political operatives of every sort and stripe, barmen and barmaids, cooks and boxers, all sorts of people having to do with the operation of trains, and a slew of people who quietly do the work of Catholic parishes in America, the vast majority of them women, who for the most part grinned when I said tart things about male dominance in the faith—"that's what we want the poor dears to think, as we run things from behind their voluminous robes," as one woman said to me, smiling broadly.

The magazine's offices were also a source of stimulation and pleasure to me, for they were on Madison Street where it met Wells Street, which was named for a soldier who died fighting the people who lived in Chicago before there was a Chicago. (His killers, impressed with his courage, immediately cut out and ate his heart, hoping for some of his valor.) Wells Street carried elevated trains, and the combination of roaring rattling trains above, and the intricate steel and iron latticework of the tracks and their pillars, and the swoop and flutter of pigeons and starlings, and the hustle of taxis and bustle of pedestrians below, and the moan of car horns and rumble of trucks, along with the endlessly changing patterns of swirling sun and fog and rain and snow, absorbed me so thoroughly that I sometimes paused for many minutes at a time on the corner of Madison and Wells, fascinated by yet another new combination of sight and sound.

Also the then-hapless Chicago Bulls played just down the street a few blocks, in the cavernous echoing Chicago Stadium, where so few patrons paid to watch them lose that the ticket-taker waved us in for free; and the famous Billy Goat Tavern was a few blocks north, and always filled to bursting with besotted reporters and commuters gulping beer before their long train ride home; and Grant Park was a few blocks south, where almost always there was a protest or a ringing speech or a peripatetic madman or a busker of startling skill; and Union Station was a few blocks west, with its vast marble Great Hall, bigger and lovelier than any cathedral I had ever seen; and the Chicago River was just west too, a river never without surprise, for I saw boats and people and animals and many other things floating or swimming in that slow dark green murk, on their placid way into the lake; one time even a policeman, who dove from the Clark Street Bridge to save what he thought was a child, but which turned out to be a small dog wearing a tartan sweater.

*

If I have given the impression that Mr Pawlowsky was frail or languorous I have done badly, for he was active as a bird around the building, fixing this and that, replacing worn and battered things, tinkering steadily with plumbing and electrical conundrums, spackling and grouting and plastering and washing and painting seemingly all day and often at night; many times when I came in late from work or from rambles in the city I would hear or see him quietly at work, usually accompanied by Edward, especially if the matter had to do with carpentry, at which Edward was gifted, according to Mr Pawlowsky; also Edward was deft at carrying boards and tools up and down stairs, and one of the first hilarious moments I had in the building was watching our youngest resident, a boy of six named Azad, gape in amazement as Edward managed two six-foot oak timbers, a red steel toolbox, and a bucket of lost-head nails all the way from the basement up to the roof.

Active as Mr Pawlowsky was in and around the building, however, I saw him more than a few feet away from the building very rarely. I had begun to be curious about how he and Edward procured food, and how he got all the necessary materials for building repair without a truck, and if Mr Pawlowsky ever went to the doctor, or church, or a ball game, or a pub, or Navy reunions down on the Pier, and had he ever been married, and did he have kids, or what?

In short I was curious, or rude, and I was awkward or

honest enough then to simply knock on his door and ask, which I did one crisp lovely Saturday afternoon before Thanksgiving, when you could feel the first whip of winter in the air, and the sure prospect of snow. As I remember it was one of those Midwest autumn afternoons where you could faintly smell burning leaves somewhere, and hear various college football games from Illinois and Indiana and Wisconsin and Michigan and Iowa on various radios, and hear geese honking overhead, and trees were almost wholly naked, and even teenagers were wearing jackets, and that morning at the grocery store there had been a learned discussion at the meat counter about hunting permits and deer season and deer camps and what wines go best with venison.

Edward opened the door, and again I found Mr Pawlowsky shivering under his old faded blue Navy blankets. I apologized for intruding and made to withdraw, figuring he was suffering from his recurrent malady, but he was in a cheerful mood, pale as he was, and called me back over to sit and talk, while Edward went off to the grocery store for coffee beans.

Even though I was in my first few months as a professional journalist I was already experienced enough to approach a big question sideways, or sidelong, so instead of coming right out and asking him about love and marriage and children and family I asked him about his provenance and childhood and early chapters, figuring that would loosen him up enough and get him talking freely— appetizing talk before the main meal, as it were.

"'I am an American, Chicago born, Chicago, that somber city, and go at things as I have taught myself,' as our great urban chronicler Saul Bellow wrote," he said, smiling, "and to date I have departed the city just once in this life, to take the train to Iowa, to make sure it was there—this was when I was young, and not altogether sure there really was anything outside Chicago, despite persistent reports. I remember disembarking from the train and walking for hours, apples in my pockets, through endless forests of corn and rustling carpets of soybeans. I cannot remember that I saw a soul that day, although the birds were profuse, and I saw deer and raccoons, animals wholly new to me, and what I later ascertained was an otter, in a small river. In the evening I took the train back to the city, enlightened. This was long before I met Edward, and it remains the longest journey I have taken solo, to date."

He told stories the rest of the afternoon, as the light slowly melted away on the street outside and dusk parked for a while and then night pitched camp; Edward came and went on various errands, carrying groceries and the mail and the afternoon edition of the newspaper; I made coffee for the three of us at one point, Edward showing me the necessary apparatus and its machinations; and all the while Mr Pawlowsky spoke of his childhood in the city, when horses and chickens were not uncommon in the streets and alleys, and fishmongers plied their trade in carts and wagons, and the city's throbbing engine was the stockyards, where cattle beyond number came and went, some to be slaughtered and sold piecemeal, others to be shipped farther on in every direction and across the oceans; the city swirled with smoke from mills and factories beyond number; the snap of gunfire in the streets was not unknown, as ruffians fought the police, themselves often worse ruffians; and the lake was alive with barges and steamers and ferries and workboats of every shape and description; "and the city was such a magnet for people from all over the world that there were thirteen different languages spoken in our neighborhood," said Mr Pawlowsky; "I know the number exactly because my brother Paul and I counted them one day, measuring in four blocks in every direction from our apartment, and including our building, in which there were five languages, basically one per floor: Polish on the first floor, where we lived, Russian on two, Gaelic on three, Greek on four, and Scandinavian in general on the fifth floor, from Swedish and Finnish to an Icelandic family, the Peturssons, lovely people who made an extraordinary cured salmon dish that I can taste even now on particularly cold days. And there were hats and caps everywhere when I was a boy, and cars became more common. There were the years of great poverty, of course, during which people indeed did sell apples on corners, and line up by the hundreds in hopes of a single job, and line up for charitable soup, and families doubled up or even tripled up in apartments, as they lost their lodgings. I saw all that, yes, and I well remember walking in a crowd of thousands of children to the house of the city's school chief to ask for food, although I was just along for the fun of it—a friend ran by as Paul and I were on our front stoop and he called to us and we ran after him. But in general our childhoods were pleasant, if pinched, Paul and me; mostly, when I put my mind to it, I remember voices, and angles of sunshine and rain, and animals— the fishmonger had a mule I was especially fond of, as he was not at all recalcitrant or sour-tempered, as so many of his brethren seem to be."

Thus spake Mr Pawlowsky at eloquent length, and by the time I stirred myself from my chair and rose to make my own small dinner it was full dark. Not until late that night, as I was falling asleep, did I realize that Mr Pawlowsky had never mentioned anything about his family other than his brother Paul, nor had he gotten the story of himself even into his teenage years. For a moment I was disgruntled, feeling as I did when I was outplayed at chess, but then I resolved to keep asking questions; even then, in the first flush of my career as a journalist, I sensed the irresistible lure of inquiry, the power of an invitation to fill an ear, the open arms of silence welcoming story. I fell asleep in the sure knowledge that there would be many moments to come in which I could tease Mr Pawlowsky's story out from behind his dignified reserve; and I could also, if necessary, resort to Edward, who knew much and forgot nothing.

6.

I WENT ALL THE WAY HOME to New York City for Christmas, taking the Hoosier State train through Cincinnati and Indianapolis (I was crazy for trains then, and at one time or another took the Zephyr to Denver, and the Ethan Allen Express to Vermont, and the Hiawatha to Milwaukee), and it was a wonderful time, crammed with laughter and chaffing and intense basketball games with my many brothers, but when I got back to my apartment I was washed with loneliness for the first time since I had come to Chicago.

I tried to run it off, dribbling my smooth shining basketball ever farther and faster along the lake, along the slippery paths cleared through the snow, and extending my brisk alley explorations much deeper into the west side of the city, which seemed to stretch all the way to Iowa; I tried to walk it off, twice walking home the four miles from Madison Street to the apartment building; I tried, one night, to drink it away, getting all the way to a fourth whiskey at the pub around the corner until Raymond the barman stopped pouring and asked me what was wrong and sent me home with an off-duty policeman who told me jokes in Gaelic and smelled vaguely of rain.

I even, for once, accepted a social invitation, to a weekend barbecue on the Iowa border, but once there I found the desperately witty banter too much to bear, and drifted off into the cornfields, where I got so helplessly lost that I finally hitched a ride back to Chicago from a carload of burly muddy football players on their way back to school from a pig roast.

It was Edward finally who roused me from my brown study, with another expedition to the South Side, this time to a tiny subterranean blues club named for its proprietress, a large calm woman named Theresa, who seemed to know Edward, and waved us into the murk without charge. It was more of a basement than a club, it seemed to me, but Edward led me to a corner where a young piano player was just finishing a meditative blues with a lovely trickling solo that had the patrons staring at him in amazement. "That was Otis Spann, you know," said the pianist quietly into his microphone. "He died eight years ago not far from here and he buried under old oak trees not far from here and we going to play Otis all night long like praying. Otis was the best of us all. He a wonder of a man. God gave that man a heart unlike any heart ever was. He was a beautiful man. He died so very young. He only forty when he died. Anybody ever to hear Otis play, you different ever after. A piano player to hear Otis for the first time, that was the end of the piano player you used to be and the beginning of your new one. This happened to me. So tonight we going to play Otis as long as Theresa let us stay here. We maybe play 'til morning if she let us. We going to *pray* on the piano. We begin with 'Someday' played slow and low so you feel the blues at the bottom of your bones," and he closed his eyes and began to play again, and the music was so lean and sobbing and sweet and sad, so slow and haunted and resigned, with a hint of thorny endlessly patient weary bemused endurance in it, that I *did* feel it in the bottom of my bones; and I had the odd feeling that I had always known this music somehow without ever actually hearing it before, that it had been waiting patiently for me, so to speak, and now we were friends, and would always be so; we understood each other somehow, we thought and dreamed in the same language, and it had nothing whatsoever to do with skin color or gender or occupation or avocation, or any of the other things by which we define and categorize and wall ourselves off from other people. This music was bone music, music that you either felt very deeply, inarticulately deeply, or you did not. I had the sense that you could enjoy it on the surface, with its propulsive rhythm and repetitive pulse, its predilection to chant and litany and tides of chorus, without *loving* it, in the way that you could enjoy pop and folk and ethnic music here and there, usually married to an occasion or event; but even before the young piano player finished the song I was utterly and completely and forever absorbed by the blues, and have remained so ever since.

★

Actually meeting Miss Elminides finally had piqued my curiosity about her, and between Edward and Mr Pawlowsky I learned a great deal. Edward was of the firm opinion that she had taken up residence ten years ago, not six, and even at that time she was in the habit of riding the bus, destination unknown, although Edward believed she was a teacher, from various mannerisms and accoutrements and habits, and even the way she carried herself. She had a firm but gentle mien, always willing to listen but brisk and impatient with her time being wasted; she had a preternatural sense of people lingering or waiting in the hall, about to knock on her door; she was apparently erudite in geography, topography, cartography, history, navigation, and music, if the maps and instruments we had seen on her wall were any indication; she took the bus south and west every morning, and returned to her bay apartment late every afternoon; she had the eerie teacherly ability to quell young Azad's exuberance with a look or a quiet word or even a slight decisive gesture of her hand; and occasionally, at the times that you would think matched the intense periods of a school calendar, she would lock herself in her room for days on end with large stacks of papers and folders, and subsist, apparently, on nothing but coffee and honey and olives, if Edward's sure sense of smell was to be believed.

"You see his line of thinking here, and there is a lot to be said for his calculations," said Mr Pawlowsky, on a particularly starry night on the roof in early December.

"But there are, of course, many other explanations for her habits. She could be, for example, a composer, or a novelist, or an accountant, or a deft and thorough robber of banks, for which she needs to carefully scout the premises and behavioral patterns of the employees, and scour over vast troves of architectural drawings and geological surveys and city plumbing and piping maps. That could be. Or she could be some sort of spiritual visionary, the leader of a small sect of some sort, devoted particularly to maps as forms of prayer, along with the usual predilection to music that most religions evince, playing on the natural rhythms of the heart. That could also be. Or indeed she could be working for the city in some capacity, or perhaps she is the bookkeeper for a business entity of some sort, from gyro shop to music store to the reading of palms and casting of horoscopes. The possibilities are as endless as Miss Elminides' range of skills and talents, which is remarkable for one so young."

This line of talk led to a discussion of her age. Mr Pawlowsky put her in her late twenties, given the translucence of her skin and the way she walked with the effortless springing graceful step of a young deer, but Edward was sure she was in her late thirties, her youthful appearance and carriage being more a matter of admirable sleep patterns, balanced diet and living habits, and the luck of the draw in the matter of heritage and ancestry. I hadn't the slightest idea, having had no experience at all then in gauging the age of women; and later this was to prove a skill I never could acquire; in the years since my time in Chicago I have regularly embarrassed myself and others in underestimating advanced age and overestimating that which is less so; never to the point of mortification, thankfully, but occasionally to hilarity, and once to tears.

What I remember best about that December night on the roof, though, was not the interesting and essentially detective discussion about Miss Elminides, but my first intimation that she loomed large in Mr Pawlowsky's affections, more than he was willing to admit, and more, perhaps, than he knew. As that night wore on, and Edward made sure to draw our attention to the wonderfully clear outlines of the constellations Andromeda and Pegasus (they share the star Alpheratz, as he noted), Mr Pawlowsky, perhaps unbuttoned somewhat by the astonishing clarity of the stars, spoke ever more warmly about Miss Elminides, about her grace and kindness, her unassuming but attentive authority with the building, her meticulously honest handling of taxes and city inspectors, her lack of false or tinny morality about the businessmen who lived two by two on the second floor or the tailor and the detective who lived together in 2B, her quiet extension of credit occasionally to trustworthy residents who were caught short for one reason or another, her adamant refusal to pay nominal protection fees to local ruffians despite the very real possibility of material or physical assault, her smiling willingness to allow Mrs Manfredi's weekly bakery to operate illegally in the basement once a week, her careful management of her apartment (he had never had to repair or replace anything in her rooms, in the six or ten years she had lived there), and various other adulatory remarks. Finally, along about midnight, he stopped, perhaps having sensed that he was revealing more than he wanted to, and we went off to our rooms. The next day, though, Edward pointed out that Andromeda, the loveliest of young women in ancient Greek lore, was saved from a monster's maw by Perseus, a man of the sea.

★

A week later it snowed for the first time, a light dusting on a Saturday and then a solid couple of inches the next day, and it was exactly the sort of gentle drifting opening snowfall that everyone enjoys and runs out into and spends the whole day savoring—snowball fights, tiny snowmen laboriously built by children and their puffing dads, kids making snow angels in fields and lots, people taking endless lovely photographs of snow sifting into the lake, dogs whirling and snapping at snowflakes, shopkeepers grinning as they sweep snow away from their front doors with brooms; they wouldn't be smiling later, when they had to wield snow shovels against wet heavy onerous tons of grimy grainy snow, but for the moment they stood smoking cigars and laughing and calling insults all up and down Broadway and Halsted Street, brandishing their old brooms like staves or wands.

Then there was a last gasp of autumn, a brief flicker of wavering light, a few days when it was almost warm in the thin sunshine, and I noticed a flurry of old folks, wrapped in overcoats and scarves and mufflers and baboushkas, basking on benches along the lake all the way from Dog Beach to Oak Street Beach; it was like they were storing up as much heat and light as they could before they battened down for the winter in their tiny apartments, drinking tea and listening to the radio and reading newspapers in the tongues of old countries, or the labor union newsletter, or the shipping news, or the racing form, or the police log. Some of them I recognized, as I ran past dribbling my gleaming basketball, their heads turning slowly like turtles as they heard the ball approaching, their eyes glued to its glow as I went by, their heads turning slowly to watch me fade into the distance, their faces faintly disapproving except for some dim sweet memory of the days when they ran too, through woods or fields or streets; but most of them I had never seen before, and I wondered if they were like cicadas, emerging from their burrows once a year at a set time, or like alewives, compelled once a year to gather on the shore of the lake.

But then it *really* snowed—all through Christmas week and past New Year's Eve and into January, when it finally slowed and then stopped just before the Feast of the Epiphany. By then there was so much snow on the street that parked cars were completely buried and people put pink rubber balls on the tips of their radio antennas to mark where their cars were. The city plows never came at all, the buses stopped running, I couldn't dribble my basketball *anywhere,* and people walking to and from the grocery store and the pub had worn a narrow trail down the middle of the street, maybe five feet above the asphalt. The pink balls marking parked cars were about at knee height, most of them new but a few the loveliest faded pink, the color of shyness.

The radio and television and newspapers roared with indignation over the stalled plows and poor planning and corrupt machinations of oleaginous politicians, and that epic snowstorm, it turned out, was a hinge point for Chicago politics, because the mayor at the time, the Machine's chosen man, heir to the gruff blunt Richard Joseph Daley of sainted memory and criminal record, was so damaged by his failure to plow the streets and collect garbage during the storm that he was soundly defeated in the spring Democratic primary elections, the first time the Machine had been defeated in a century in Chicago, and the new mayor was, gasp, *female,* the first time the city had ever had a person with a bra running City Hall, that anyone knew.

But the image I retain from the storm has to do with Edward. The first sunny day after the storm ended I was walking atop the snow to the gyro shop around the corner when I noticed Edward inspecting each of the pink balls on car antennas along the street. He went up and down the street, inspecting each one, until he found the one he wanted. I watched as he removed it deftly with his teeth and buried it a few feet away, digging a couple of feet down into the snow to be sure it would not be found for weeks. I wondered if there was some quiet enmity at work there—if the owner of the car had in some way bruised or insulted Mr Pawlowsky or Edward or Miss Elminides—but when I asked Edward about it, a week later when the snow had receded somewhat, he stared at me blankly as if he hadn't the slightest idea what I was talking about.

7

INCREDIBLY, A FEW DAYS after the tremendous snow-storm that lasted for nine days and was the biggest snow-storm in Chicago for fifty years, it snowed *again* for several days, even harder, and this time the city pretty much shut down altogether. Not only were streets unplowed and garbage uncollected, the *Tribune* and the *Sun-Times* undelivered, the benches along the lake unpopulated by old folks in baboushkas, dogs unwalked and crows unable to collect their usual tribute of smashed squirrel parts, buses canceled or so crowded with people in immense parkas that some passengers were never able to disembark at all and had to live in the back of the bus for days at a time making coffee over small brushfires, but this time the older residents in our building were essentially screwed, as they could not make their way to the grocery store or the bank or the doctor. The rest of us worked in rotations to cut a narrow path high in the snow over the street again, but two days passed before I even thought of people like Mr McGinty, who was ninety-nine years old and had fought in the American war against the Filipino people when he was brave and stupid and twenty, as he said. Mr McGinty lived in the first floor near the alley, and in good weather he could shuffle out into the alley where he had a battered table and chairs for chess, but with something like eight feet of snow drifted up against the back door, egress even for someone pliable like young Ovious was out of the question.

But here too I learned a lesson from Edward; it turned out he had quietly been shuttling back and forth to the grocery store with loads of food on his back for the older residents. He was not the biggest dog, but he was relentless, and according to Mr Pawlowsky if Edward was properly balanced he could carry not only bread and milk but two bottles of beer on his back. Oddly enough, tall things like milk or beer bottles were apparently not a problem but broad things like steaks and crabs were, for reasons that eluded me; Mr Pawlowsky thought it had something to do with Edward's center of gravity. I did see Edward once returning from the store, where he must have had a line of credit payable after the melt; he was completely submerged in the snow, through which he moved like a dogged submarine, and all I could see of him was the tip of his tail, and the upper halves of two bottles of red wine. For a moment I had the feeling I was watching a tiny steamer on the lake with its two funnels, but then Edward came up for air for a moment, and saw me in the window. I waved and he smiled and then he submerged again and the bottles slowly approached, looking for all the world like they were walking hesitantly through the snow themselves.

★

It was when this vast and epic snowstorm finally melted away that what Mr Pawlowsky came to call the Awkwardnesses began. There were three Awkwardnesses that winter and spring, and they were not all resolved until August, as if the roaring heat and searing light of a full high Midwest summer by the tremendous lake was necessary to turn them finally to ash and memory.

The first was the Affliction—every single being in the building got terribly sick, essentially one by one, and while official diagnoses ranged from influenza to pneumonia to bronchitis to sinusitis to rhinitis (or "whinitis," as Mr McGinty said of Ovious, who was the sort of patient who moaned loudly all day and night), everyone had roughly the same symptoms, and took the same long weeks to return shakily to a semblance of health, and lost the same amount of weight because he or she lost all appetite and subsisted on water and music and Bulls games on the radio, and looked as wan and emaciated when he or she walked to the lake for the first time since he or she had been felled, and breathed in the sharp stinging restorative air that sometimes held a zest of spruce in it if the wind was from the northeast, where the great deep dark brooding forests of Michigan's fabled upper peninsula had held their ground since the glaciers retreated ten thousand years ago.

The Second Awkwardness also began in January, with a visit from two members of the Gaylords gang. This was the same organization that had sent a scout to the building

before, inquiring as to our desire to purchase fire insurance; in that instance the lone Gaylord had lost the top
half of his left pinky finger, and had not returned. But on
the last very cold day of January there he was again on the
porch, nine-and-a-half-fingered, this time accompanied
by another burly Gaylord, and Edward pointed out an
idling car with two more scowling Gaylords in it parked
up the street.

There were many street gangs in Chicago in those
years, of course; every city of size has its human vermin, loudly asserting neighborhood pride and defense
of helpless women and children and old folks against the
depredations of other gangs, even as they rape and steal
and murder and terrify and drug and assault and batter
the innocent; every culture hatches its rapacious young
warriors, and either bends them to the larger plunder
and the greater maw of international war, or leaves them
to knife each other in dim alleys until such time as they
are dead or imprisoned or beaten in their turn by the
forces of the law; and on the north side of the city alone
in those years there were the Popes and the Imperials, the
Royals and the Jousters, the Latin Kings and the Latin
Eagles, the Playboys and the Ventures, the Deuces and
the Cobras, and many more. All jostled for territory, all
were entrepreneurial in nature, all raised money in sun-
dry and various ways. The Gaylords, while trafficking
in the usual squirm of drugs and guns and sex, had developed a thriving side business in insurance, as they
called it, or protection-racketeering, as the police called

it; and here they were again on the front steps of the building, on an afternoon *grimacing with snow,* as Mr Pawlowsky said later.

But here again I learned a lesson about Edward, who had not forgotten his previous conflict with the Gaylords, and who had planned carefully for their return. Even before the Gaylords knocked on the door, the street began to fill with dogs. They came from both ends of the street, and emerged from the alleys north and south, and they were utterly silent; not one barked or growled or snarled, though they all looked grim. A dozen or so surrounded the idling Gaylord car, pressing so close that the doors could not be opened; the rest—and there were at least sixty or seventy of them, of every shape and species, from bulldogs to the tremendous wolfhound who lived with the rabbi at the temple—pressed close to the front steps of the building.

I had been watching all this from my window, from which I could see the front steps, and I turned to say something in amazement to Edward, but he had vanished; and just then the front door opened and Mr Pawlowsky stepped out and said something quietly to the two Gaylords, who looked around and then walked carefully down the steps and back to their car, the sea of dogs parting silently to let them pass. The car moved slowly into the street and started west toward Broadway but then stopped because again the dogs had massed around it, again without the slightest sound; it was this silence that was most frightening, somehow, and for all the oddity

of the scene itself it is that eerie dangerous silence I remember to this day. After a moment the dogs fell back
and let the car leave. A minute later every dog was gone
and the street was as empty as before.

I had strained to see if any of the dogs in the street
conducted or commanded the others, or if signals were
communicated from Edward to them in some ascertain-
able way, but I had seen nothing I could understand as a
message, and Edward, when I appealed to him for an explanation, declined to clarify the matter. Mr Pawlowsky
was only slightly more forthcoming, saying only that ruffians were a regular and unfortunate aspect of life in the
city, and that while he understood the urge to cohere in
small bands of like-minded companions, he did not see
any reason to accept what amounted to an invitation to
violence, especially since he had himself been in a violent organization; and though he was now retired from
the Navy, he could at need, as he had explained gently
to the Gaylords, summon former professional companions to defend the building and the street, and his advice
to the Gaylords, and to any other entrepreneurial bands
they might be in contact with along these lines, was to
consider the area between Broadway and the lake, from
Belmont to Addison, as territory protected by the United
States Navy, as well as other shadowy but formidable entities whose identities he was not at liberty to divulge,
but whose agents took many forms, as perhaps they had
noticed today.

★

Some mornings I would get up crazy early and take the very first bus downtown along the lake—the Sound Asleep Bus, as its driver called it. This was Donald B. Morris, whose name I learned on the first dark morning I boarded the bus; I had forgotten to get tokens, and had not a cent on my own personal person, but I greeted the driver in an ingratiating way, and began to mumble something about not having a cent, and he smiled and said his name was Donald B. Morris, and I was welcome on the community of the bus, and he would cut me slack twice but not more than twice, was that clear? I said yes sir and he said Don't call me sir, son, my name is Donald B. Morris, and I believe there is a seat right rear window for you. No one like that seat because the hump of the wheel there and some trick of the engine make it too hot for comfort but you young and can bear the heat. On this bus we are a peaceful people and there is no loud music or any of that. Generally on this bus people sleep until we arrive downtown. Your ride is my treat this morning. Next time the *last* time I treat. Also do not board the bus and ask passengers for change. That is not done on this bus. When you are seated we will proceed. Estimated time of arrival at Dearborn Street is twenty-two minutes. Pleasure to have you aboard. If you look out the left side the bus you will see the sun coming up over the lake in about twelve minutes. Do not stare directly at the sun. My advice is look at the lake in *front* of where the sun come up. Such a shimmer is rarely seen. Here we go.

Partly because Donald B. Morris was such an interesting man, and for reasons having to do with work, I
began to take the Sound Asleep Bus fairly regularly in
February, rising at five in the morning and showering
hurriedly and then trying to time my sprint to the lakefront for exactly 5:39 for Donald B. Morris's punctual
arrival at 5:41. After a few rides I was granted a seat directly behind Donald B. Morris, which I took to be a
great compliment, although it might also have been the
case that I was the only person actually awake on the bus
except for Donald B. Morris, and he rather liked having
someone to talk to; everyone else got on the bus, went
to their usual seat, and fell asleep so thoroughly that
Donald B. Morris would have to go and gently wake
most of them when we arrived at Dearborn Street.

Donald B. Morris, it turned out, was a gifted and
amazing monologist, and the pattern of our conversations
was set early on: I would ask a brief question and he
would sail off on an erudite and endless commentary
on religion, politics, history, the Chicago transit system,
music, natural history, plumbing, and most of all football, especially his beloved Chicago Bears. It was a near
thing, I discovered, between religion and the Bears for
which thing he loved most in life, and I learned to switch
him back and forth between them with a question if
he got too monomaniacal about one or the other. His
speeches about the Bears were often hilarious, and featured every sort of scandal and crime and peccadillo and

misdemeanor—it turns out that bus drivers, like policemen, know everything about everyone, especially their
vices—but his religious talks were even more interesting because they would occasionally soar up and away
in the most amazing fashion. Some combination of the
early hour, and the sleeping passengers, and the slow
rising of the sun from the lake, and Donald B. Morris's
indisputable imaginative gifts, sometimes led him to say
things that bubbled up from somewhere deep inside him,
and caught him as unawares as me; for example one
morning he told me he had been in the war, and had
been saved from death by a horse where no one had ever
seen a horse before, and that this horse was, he was absolutely sure, sent to him by the woman some people call
the mother of God, although he himself was of the opinion that She was herself in some way *also* God, because to
put gender on God is just silly, gender is a human being
thing, and God is no human being, total respect to the
Jesus people. Now young Jesus, who was an Arabic boy,
we forget, may well have been *sent* by God, and he may
well have been some *part* of God also, or *infused* by God,
or *was* God wearing human being *skin* for a while, but to
say, well, Jesus the *only* form of God, all the other *possible* forms of God no way could they *be* God, well, that is
just silly, and arrogant too. How the hell we know what
shape God taken over the millions of years since universe
was sneezed into being? Hey? Who knows the shapes
and songs of God? Not one of *us,* and that is for sure.

Better to pay attention and see if you can see some of the fingerprints where God was or is. Like for me that island with the horse. But here we are at Dearborn Street. Watch your step. God bless. Go Bears.

8.

THERE WERE SO VERY MANY THINGS that were riveting and amazing about Chicago to me that year—remarkable people, the deep sad joyous thrum of the blues, my first serious excursions into dark wondrous jazz clubs, the vast muscle of the lake, the mountainous snowfall, the cheerful rough rude immediacy of the bustle and thunder of the city at full cry, the latticework of the elevated train tracks, the deep happy mania of Bears fans, the thrill of being paid for work rather than paying for ostensible education, and so much else; but I suppose what absorbed me most, in those first few months, was the sheer *geometry* of the city, its squares and rectangles, its vaulting perpendicularity, its congested arithmetic; I took to roofs and fire escapes more and more that winter, climbing up not only on my apartment building roof but on the roof of my office building (nine storeys) and the occasional hotel, given the chance while sentenced to meetings for this and that. I summited the Blackstone, on Michigan Avenue (twenty-one storeys), and the Palmer House, on Monroe Street (twenty-five storeys), and the Burnham, on Washington Street (fourteen storeys); I very nearly climbed atop the Chicago Stadium, the huge old boxy castle where the Bulls played, but chickened out due to ice on the roof; and I got as high as I could in the Hancock building, which was a thousand feet high, by slipping out onto the roof through a service door and briefly contemplating the meticulous jumble of the city far below.

All my life I will remember those few minutes a thousand feet in the air over Chicago; I could see where the city ended to the west, and turned to fields of snow and stubble; I could see north and south where the city vaguely morphed into Indiana and Wisconsin; and best of all I could see how the tremendous lake, stretching far out of sight to the east, held the city in its immense cold gray hands. I had expected to be amazed by the incredible welter and shapely chaos of the city below me, the countless jostling structures shouldering and crowding against each other, veined by streets and alleys, stitched by train lines, dotted with floating gulls and crows like scattered grains of salt and pepper, but I had not expected to be so stunned by the lake. It had never occurred to me that something could be far bigger and stronger than the city, but this was inarguably so, and I walked home that night along the lake, marveling at it, and a little frightened too.

★

Miss Elminides remained a shadowy and elusive figure to me deep into the winter; no matter what time I arose and ran for the bus, or slept in and sleepily shuffled down-stairs for empanadas and the papers and the mail, I never saw her going to work or in the hallways; and no matter what time I came home from work, or dashed in and out on the weekends with my basketball or on my late-night adventures in pursuit of music, I never saw her coming in or out, although often I could see her bay windows lit from within. The only time I saw her, it seemed, was when she wanted to speak to me, and this always hap-pened in the lobby by the mailboxes; I would be reach-ing for my thin scrabble of mail, when she would suddenly appear at my shoulder, murmuring gently about a jazz club I really should investigate, or a gyro shop on the west side of the city where the spanikopita had healed two children of serious diseases, or the train schedule to White Sox games, which were only two months away, hard as it was to believe in baseball in the marrow of a Chicago winter.

After a while her illusory presence began to seem amaz-ing to me and finally I bearded Mr Pawlowsky about it one evening when he was clearing out one of the storage stalls in the basement. I remember this discussion par-ticularly for two reasons: his muffled voice emerging disembodied from behind and beneath dense layers of mattresses and boxes and jackets and clothes-hangers, and the way in which we had a gently honest conver-sation about romance without ever mentioning the word or the idea directly; a particularly male approach, I suspect, although perhaps women also have sidelong conversations in which you each row close to but never quite directly at an island between you; let alone actually *land* on it, God forbid.

He said, faintly, from behind the wall of dusty possessions, that Miss Elminides was a remarkable woman altogether, and one of her many virtues was what he would call a masterful discretion; some people might call her shy or retiring but he himself much admired the way she grappled with things as they were, when it was time to come to grips with them; for example her mention of the White Sox now, in early February, was sensible in that pitchers and catchers reported to training camp in Florida next week, so baseball is suddenly in the air, which is especially delicious given that we are in the icy snare of winter at the moment, so to speak, and what could be more cheerful to think about than hot summer days and beer and a decent outfield for once, and also what trains to take to the park when the Sox open the regular season in April? Similarly Miss Elminides mentioning a particular gyro shop; for one thing she has exquisite taste in Greek culinary matters, as you now know, so you can be sure that if she tells you to go there it will be a stunning experience, but also the fact that she told you about it is tantamount to saying there are other and deeper things to be discovered there, and she knows you are a journalist, so in effect she is saying to you there are amazing things to be found, if you take the hint, which I assume you will. So are you dating anyone or what?

He caught me by surprise, and also I was at that moment holding up my end of a huge bedstead that weighed a ton and surely once belonged to Gargantua or Pantagruel, so I was silent for a moment, and then I said well, yes and no, or properly no and yes—that I was not dating anyone seriously, but that I'd had a few dates, here and there, when I could squeeze them into my busy schedule.

Your busy schedule, came his voice from behind the bedstead, being basketball and jazz clubs and blues clubs and prowling alleys with Edward? Those are the things keeping you from romantic exploration?

I explained that basketball was the greatest of games, and invented in America, as were jazz and blues, and as a man new to Chicago I felt the need to see and feel and hear and smell and touch the bone and thrum of the city myself, fully present and attentive, undistracted and alert to idiosyncratic and unique flavor and rhythms as I could be, Chicago being, as he himself had said, the most American city of all, what with it being in the middle of the nation, and shouldered by great waters, and roaring with industry while surrounded by agriculture, a visionary city open to the world but sure of its own place and grace, king of the plains, dismissive of the arrogant flittery cities of the coasts, a vast verb of an urb, but one still built for people, one where neighborhoods were villages, and all the villages from far South Side to far north, from the far west to the Loop on the shore of the lake, threw in together to worship together at common altars, for example the Bears and gyro sandwiches and a decent outfield for the Sox for a change. And if you admire Miss Elminides so much, and she clearly admires you, and you are single and she is single, why don't you ask her out?

That floored him for a moment and I expected him to come out from behind the bedstead but he didn't and after a while his voice said quietly Did I tell you whose storage stall this is?

No.

The old lady in 3C, the lady who used to be an actress in the Broncho Billy films. She died this morning. Her name was Eugenia. She really was an actress in the first Westerns filmed in Chicago and she loved it but she married a guy who hated that she was an actress and he made her get out of the game. She put all her costumes and posters and props and stuff in trunks and boxes in their house in California and never opened them again as long as he lived. When he died she sold their house in two days and came right back to Chicago on the train with all her trunks and boxes and got an apartment here and all that stuff is in her room. This stuff is all *his* stuff that she didn't want to sell or give away but she didn't want it in her room either. I used to go up there some days to pretend to fix something and she would be happy as could be, all dressed in character from one of her movies. One movie she was the sheriff's daughter and another she was a girl rustler and another she was a wrangler and another she was a Comanche princess. All that stuff is still up in her room. She was the nicest lady you ever wanted to meet. She was in plenty more movies but I don't know their names. The only thing from the movies that she couldn't fit in her room was this horse, which is why he is down here. I don't think she had any kids, so we will have to do something about this horse. What a nice lady. Never a harsh word for anyone. All she ever wanted to do was be an actress, I guess. Let's haul the bedstead out into the alley and then call it a night. Tell me if you know anyone who needs a stuffed horse.

*

Not only did I climb to the tops of hotels and other buildings to try to see the city as a whole; I also haunted alleys then, being young and supple and swift afoot if necessary, and I made a conscious effort to cut through every alley I could find, on the theory that alleys might show me more of the real salt of the city, its undertones and foundational colors, the bones beneath the shining flesh. It seemed to me there were far more stories in and among the alleys, where I found the more unusual residents of various species, including once, to my astonishment, a badger, although that might have been someone's pet.

Alleyness, you might say, is one of the things I remember best about Chicago. For all that some things were true of all alleys—narrowness, shabbiness, the occasional rat the size of a bear, a dank dark smell you knew had been there for a century and would be there for another century—there was a curious disparity in alleys according to sections of the city, and an odd inversion of expectations. Downtown in the Loop, and in the wealthy

Near North sections of the city, where commerce was king and the brightest wealthiest residences and businesses held sway, the alleys were generally terrifying, and twice I barely evaded ruffians with knives and poor attitudes; whereas there were warm and alluring alleys in the toughest raggediest neighborhoods to the south and west, neighborhoods where no one spoke American at all except cops and bus drivers. I remember one great alley on the west side where two brothers had built a brick oven for roasting lamb right into the wall, designed in such a way that the glorious smell of roast lamb with garlic and onions drifted out of the alley and snared passersby who could not resist at all and entered the alley sometimes with their eyes closed, dimly remembering something from their childhoods, perhaps an aunt's kitchen, or a redolent church basement, or a grandfather roasting shish kebab in the back yard in the wild sunlight.

Several alleys I explored had people living in them, in lean-to shelters or even little sheds, though no domicile I saw was bigger than your average garden shed. One alley on the South Side had a tarpaulin ceiling and several hammocks strung deftly high in the air, accessible only by a fire escape ladder; that particular alley also had a beautiful little fire-pit, at which the residents cooked sausages for sale at a cart in the street. Another alley, to the northwest, had been bricked over so meticulously at either end that you could not easily tell the alley from the adjoining walls, unless someone pointed out the infinitesimal vertical line that betrayed a small door. I was curious to enter that alley but there was a deeper law at play there and the man who showed me the door walked another couple of blocks with me silently before he suggested that I forget the alley and especially the door, which I have done until now.

I suppose the one alley I think of first when I think of Chicago's alleys is one on the north side, a few blocks past the basketball court where I played with the Latin Kings and the Latin Eagles. I was walking home from a blues club one night and heard music coming from an alley and I poked in to see what was up and I found a small man playing a tiny piano the size of a suitcase. He was surrounded by children, a good seven or eight of them, and no one said a word or moved a muscle until he was finished with a long lovely song. He had a thin quavering voice and he murmured more than he sang but he played the piano beautifully and somehow the combination of his gentle voice and the clarity of the piano notes was mesmerizing. I didn't know the song but one couplet from it struck me forcibly and I sang it all the way home that night: *there's a song that will linger forever in our ears / o hard times come again no more.* Much later I discovered those were lines from a song by the American composer Stephen Foster, who died only with three cents in his pocket and a scrap of paper on which he had written the words *dear friends and gentle hearts.*

*

One day I sat with Edward and charted out who lived where in the building, from apartment 4F, which was

Ovious and his mother, down to 2A, which was the guy across from me who'd invented children's propeller hats, and when I added up residents I realized the guy who had been a sailor but not in the Navy was missing. I knew he was a resident—I saw him occasionally getting his mail from the lobby, and he got a lot of mail, more than anyone except Miss Elminides—but according to my chart he didn't have an apartment.

I went over the chart again. Fourth floor: Edward and Mr Pawlowsky, little Azad and his family, the two young women from Arkansas, Ovious and his mom, Mrs Manfredi, and the Armenian librettist. Third floor: Miss Elminides in the bay apartment, the two hermit brothers in 3E and 3D, the four businessmen in apartments 3A and 3B, and the apartment in which Eugenia the movie actress had lived. Second floor: the inventor in 2A, the Scottish tailor and the detective together in 2B, old Mr McGinty in 2C closest to the back door, the man who had once raised cheetahs in 2D, the Trinidadian cricket player in 2E, and me in apartment 2F with the big windows over the street. No sailor.

I asked Edward about this and he stared at me with the oddest combination of emotions on his long face—something like guilt and sadness and hesitation all at once—and then he led me upstairs to the roof, where Mr Pawlowsky was sweeping snow toward the drainpipes. Mr Pawlowsky looked at Edward and then at me and then said, "Well, we trust you to keep the matter private. The man lives in the basement, in two of the stalls. We fixed up a sort of cabin for him exactly like a bunk on a ship. He uses the Young Men's Christian Association in winter and the lake in summer for bathing. The YMCA was started in America by a sea captain, you know, and they keep an eye out for sailors down on their luck. He has some problems. Miss Elminides knows but no one else does. Now *you* know, but we trust you to keep it confidential. He's not in a position to pay rent and his accommodation is not quite up to city code but he's a gentle guy and there's never been a problem. Miss Elminides is of the opinion that healing will come and he will someday make up what he owes. That would be great if it happens but if it doesn't happen sometimes you just do what needs to be done. It's probably best if you just leave him alone. He's friendly enough and he says hey if you see him getting his mail but other than that probably it's best just to leave him be. He's quite handy with tools and sometimes he helps me when there's a lot of repair work to be done. He's a very fine carpenter. I would guess that he has many fascinating stories and I can see you would love to listen to him but Edward has suggested and I agree that perhaps it would be best for now to just say hey in the lobby and otherwise leave him be. I can trust you in this matter, I'm sure. Are you as cold as me? Because I am absolutely freezing, and Edward can finish the sweeping later. Let's go get some hot tea and think about the White Sox. Pitchers and catchers report to training camp next week, and this year by golly they are going to have a decent team. Bill Veeck bought them a couple years ago and when old Bill is involved with a team you are sure to see some wild and wonderful things. I think they might have the best outfield in the league this year and old Wilbur Wood on the mound throwing that silly knuckleball is going to be entertaining and then some. They'll have a game where they score eighteen runs and a game where they give up eighteen runs, mark my words. Maybe it will be the same game, which would not surprise me. Nothing about the Sox surprises me. This will be fun. You'll see."

9.

THE MATTER OF EDWARD'S age began to absorb me
greatly as February wore on, and one clear night on the
roof, as we were looking for the constellations Auriga
(the charioteer) and Columba (the dove), Mr Pawlowsky
pointed out Canis, the great dog, with a smile, and then
talked at some length about Edward.

"It is conceivable that he may have been Abraham Lincoln's companion," said Mr Pawlowsky, leaning back in
his lawn chair. "It is faintly possible. Edward has some
serious mileage on his odometer, but he eats healthy, except when he gorges on alewives, and he gets his exer-
cise, and he has moderate habits, and he handles things
without undue stress. Lincoln loved dogs and if you read
his journals carefully he was usually accompanied by a
dog like Edward, of uncertain heritage. And Springfield,
you know, is just downstate a little from Chicago—a dog
with a sure sense of direction, like Edward, could easily
make his way northward after Mr Lincoln took the train
to Washington to become president. There would be no
good reason for Edward to stay in Springfield after that
and it would be only natural for him to migrate to the

city as so many others have done, greatly to our civic benefit."

I told Mr Pawlowsky that I had many times asked Edward directly about his age and previous adventures but had never gotten more than hints and intimations in reply, and Mr Pawlowsky said, "Well, that is Edward's way, of course; he is not much for boast or braggadocio, which is admirable, though it can also be a bit frustrating when you are genuinely curious and there are no answers in sight. However I believe there is much to be discerned about his past in his present, so to speak, and that is why I suggest he may be far older than we would think. He is awfully familiar with Lincoln's letters and speeches, for example. Now, *I* read the speeches fairly often, sometimes aloud, as an act of citizenship, and also for the clear thinking and dry humor and wry cadence of the man while speaking, but I cannot say that I know whole snatches of them by heart, or can distinguish one from another within a line or two of quotation from anywhere within the text, but Edward can, and I have seen him do it many times. He is the same way with the letters, although they are not such ringing things as the speeches, and many of them are workmanlike missives, of course, having to do with policy or persuasion. Still—it's interesting to note that Edward is most versed and most interested in the speeches and letters from Illinois, rather than from the presidential years, with the exception, of course, of the inaugural addresses and the Emancipation Proclamation. You wonder if Edward is more familiar with the Illinois work because perhaps he was present when those speeches were delivered and letters written. Improbable, perhaps, but not impossible. But I am afraid we will always be reduced to speculation in this matter, given Edward's character."

★

I should say a bit more about my job at the Catholic magazine downtown, because of course in a real sense it was what allowed me to live in Chicago, and paid for my food and train tickets and basketball sneakers and small glowing whiskeys in small dark blues bars.

The editor-in-chief was a round beaming ebullient Irishman with the most glowing Irish face I had ever seen. He wore only beautiful glowing gray suits of the finest cut and cloth, an infinitesimally different shimmer and gleam of gray every day. He called me into his office at ten in the morning of my first day on the job and informed me tersely but cheerfully that we did not use the words *hopefully* or *unique* in the magazine, nor did we say such silly things as *it remains to be seen* or *on the other hand,* nor did we respect ostensible religious authority overmuch without cause to do so, nor did we take an unnecessarily confrontational attitude toward the hierarchy and its agents and minions, but rather we tried to walk a road in which clarity and humility were our recurring signposts. Also the office was not a drinking club, a fraternity, a lunch group, a refuge for the sleepy, a sinecure, a stepping-stone, a competition, a love-nest, a dating service, a source of free office supplies, a meeting-place for those with soaring literary aspirations, a coffee shop, a revolutionary cell, a nest of religious anarchy, a coven of apologists, a café for free telephone calls, or a place where such things as dungarees and shirts sporting the names and logos of colleges or athletic teams or musical ensembles were welcome. I was expected to bring my intelligence, diligence, honesty, creativity, and curiosity to work every morning by eight and wield those admirable and God-given tools until four. I could come in earlier and leave later if there was sufficient reason to do so but no undue credit would be given for extra hours when the coin of esteem was creative and trustworthy production. "You get two weeks for vacation and you must stagger your vacations around the vacations of the rest of the staff. See Mr Mahoney about vacation schedules. You get ten paid sick days a year. If you honestly require more than ten days to deal with illness or grief we can negotiate something depending on your trustworthiness and the nature of the affliction. See Mr Mahoney about that. We do not play radios or musical instruments in this office. We do not drink alcohol in this office. We try to maintain a professional appearance within reason. We often have visitors of every sort and stripe from cardinals to members of many other faith traditions in this office and we treat them all with respect and we do not make scurrilous remarks disguised as jokes. We once had a man who did exactly that and he did not last. As regards paychecks, monies withheld for tax and insurance purposes, pension funds if any, advice on commuting in and out of the city by train or bus, and any other matters of that sort, see Mr Mahoney. As regards ideas for the magazine, see me. As regards possible writers and photographers for the magazine, see me. We do not publish poets and we generally steer clear of artists. We do not publish fiction, knowingly. As regards complaints and diatribes about what you write, see Mr Mahoney about our form letters in response. If a personal response is required above and beyond our form response, I will handle that. We once had a woman who liked to write her own responses to complaints and diatribes about her work and you would be shocked at the language she used, and her a woman of the cloth, too. A Dominican sister. The Dominican sisters are a tough bunch, with skins like tree bark and a capacity for brawling, in my experience. We do not make jokes in print about the various charisms and characters of the Catholic religious orders, even the Jesuits. That Dominican, by the way, once punched out a cop who was beating a helpless drunk with his truncheon. This was right on the corner of Wells and Madison. He was a burly fellow, too, and she dropped him with a flurry of jabs that would have done a middleweight proud. Knocked him right out cold. He went down like rocks thundering from a truck. Remarkable woman. Do you have any questions?"

"About the nun?"

"About the magazine and your duties."

"No, sir."

"Better get to work, then."

"Yes, sir."

"God bless."

"Thank you, sir."

"Remarkable woman."

"Yes, sir."

★

Mr Pawlowsky had often told me that he had only once in his whole life been outside the city of Chicago, to the Iowa border to the west, from which vantage point he gazed out over fields of corn and soybeans, and admired tractors and silos and church steeples and railroad towers, and delighted at small stands and copses of trees around which the fields flowed like dark corduroy rivers, and smelled the rich dense redolence of it all; but then one day when we were on the roof talking about how farmland was gently lovely even though some people ("mostly automobile drivers and young people trying to convince themselves, not to mention others, of their own sophistication," he said) sneered and called it flat and boring though it wasn't at all, he suddenly said, "But I was often on the lake in ships and boats, of course, so I suppose I was outside the city much more than I thought," and off he went on a long peroration about his life on the vast inland sea we could just see, roiling and gray, from our chairs on the roof.

"We went out on rafts, in the beginning, just like Tom Sawyer and Huck Finn," he said. "My friends and I built rafts of varied quality out of anything we could. The prospect of being afloat was irresistible. I think I was perhaps six years old when I first went out on the lake. I had a friend named Raymond. His father drove a truck delivering goods on wooden pallets, and he built us a sturdy little raft, perhaps six by six feet, with three paddles also of wood, and he waded into the lake with us on the raft and then gave us a shove and we were away. I don't think I'll ever forget that feeling the rest of my life. It was a calm summer day and the lake murmured as we edged away from the shore. I remember the look on Raymond's father's face—worried and pleased and concerned and proud and worried. Raymond was nervous but I was delighted. I kept looking for fish. Raymond kept looking for tankers. He was afraid we would be run over and there would be nothing left of us but splinters. I remember I saw three enormous fish pass below us in a sort of arrow formation, going south toward Indiana. To this day I can see them if I close my eyes. Perhaps that was the moment I joined the Navy, in a sense. I think that they were sturgeon, although there are also very large salmon in the lake. After that I was on the lake as often as I could possibly be. I went out in canoes and rowboats and skiffs and ketches and catboats and sloops and motorboats and old historical schooners and brigs and steamboats and scows. I got summer jobs as a crewman on barges and freighters. When I was in my teens I was on the lake every single day I was not in school, I bet. My parents did not mind as long as I had a job. My father said as long as I was earning money for the family from honest work I could be on the lake or the moon or

on a dirigible for all he cared. Finally when I was eighteen years old I went down to Navy Pier and joined the
United States Navy. I don't think I was ever so proud
and happy as I was that day. Although it is ironic to note
that I never once went out on the water in my official
capacity; never was there a more landlocked Navy man
than me. But I was out on the lake every other moment
I could spare. Even during the war I owned a catboat
with Raymond and we were out on the lake at every
chance we got, until Raymond went overseas. He left a
letter under the thwart of the boat for me, giving me his
half of the boat if he didn't come back. He didn't come
back. I found the letter a few weeks after his father told
me about Raymond being killed in New Guinea. His
father came down to the Pier to tell me. I'll never forget
his face. It was like a mask whereas it used to be a face.
He asked me if he could see the catboat and I took him
down to the end of the pier where Raymond and I kept
the boat in a little secret slip we had built in the shadows. He stared at the boat for a long time and then he
said Raymond left you a letter somewhere in the boat.
He said Raymond was the love of his life and he would
never see him again and he could not stand even thinking about never seeing him again. He said he remembered the day he waded us out into the lake when we
were little and handed us each a paddle and gave the raft
a good shove and watched us paddle away and he was
scared and happy and proud and worried. He said now
that there were some nights that he could not sleep at all

and all night long he waded with us out into the lake and in the morning it was all he could do to get out of bed and shower and have coffee and pretend that life meant anything at all anymore. He said that he wished me the best with the boat and he asked that if ever I needed to sell it that I come to him and he would buy it for whatever price I asked. For a while after the war I kept the boat, and took it out a good deal, ostensibly fishing but not really, but it wasn't the same boat without Raymond in it, and eventually I sold it to Raymond's father. I wanted to just give it to him in memory of Raymond but he insisted on buying it. It had something to do with pride and pain. I was uncomfortable taking money but eventually we agreed that I would give him the boat and he would give me the collected speeches and writings of Abraham Lincoln, which is the lovely set of books you see in our apartment. I would treasure them anyway for the humor and genius of the author but I treasure them the more because in my view Raymond owns half of them. In my estimation I own the ones up to the presidential years and Raymond owns the presidential years. Edward is of the opinion that it is the other way round, as Raymond was older than me by a few weeks, and has the right of primogeniture."

10.

IT WAS ALSO EDWARD'S CONSIDERED opinion that Mr Pawlowsky and Miss Elminides were made for each other, that they enjoyed and were stimulated by the other's company, that they both secretly harbored affection and romantic interest in the other and had done so for years without the slightest productive action along those lines, and that hell would freeze over before the two shyest human beings in the city of Chicago would ever so much as shuffle an inch toward the idea of actually asking the other to have tea or coffee or lunch or dinner or go to a movie or a jazz club or even God help us all go for a walk together along the lake, how hard is *that,* to walk together along the lakefront, watching the gulls and savoring the gentle music of the waves? You don't even have to *say* anything or walk arm-in-arm or hold hands or have a destination, you can just shamble along and enjoy the crisp wind, how hard is *that?*

But no.

I had noticed that Mr Pawlowsky spoke of Miss Elminides with respect and almost a proprietary reverence, and that Miss Elminides, in the few brief conversations

I had had with her, spoke of him with a grave courtesy and hint of humor; she had, for example, once listed all the things in the building that Mr Pawlowsky had repaired or renovated or rebuilt, from doors to windows to cabinets to shelves to ceilings to walls to stairs to mailboxes to the roof to the epic boiler in the basement, and she had concluded her litany by saying, again gravely but with the tiniest flash of something in her face, that Mr Pawlowsky had in fact rebuilt the building in toto over the last few years, an amazing thing to say, a remarkable accomplishment which her grandfather would have much enjoyed for the odd humor and amazement of it, not to mention awe at the sheer amount of quiet dogged work involved, and work done by one man alone to boot, with total respect for Edward's role in lugging tools and lumber up and down the stairs, for which she was very grateful.

It wasn't that they didn't talk to each other; indeed they did, morning and afternoon and evening, for one reason or another; but their conversations were always stilted and formal, and each addressed the other as Miss and Mister even after years of daily discourse, and they seemed to carefully stay within established boundaries, subject-wise; the building, the neighborhood, the weather, the lake. Miss Elminides had no interest whatever in actually watching the Bears or the White Sox or any other sporting proposition; Mr Pawlowsky, while interested in Wes Montgomery's guitar, evinced no interest in actually playing a musical instrument; neither of them seemed to care overmuch about politics or popular culture or the making of money, the usual seas on which Americans sail; neither was particularly absorbed with food or alcohol, and both seemed generally content to live quietly and contemplate home repair and Abraham Lincoln, in Mr Pawlowsky's case, and maps and musical instruments, in Miss Elminides' case.

In March, as the snow finally began to subside, I suggested to Edward that perhaps it was our responsibility as their friends to gently nudge them toward seeing each other in a new light, as it were; to gently intimate to them that their dignity could be both at once wholly admirable and a sort of prison; to hint that their courteous reserve could and maybe had slipped infinitesimally from virtue to habit.

But Edward declined, dismayed by the very idea of matchmaking; and as he noted, there is a selfish aspect to setting people up on dates, and pushing them together not of their own volition, and arranging matters so that people are thrown together in the social ramble, with no routes of escape; it's almost cruel, not to mention often awkward and uncomfortable public theater in which the principal actors have not sought or prepared for their roles. He was adamant about this, and I was uncomfortable enough about it myself, so we agreed to do nothing but hope for something like a thaw in their formality, a warming of their friendship, the serendipitous opening of new windows in their affections; which indeed did come, but not until spring turned to summer, on the weekend the White Sox took three in a row from the Oakland Athletics and rose to first place in the west.

*

The Third Awkwardness, the most serious crisis in the history of the apartment building, began in the middle of April, with a letter to Miss Elminides from the City of Chicago. According to the city, the building was in epic arrears tax-wise; property taxes had not been paid for the last two years, and repeated inquiries to the trustees had gone unanswered. The city then sent a second letter, announcing a new assessment of the building's worth, and thus a new charge attached to the taxes already in arrears. A third letter announced a rise in water rates; a fourth letter announced a new charge for building inspections; a fifth letter announced new building codes from which no buildings whatsoever would be released, so as to protect against the illegal sale and trading of permit releases, as if such things had ever happened in the city of Chicago in living memory. A sixth letter announced a new scheme for sewer connections, which doubled the rates for connection for both residential and commercial properties. A letter came from a bank noting that a routine analysis of title status had discovered no extant registered title for the building; could Miss Elminides come to the bank and elucidate the matter, with documentation? A letter came from a second bank, inquiring as to a lien on the building, resulting from a series of loans issued through a now-defunct bank in Greece, of which investigators could find no legal history whatsoever.

Could Miss Elminides come to the bank and explain the lien and loans? And finally a letter came from the United States Post Office, reporting a slew of returned letters addressed to the trustees of the building; according to their postal colleagues in Greece, the address for the trustees there was a boathouse, and a note pinned to the door of the boathouse directed all mail to Miss Elminides in Chicago. Could Miss Elminides stop by the post office on Dearborn Street and illuminate the mystery of the boathouse?

And this was not all. The weather turned bad, and torrents of rain fell; it grew eerily and uncomfortably cold, with mean slicing snarling winds off the lake; sleet poured down at dusk three times in four days, and cars skidded and skewed everywhere; a barge, disoriented in the storms, drove directly into Dog Beach and sank, with only the tip of its bow visible the next morning; a police horse slipped on the ice and broke its spine and had to be shot on the spot by its weeping rider; an alderman who was about to be imprisoned for defrauding a Catholic grade school of its auction proceeds was mysteriously reinstated to office, whereupon he devised incalculable new thefts from children; the icy rain choked and hammered the first sprouts of corn and soybeans outside the city, causing farmers and their families to lie awake worried and frightened in the nether reaches of the night; the wooden fence built by hand by Abraham Lincoln behind his house on Jackson Street in Springfield fell down suddenly, section by section, as if it was being flattened by a huge invisible hand; and Edward grew so sick he could not rise from his bed, or eat, or drink tea, or even, after three days, open his eyes.

On the first day Edward was sick Mr Pawlowsky assumed this was Edward's annual spring cold, which usually presented itself on April 15, the day Lincoln died, and arrived with the same calendric precision as his annual autumn cold, which always arrived on September 22, the day Lincoln informed the known universe that in one hundred days he would thereafter forbid the sale of human beings in America by virtue of the color of their skin, and free those who were enslaved to others by virtue of the color of their skin, and thereafter make illegal the possession of human beings by other human beings for any reason whatsoever. Edward had himself speculated that perhaps his autumn cold came to him because the Emancipation Proclamation was a proximate cause of Lincoln's murder, so that September, which was usually a sunny and lovely month in Illinois, had the virus of disaster and loss in it, and some residents, especially those who may have been close companions of Mr Lincoln, were afflicted by sadness in September, and felled by the knowledge that what was spoken in autumn would reap blood come spring. But even Mr Pawlowsky, who usually agreed with Edward on speculative matters, thought this was overblown, and considered that Edward was just particularly susceptible to the first-month-of-school colds that every schoolchild in the city came down with by the end of the month.

But this time Edward did not recover quickly, and his breathing grew ragged and desperate, and by the third day he could not rise from his bed, or eat, or drink tea, or even open his eyes. Miss Elminides came up and sat by him and read to him, as did Azad and his sister Eren from next door in 4A, and one by one most of the rest of the residents came too, some shyly standing in the doorway and murmuring their respects and best wishes, and others coming in and kneeling down and whispering or even singing to Edward; but he did not respond, and Mr Pawlowsky began to grow quietly frantic.

Miss Elminides summoned an animal doctor, a tall cadaverous man who conducted tests and took blood and stool samples and left small jars of bright elixirs that Edward could not swallow. The four natty businessmen in 3A and 3B sent a friend of theirs who was a nondenominational healer, a gentle gaunt man who spent a whole afternoon with Edward and then withdrew silently with a face of terrible sadness.

On the fourth day I was at a conference of editors and printers and such deep in the country, and got back to the apartment building quite late; I ran up the stairs to 4B, taking them two and three at a time, and knocked very gently; there was no answer, but the door was slightly ajar, and I poked my head in and found Mr Pawlowsky sitting in the dark, under his Navy blanket. Edward was motionless in his bed. I knelt down as quietly as I could to feel Edward's chest and he was still breathing but very slowly, like each breath was being excavated from some deep ancient cave inside him where he refused to die.

Mr Pawlowsky had not said a word as I knelt there but I could see his huddled face in the moonlight and I stood to say something but he raised his hand and said quietly, "I have been reading Lincoln to him. I think it helps. I think he hears me. I think he knows the words so well that perhaps it gives him pleasure or hope. The speech from the train at Springfield, when he left everything he knew and loved. 'Friends, no one who has never been placed in a like position can understand my feelings at this hour, nor the oppressive sadness I feel at this parting,' he said. Probably he had removed his hat and was holding it in his hand. 'For more than a quarter of a century I have lived among you, and during all that time I have received nothing but kindness at your hands.' Some say he spoke from the last car on the train and others say he was standing on the platform before boarding the train, which was waiting for him, but to me this is an immaterial detail. 'Here I have lived from my youth until now I am an old man.' He was fifty-two years old, my age. 'Here the most cherished ties of earth were assumed. Here all my children were born and here one of them lies buried.' That was Eddie, who was four years old when he died, although his son Willie was also born and died in Springfield, only three months old; it is interesting that he does not say two of them, you wonder if he and Mary just did not talk about Willie because he didn't live very long. 'To you, dear friends, I owe all that I have, all that I am. All the strange checkered past seems to crowd now upon my mind. Today I leave you . . . for how long I know not. . . .'"

11.

THE WHITE SOX OPENED their home season at Comiskey Park in April that year, against the Boston Red Sox, after three games in Toronto against the Blue Jays. I had planned to go to the home opener with Edward and possibly Mr Pawlowsky, and there had been talk in the lobby about a few other residents coming with us, even though it was a Wednesday—the cricket player from Trinidad was particularly interested, as he had never seen a baseball game, and was curious about "cricket's spawn," as he said. With Edward so very ill, all plans were canceled, but as several of us had taken the day off from work for the game, we drifted up to 4B to sit with Edward and listen to the game on the radio.

It was a sunny day but windy, I remember, and Edward was covered with two Navy blankets. Mr Pawlowsky made tea for everyone, and we got to talking about Edward and all the gracious things he had done for people in the building and the neighborhood (he had several times saved crows and jays from being hit by cars, and more than once edged a child away from traffic "with the most insouciant grace," as the detective said), and we lost track of the time. It was the man who had once raised cheetahs who looked up late in the afternoon and said "the game!" at which point we realized that not one of us had thought to bring a radio. I stood up to go get a transistor radio, but then something happened that I have never forgotten; and indeed I still think of it sometimes, on late spring afternoons, at the hour when baseball games are in their penultimate innings, inching toward dusk and empty outfields, across which ticket stubs and popcorn boxes skitter in the wind, and the last vendors are locking up their food carts, and the gates to the park are being padlocked until tomorrow, when there is a doubleheader, with music between games, possibly a barbershop quartet, or a boys' choir from deep in the farmlands, winners of a competition for choruses specializing in music having to do with America's oldest game.

Before I could take a step to get a radio, the detective said, "Wait," and we all looked at him, partly because he was a quiet man, somewhat shy, and this was the first firm declarative statement we had ever heard come from his lips. No one knew him well; he had lived with the Scottish tailor in 2B for two years, they were quiet and retiring men, and no one knew the nature of their relationship, or even the nature of the detective's business, other than what he said of himself, that he was a private detective; whether past or present we did not know. Neither tall nor short, fat nor thin, shabby nor well-dressed, handsome nor awkward, he was something of a cipher; but it was the unspoken ethic of the building that no one pried or speculated overmuch on occupation or avocation, relationship or politics, religion or money. For my own part I had wondered about him and the tailor, as I wondered about the four businessmen in two rooms and the two adjacent hermit brothers on the third floor, and Ovious's mother on the fourth floor, a woman no one had ever seen except Miss Elminides; but something held my tongue, when I wanted very much to ask Mr Pawlowsky; and I already knew, after only a few months in the building, that asking Edward about any other resident would only earn me that silent half-smile I knew too well.

"Wait," said the detective again. "I'll tell you the game. Open the window about four inches. That will be enough for me but not enough to give Edward a chill." The man who had raised cheetahs was closest to the window and he opened the window. No one spoke for a moment. I remember that I heard a gull screech by the lake, and that Edward twitched when the gull screeched.

"Ken Brett on the mound for us," said the detective, who was staring at the ceiling. "Lefty. He's not nervous. He's surprisingly confident, even facing a lineup like Boston's, with Jim Rice and Carl Yastrzemski and Dwight Evans. The leadoff batter for Boston singles to right, but the next guy hits into a double play, and Brett gets Rice to ground out. His confidence rises even more. Big crowd. There are kids from Indiana sitting in our seats. The usher just glanced casually at their tickets and they are over the moon feeling like they put one over on authority. They are cutting school today. I think they are from Mishawaka. One of them just secretly ate a bright blue pill without telling his friends.

"Ralph Garr leads off for us. He's in left, Chet Lemon in center, Richie Zisk in right. This is the best outfield we have had in years. They all might hit twenty homers this year. Decent infield, decent pitching, but this might be the best outfield in the league. Garr singles and scores on a double. Oscar Gamble is the designated hitter today but they will have to make room for him in the outfield. We have four all-star outfielders this year!

"The Red Sox get a run back when Yaz doubles but we score four more in the bottom of the second behind solid shots from Lemon and Garr and superb baserunning from Oscar Gamble. You should see the Afro on Oscar this year! It must be a foot tall easy and his hat flies off at the slightest movement! A run for Boston in the sixth, but otherwise it's groundballs and flyouts the rest of the way. Lovely day, warmer than you would expect, but blustery. Richie Zisk hits the ball hard all day but gets caught stealing and grounds into a double play. The kid who ate the pill throws up in the bathroom and faints and his friends come and find him and clean him up and walk him out to the parking lot and miss the last two innings. For one of his friends this is the very last straw and he never speaks to the kid again. Two hits apiece for Lemon and Garr, three hits including a triple for Jorge Orta at second base, Brett goes seven innings for the win. Much of the talk in the press box after the game is the

two terrific throws from the outfield to nail Boston run-
ners at third; Zisk threw out George Scott from right
field, but of course George is the slowest guy in baseball. He might weigh three hundred pounds, although
Boston says he weighs two hundred. If he weighs two
hundred I am the mayor of the City of Chicago. Little-
known fact: George actually did grow up picking cot-
ton in Mississippi, and wanted desperately to play pro
baseball so he could take care of his mother. Also in the
stands today, and hanging around the field afterwards, is
a kid named LaMarr Hoyt. We just got him in a trade
and he's headed to the minors to pitch but there's something about this kid that feels like he's going to be great.
If we could get a real true honest to God ace on the
mound we could take the pennant. I don't think this kid
is going to be ready for another year but you remember
that name, LaMarr Hoyt. Big friendly kid who will pitch
like hell, I think. You should see him staring at the field
like he is hungry for it. Another big old Southern boy like
old George Scott. Finally a clubhouse boy comes to get
LaMarr because he is going to miss the bus to the minors
and that will wrap up today's broadcast, gentlemen. I am
sure I speak for all of us when I say Edward is in our
prayers," and we all got up quietly. Mr Pawlowsky was
asleep under his blanket. The detective gently closed the
window and I knelt down and made sure Edward was still
breathing and then we all left, quiet as altar boys.

The next day on my way to work I got a copy of the
Sun-Times newspaper and indeed the White Sox had

beaten the Red Sox 5–2, before a packed house, with Richie Zisk throwing out a lumbering George Scott at third base. I never did figure out how the detective did what he did. Months later the man who had raised cheetahs said to me that he thought the detective had heard a radio or television broadcasting the game faintly through the walls or the window, maybe that's why he wanted the window open so he could hear it better, but neither Mrs Manfredi in 4C or Azad and Eren and their parents in 4A had a television, and I had been sitting closest to the window and never heard a radio. To this day it is a mystery. LaMarr Hoyt, by the way, threw his first pitches for the White Sox two years later, and went on to become the best pitcher in the league for two years. For years every time I saw his name in the box score, or Oscar Gamble's, or Richie Zisk's, I would suddenly be back in Mr Pawlowsky's apartment, staring at Edward deathly ill and terribly still under his blankets, listening to the quiet detective tell us the opening game of the season.

12.

SOMETIMES, EVEN NOW, years later and far away, on steel-gray days when the wind whips and I am near large waters, I feel a bolt of what I can only call Chicagoness, and I remember, I remember . . . what? A certain Chicago of the mind, I suppose. And sometimes then I sit by a fire and remember aloud—to an understanding friend in a pub, maybe, or to my children, when they were young and liked to hear stories of my unimaginable past, or to the woman who married me, who knows that we are made of many moments, some fleeting and some scraps and shards and tatters of dreams.

So I talk about the way buildings crowded the streets in Chicago, and the sidewalks were narrow and buckled in the oldest parts of the city, and how stores and shops leaned in eagerly toward the street, almost reaching for their customers. And the swirl of snow along the lake, eddying and whirling and composing drifts deep enough to hide a horse. And the way the cops and the hookers and the gangsters and the shadow-men, as Mr Pawlowsky called the denizens of the alleys selling drugs and lust, all knew each other and communicated in nods and codes

and gestures and the deft signals of their vocations and
avocations. And the bone-chilling cold, and shuffle of
boots leery and weary of ice, and the groan and sigh of
buses coming to a stop, and the whir and whine of evening traffic along Lake Shore Drive, and the roar of the
bitter frozen crowd at a Bears game, and the smell of
sausages and kielbasa and onions and beer at games and
carnivals and festivals and street fairs, and the growl of
the blues in the murk of the clubs, and the rattle of pad-
locks on whole streets of fenced-off abandoned houses
on the South Side, and the sight of whole huddles of
morning commuters in vast parkas at train stations, looking like so many brightly colored bears clustered for
warmth on the merciless tundra. The vault and soar of
skyscrapers downtown in the Loop, and the smell of
urine and asphalt in the alleys among them; the shriek
of trains leaning into the curves of elevated tracks near
Wabash and Wacker; the red kiosks for the *Sun-Times* and
blue for the *Tribune*; the infinitesimal sneer of elderly
white waiters in the oldest hotels as black couples arrived
for their dinner reservations; the relentless river of corruption and payola, bribes and payoffs, quid pro quo and
secret deals, hush money and baksheesh, zoning amaze-
ments and construction chaos, union violence and alder-
manic greed, mayoral games and senatorial sin, filling the
air everywhere you turned; and one thing I remember
with amazement about Chicago is that everyone knew
everything *before* it was splayed lurid and naked in public;
you never saw a city so filled with knowing as Chicago

then and probably now; but for all the sure knowledge that the mayor was a thief of epic proportion and the state senator on the take, the police commissioner a thug and the cardinal a man with a mistress, I do not remember that anyone was in the least resigned or cowed; it was more like you knew the score and worked around it, you assumed the worst but sought out and esteemed the best where you found it; and that was, as far as I could tell, on your street, in your neighborhood, among the shopkeepers and cops and nuns and bus drivers and carpenters and teachers who composed the small vibrant villages that collectively were the real Chicago.

Perhaps this is true of every city, but it was certainly true of mine then, that what the world saw—the throbbing commerce of downtown, the legendary professional sports teams, the beginning-to-be-famous comedy and theater troupes, the renowned restaurants, the notable universities, the glittering stars of music and literature—was not at all the real city, and was only the thinnest of gloss and sheen on a rough grace that was the actual bone and music of the place. I suppose that is what I try to talk about, when I sit by the fire and talk about swirling snow, and patient policemen, and tough small smiling nuns, and the smell of roasting lamb and garlic around the corner, and the rumble and thrum of the lake at night, and the grumble of buses, and Edward and Mr Pawlowsky, for those were the things and the souls I found and savored, when I was a young man long ago, in Chicago.

★

Edward recovered. It happened this way. On the day after the White Sox beat the Red Sox to open their home season, the sixth day of Edward's terrible illness, the alewife run began in the lake. It began before dawn on the thirteenth of April and continued all day and all the next day as countless thousands of small gleaming fish approached the shore from the deepest parts of the lake where they huddled in winter. Once they were in warmer shallow water the female alewives released their eggs beyond counting and the male alewives loosed their seed beyond numbering and some eggs were fertilized and many were not and many sank into the depths to be eaten by other beings or to huddle in protected spots on the bottom and grow unto maturity and also someday rise and spawn anew. So many alewives were thrashing in the shallows and spawning and dying that they attracted a tremendous army of predators among them gulls and crows and cormorants and jays and larger fish of every kind and human beings, and along the shore of the lake there was a surge and whirl of life and death beyond my capacity to tell. People ran down the street carrying clanking buckets and old nets and nets made out of window screens. One man ran down the street pushing a wheelbarrow with a snow shovel poking up out of the barrow like a strange sail. A woman ran down the street in a yellow rain slicker and yellow rain boots carrying a laundry bag on which was stenciled PROPERTY OF COOK COUNTY JAIL.

It was the shrieking of gulls at dawn that caught Mr

Pawlowsky's ear, he said later; he recognized the mania-
cal thrill, the call to arms, the summoning of the troops,
the trumpeting of silvery meat beyond measure; and he
leapt out of bed and dressed in his oldest raggiest clothes
and ran downstairs to Miss Elminides' door, and tapped
very gently, and when she opened the door, knowing his
knock, he said the run! the run! He leapt back up the
stairs and picked up Edward and wrapped him in a Navy
blanket and went downstairs and when he got to the
lobby Miss Elminides was there with two nets and two
big white plastic buckets. "She was all in black, with a
watch cap pulled down over her eyes," Mr Pawlowsky
said later, "and for a moment I thought I was back in the
Navy on some sort of clandestine operation, and then for
another moment I thought I was going to faint because
she looked so beautiful and mysterious, but then I got a
grip and we ran down the street. It was too early for real
traffic so we got across Lake Shore easily and climbed
over the seawall. Miss Elminides held Edward for a moment while I got the nets and buckets ready and then she
handed him down to me and I carried him to the water.
There was no one else there. It was just after dawn, you
know, when the sun doesn't have any gas in it yet. There
was no wind and the lake would have been still as a pond
except for the incredible turmoil in the shallows. Maybe
this was a regular run but I have never seen so many fish
at once and I think this might have been a record run
but who keeps records of that? I stood there with Edward in my arms and he heard the thrash of fish and he

opened his left eye. Miss Elminides said something gentle to him and he opened his other eye. Then I just walked into the water with him. I didn't think about how cold the water would be or how I should have by God worn waders or anything like that. It just seemed like the right thing to do so I did it. I got about waist deep and the fish were everywhere around us paying no attention to us at all. I bent my knees a little and tried to hold Edward as close to the water as I could without him getting soaked and the fish were zooming and swirling right in front of his nose and then he moved his head. That was the first time he had moved a muscle in days. Then he opened his mouth and by God a fish jumped right into his mouth and he sort of shivered and then he started snapping left and right for them and Miss Elminides made a sound behind me on the beach and I don't know if she was laughing or crying. After that Edward was fine. I bet he ate fifty alewives in fifteen minutes and when I carried him back to the beach he felt a little bit heavier. We wrapped him up in another blanket and Miss Elminides sat with him while I harvested as many fish as we could carry and then we staggered back up to the building with the buckets. By then the sun had some heat in it and it turned out to be a really beautiful day and Edward was on his way back. He was thin and shaky for another week or so but after eating the rest of the fish he was pretty much himself again. Great day. Miss Elminides and I had two fish each that morning, with eggs and toast and cups of coffee, but we gave all the rest to Edward. *Great* day."

★

I didn't spend *all* my time in the apartment building or at work downtown at the magazine or playing basketball with the Latin Kings and the Latin Eagles or rambling about the city chasing blues and jazz in dark cool small obscure shabby clubs; I did actually pursue romance, to a minimal degree, though I was shy and unprepossessing physically and generally penniless, and I suppose I should be honest about those misadventures, for one of them would eventually lead me away from Chicago, never to return as a resident, though the city has stayed resident in me.

I mooned ineffectually after two young women in the magazine office, one in circulation and one in the mail room, though to neither did I speak a word, content only to glance and dream, imagine and speculate; and now that I am older I think we do not celebrate silent mooning enough, or see it for the essentially healthy imaginative apprenticeship it is; for every young man, and I would guess every young woman too, lives many secret lives between the ages of fifteen and thirty, and only slightly fewer thereafter, no matter your age and stage; and maybe that is healthy and nutritious, that we savor and appreciate the idiosyncratic charm and unique energy of people we meet, while knowing full well we will never ask them out, or make love to them, or even speak to them, or do more than observe and savor and appreciate their charism, and admire its existence, much as you would celebrate the accomplishments of a fine athlete or superb musician from afar, though you will never have even the briefest of acquaintances; or maybe I am rationalizing furiously here, to fend off the all-too-accurate charge that a man with any shred of courage would have struck up a conversation with Maria in the mail room and Clarissa in circulation, and at the least afforded the young woman in question the small pleasure of knowing she was held in high esteem by even such a being as myself.

But I did not.

Also I mooned after the extraordinary creature who ran the register at the gyro shop on Broadway on weekend afternoons. Her name was Leah, although the old man slicing lamb for gyros called her Hypatia for some reason; she was the loveliest dark-haired dark-eyed lean gentle silent glorious female being I had ever seen then, but she was also seventeen years old, and I was five years older, and five years between ages when you are young is twenty years between ages when you are older; why is that, that a man of fifty might easily woo and wed a woman of thirty, but a man of twenty-two, gazing raptly at a stunning Greek girl of seventeen, soon finds himself being glared at by a stern man with a huge knife? Why is that?

Also I mooned after a young woman on the Sound Asleep Bus, the dawn bus driven by Donald B. Morris, although in all the time I rode the Sound Asleep Bus she never once was awake, but slept soundly in her long camel coat the color of fawns, with her brown cashmere scarf and her long brown boots and long brown hair and long brown eyelashes closed firmly over what I could only imagine were lovely liquid brown eyes; but she boarded the bus before me in the morning and I left before she did, and for some strange reason I never did wait there by the Picasso statue on Dearborn Street to see her disembark, let alone greet her with a smile, or offer to buy her a cup of coffee, or just walk alongside her, bantering wittily, as she walked to work in those beautiful brown boots.

I did not.

The occasional riveting woman in a jazz club, sitting alone and mysterious; the occasional woman on the train, glancing at me curiously just as I glanced at her; the woman who stopped to watch a basketball game in which I was playing; that sweet soul picked up a loose ball that had rolled to her feet, and held it for me as I jogged over, and handed it to me with the most brilliant shocking sudden sidelong smile, which rattled me so that I was terrible the rest of the game, and was roundly chastised for poor play by the captain of my team afterward, the quiet slip of a boy called Bucket with tattoos and earrings, who hardly ever spoke, although he did that time, to the amusement of the other players; and by the time I looked up, after apologizing to Bucket for being so distracted, she was gone.

But I did meet a woman that year, and a portentous

meeting it turned out to be, for finally she was the reason I drove away from Chicago one crisp cold sunny morning, deeply excited and deeply saddened at once.

I met her on the train; she was returning to the college I had attended; I was on my way to visit my dear and headlong friends there, for an annual campus basketball tournament in which I would play as a ringer; we struck up a conversation, and exchanged addresses, and sat together for the last hour as the train wound south around the shore of the lake, past steel mills and cornfields; and so began a longer denser conversation that would lead eventually to me resigning from the magazine, and giving up my apartment, and trying not to weep as I sat one last night with Edward and Mr Pawlowsky on the roof, and packing my worn shiny basketball and sneakers and books and few clothes into a borrowed car at dawn, and driving slowly down the street, toward the lake, into the sun, and then south along the lake, and then east to Boston, because she had gone there, and she invited me to be there too.

That we did not last very long as a couple after that is immaterial here; what matters here is that during my time in Chicago I met the reason I would leave it. You cannot edit your life, and even if I was today offered the chance to never meet her, and so not leave the city I loved, I would decline, for life is a verb, life swerves and lurches no matter how cautious and careful your driving, and I would not be who I am, surrounded by those I love most in this world, had I not left Chicago when I did.

Still, though, whenever I remember driving down the street at dawn, toward the lake, into the sun, it makes me sad, for that was the last time I ever saw Edward and Mr Pawlowsky and Miss Elminides, and even then, even so young, even so muddled, I knew a great sweet deep thing was ending that would not come again, not in that way, with those beings; and as I turned south along the lake, the city reflecting the first glare of dawn, I cried. I tried not to cry; crying was uncool; but I could not stop, and I cried all the way through the South Side of the city to where the Calumet River empties into the lake, and Indiana begins.

13.

IT WAS THE DETECTIVE who patiently worked back from the many dark greedy grasping fingers of the Third Awkwardness to its single root, a man named Giannis. It was Giannis whose last known mailing address was the boathouse in Greece, the one with a note pinned fluttering to the old wooden door. It was Giannis whose father had been the sole trustee named to watch over Miss Elminides' trust fund and its attendant titles and fees. It was Giannis whose father had for many years carefully paid every bill and fee and cost having to do with the apartment building and its operation. It was Giannis whose father, while never setting foot once in the United States of America, had paid city and county and state and federal taxes, electricity bills, heating bills, water bills, fees for inspections, and all bills having to do with all the repairs that Mr Pawlowsky had performed in the last six years as building manager. It was Giannis whose father paid Miss Elminides' health care premiums and fees, who established a healthy retirement fund, and who had bought and refurbished the boathouse, on a beach, on the chance that Miss Elminides would prefer ultimately to live in Greece and not in Chicago. It was Giannis whose father had died instantly when struck by a bus in the streets of Alexandroupoli, and Giannis who pawed through his father's papers greedily that night, before his father's attorney came in the morning to put his papers in order, and Giannis who found all the details of the trust, with its meticulously maintained account books and account numbers and codes, and Giannis who in the first few minutes the bank was open the next morning, drained the trust of every penny he could, forging his father's signature to every document possible, a signature he had forged many times before on many checks. It was Giannis who left Miss Elminides' address pinned to the door of the boathouse, right after he ransacked the boathouse for anything he could sell instantly as he made his way east and south across the Hellespont into Turkey. And it was Giannis who crossed the Hellespont by boat that evening just after dusk, not far from where Miss Elminides' grandfather had swum the passage, and once safely in the Turkish city of Çanakkale, found a man who sold him a chunk of hashish the size of a baby's fist. So it was that for the first time that money that was earned by Miss Elminides' grandfather, and saved for her in a form that he thought would be safe forever from predation, did not go to her, but instead went to a sergeant in the Turkish Land Forces, who bought a crib for his new granddaughter, whose name in Turkish was Radiance.

★

We heard all this while sitting on the roof. It was a warm late afternoon. Edward was asleep with a Navy blanket over him. Miss Elminides and Mr Pawlowsky were sitting together in folding lawn chairs. The detective was sitting on the copper coping Mr Pawlowsky had built around the chimney. I was sitting against the wall soaking up the sun. No one spoke for a while and then the detective said he was awfully sorry to be the bearer of such tidings and Miss Elminides stood and shook his hand and said thank you so much for your hard work, Horace. The detective asked after plans for legal redress and restitution, and Miss Elminides said she would have to contemplate things for a while, and the detective said he would be happy to do whatever was required as a gesture of thanks and respect, and Miss Elminides said thank you, Horace, that is most kindly of you, and I am honored. The detective bowed and went downstairs and Miss Elminides sat down in her lawn chair and no one spoke for a moment and then Miss Elminides began to cry quietly and I gathered up Edward and went downstairs. After I tucked him into his bed I thought about reading Lincoln to him for a while but sometimes you can just feel where being kindly slips over into being intrusive and I tucked him in tighter and went down to my apartment and got my basketball and dribbled up along the lakefront for miles. I ended up so far north that I had to catch a bus back home, borrowing the fare from a large man who was amused I was carrying my basketball and who told me he too had been a baller, long ago and far away now, son, but dear Lord your ball has seen some *service*, it's worth the fare to me just to see a ball so shiny with use, yes it is. You can pay me back by taking one hundred shots with your left hand next time you practice. I never did work on my left hand and I surely should have done so. We all be better in life did we use both hands equally, yes we would.

★

Near the end of April it snowed one more time for an hour, just to get the last word in the argument with spring, but it was just a thin scatter of fat flakes, and the snow melted as soon as it touched the ground. After that the weather was instantly summer, and given the warm dry days and lengthening light, I spent many early evenings on the basketball court up the street, the one on the dividing line between the territories of the Latin Kings and the Latin Eagles.

One evening we finished an intense game and there were a few minutes when guys sat around pondering whether to go one more or let it be, and I got to talking to Bucket and Monster. Monster was the muscular rebounding machine who hardly ever spoke and never ever took a play off and set picks firmly but fairly and never ever trash-talked or cursed. Bucket was the slim slight kid with tattoos and earrings who was as quick as a cougar and could score at will although he much preferred to pass and did so with flair and an uncanny knack for angles no one else could see. We were sitting on the asphalt leaning up against the school wall and I mentioned that a friend of mine was in some trouble and could I ask their advice on financial matters?

"We not the best counselors in money matters," said Bucket. "Got to have money to talk money, and I have no money, and Monster have no money. None of us have money. Not My Fault *say* he have money and he wears *chain* like he have money but he have no money. He have *air* for lunch and dinner, that boy, but good luck getting him admit that. His *pride* taller than he is."

I explained that my friend, or properly a friend of a friend, had been thoroughly robbed, and now she was in the hole for many debts.

"Who rob her?"

"A man in another country far away."

"Who own the debt?"

"The City."

They turned to look at each other and Monster shook his head sadly and Bucket said, "Oh man you screwed. City the biggest robber of them all. City reaches for everything it can think of and good luck dodging them bills. They charge you for the air you breathe and the color of your shoes. They charge you for being left-handed and sneezing too loud. Your friend up a creek, man. City never forget, either. And all uniforms work for the City, man. You have a fire in your house and the firemen come they *might* put out the fire if you pay your 'lectricity bill first and deposit down on your water bill. Cash too, with extra for processing charge, you know? Way it is. City is king and king don't play. You can *try* to dodge the City but good luck with that. We had a friend tried to dodge the City and pay no bills and ask no services, and he now in Joliet jail. City did *not* like him trying to duck the game. The City is the man and you must pay the man. You really be a friend to this friend you better find some serious money. Don't even *talk* about talking about it. You got to find *money*. Money is what the City eats and you better feed it or your friend be in Joliet jail too, man. You don't want that. Listen, one more game to fifteen, we got just enough light, us three against Not My Fault and his boys full court, what say, you in?"

★

Miss Elminides was able to hold off the City and the banks during the month of May by draining her own bank accounts and selling her instruments and maps; it turned out that they were far more valuable than anyone knew, some of the instruments made by famous luthiers or previously owned by famous musicians, and some of the maps of substantive historical or artistic value. I learned this from Mr Pawlowsky, who had the impression that the maps and instruments had also been gifts to Miss Elminides from her grandfather, perhaps as quiet hedges against just such a day. She also apparently sold some clothing and some or all of the lean wooden furniture I had noticed in my moment in her apartment; Mr Pawlowsky said her apartment now was filled pretty much with light and nothing else, although if anyone could make rooms of such sparse severity look inviting and graceful it was Miss Elminides.

Also in May another letter came from the City, accusing Mrs Manfredi of running an illicit commercial enterprise in a residential zone, but this effort backfired completely on the City, for Mrs Manfredi was furious, and not only did she storm City Hall with fire and brimstone and bags of redolent empanadas for her alderman and his aides and the new mayor and her aides and the secretaries and photographers and newspapermen covering her attack with great high glee, but she also, in a brilliant stroke, went to a famous *Daily News* columnist, who knew a glorious small-brave-soul-against-greedy-bureaucrats story when he saw one, and wrote a scathing hilarious column that so embarrassed the City that another letter came forthwith, not only withdrawing the charge of illicit commerce but enclosing a check as payment for "procedural errors." Mrs Manfredi, knowing full well that Miss Elminides would not accept the check directly, gave it to Mr Pawlowsky, who would know how to apply it to the Third Awkwardness.

As Edward pointed out later, this episode might well have been the hinge upon which the defeat of the Third Awkwardness swung, for Mrs Manfredi, flush with success and grim in her pursuit of profit as vengeance against the City, then struck a deal with the owner of the gyro shop on Broadway to sell her empanadas daily rather than weekly, and she tripled her production; which elevated spirits in the apartment building, for now the extraordinary scent of her culinary genius wafted up from the basement six days a week, and elevated *my* spirits, for now

I had an excuse to pop into the gyro shop religiously every Saturday and Sunday, ostensibly to buy bags of those magical empanadas but actually to gaze worshipfully upon Leah (or Hypatia), as she rang up purchases, and spoke tartly to her father in Greek, and laughed at sallies issuing from the invisible cook in the kitchen. I cannot remember now if she ever even looked at me, or said anything to me other than *thank you* when I turned to leave the shop, but at that age and stage I was not especially interested in actually getting to know the person, as much as I was interested in worshipping the idea of such grace and loveliness loose in the world, and incarnated in such an extraordinary vessel; it was enough and more than enough for me then to simply say *six empanadas please,* and watch happily as she turned to fill the bag, and then turned back and said *two dollars, sir,* and I would say *these are the greatest things ever baked in the history of food,* and she would smile and not say anything, and I would turn to leave, and she would say *thank you,* and I would say *no, thank you,* and I would walk out onto Broadway filled with joy, and pleased at the state of the world at present; a world which grew even better as I slowly ate the empanadas, savoring every bite, on my way home.

*

The month of May, then, was something of a respite or lull, and Edward, now wholly recovered and nearly manic with unspent energy, decided to show me every single obscure or little-known or essentially unknown cool place in the city of Chicago. We went to the house where Walt Disney was born, on the west side of the city between Blackhawk Park and Mozart Park. We went to the building on Cottage Grove Avenue on the South Side where Chess Records began. We went to DeKoven Street on the South Side, the street where a vast epic awful titanic fire in 1871 burned three square miles of the city and wiped out people and streets and churches and tenements and the Chicago Cubs' first ballpark. We went to the Krause Music Store on Lincoln Avenue, which Edward loved not for the products sold there but for the unbelievably ornate terracotta façade, which indeed was remarkable and something you could gaze at raptly for hours, which we did. We went to the old Peerless Films building on West Argyle Street, where the lady who had lived in 3C, Eugenia, had acted in the Broncho Billy Western movies, and we left a glove from one of her costumes there, as a sort of offering or prayer or memento. We went to the intersection of Michigan Avenue and Wacker Drive, where old Fort Dearborn was, which is where the Potawatomi people who had lived there for thousands of years fought back against the new people who were taking all the land and animals. We went to the Navy Pier so Edward could show me the hut in which the teenage Mr Pawlowsky had clerked during the war. We did not go to any places famous because of criminals like John Dillinger and Al Capone. We did go to Ellis Avenue on the South Side where the first nuclear reaction on earth occurred in a secret chamber under a football field at 3:25 on the afternoon on an autumn day in 1942. We went to the streets where the great musicians Paul Butterfield (south side) and John Prine (west side) and Lee Loughnane (north side) were born; Edward just adored Loughnane's trumpet style. We went to the street where Shel Silverstein was born, on the west side, and to the street where Bob Newhart was born, on the south side, but not to the street where Ernest Hemingway was born, on the south side, because Edward considered Hemingway the sort of writer who was more famous for his escapades than for his work, which was a shame, because he was a very fine short-story writer, and ought to be remembered that way. And we did go to the street where Saul Bellow was raised, on the west side, even though he had been born in Montreal; but still, Edward considered him to be a Chicago man through and through, and so worthy of a visit, much as we journeyed all the way up into the north side to Waukegan to walk on the street where Ray Bradbury had run and laughed as a child; it was Edward's opinion that other than maybe Samuel Clemens of Missouri, there was no finer writer ever born in this country than Ray Douglas Bradbury, who said himself that his whole childhood was running to the library and the lake and the wooded ravine where anything could and did happen, and he learned to "live feverishly," as he said. That trip way up to the north side to walk on Ray Bradbury's street, I remember, was the longest of our adventures, and by the time we got home that night it was long past dark, and Edward was sound asleep next to me on the bus, and I carried him up our street in my arms, marveling at the crystalline stars and the moon as thin as the blade of a knife in the sky.

14.

AT WORK I SPENT MORE and more time with Mr Mahoney for various reasons—he and I were involved in a series of stories reporting on parish life by American regions, trying to piece out how much regional culture affected religious practice, and also he had become my de facto editor for the occasional "think pieces" I was trying to write—and I found myself more absorbed every day by how his exterior belied his interior; how his costume and manner, both austere and gravely polite, were some sort of disguise or jacket or vessel into which the wit and humor and riveting inner life of the man were poured, for reasons of his own; it was almost as if he was so bursting with stories and ideas and energy that he had to carry himself carefully in his dark suits and dark fedora hat and meticulously knotted dark tie and dark shoes, looking more like a funeral director than a journalist, although twice that year, when he had to penetrate cordons of policemen and officious priests and aides-de-camp at gatherings of cardinals and bishops and monsignors, he wore a press pass in his hatband, and suddenly looked as jaunty and confident and comfortable as Ring Lardner at a racetrack.

The more time I spent with him the more I caught the wry amusement and entertainment behind his gravitas, the exuberant youth still capering inside the gaunt pale courteous dignity of the older man; and one by one, as we shared sandwiches in his office, or walked to noon Mass at Assumption Church on Illinois Street, he told me remarkable stories of his adventures. At age twenty he had heard Hitler speak from an upper-storey window in Berlin, to a worshipful crowd in the street; that was the first time, said Mr Mahoney, that he saw how one person could sway others by mere cadence and rhythm. At age thirty-five he had somehow been involved in the war in Burma, although all he would say of that time was that it taught him why poetry mattered. He had been a close companion of Thomas Merton, had corresponded with Flannery O'Connor, and had twice filed lawsuits against the current Archbishop of Chicago, the powerful and vengeful John Patrick Cody, for theft of church property, to wit more than a million dollars of hard-earned donations from the penurious faithful, and for violation of his priestly vows, to wit taking as mistress one Helen Wilson, widow, and lavishing upon her and her children additional funds contributed by the penurious faithful, some of them so poor that they did not have enough food to eat and clothes to wear or money to pay the rent. Neither lawsuit had made it to trial, and both efforts had enraged the Cardinal, who had several times tried to have Mr Mahoney fired from the magazine; but the magazine was run by an independent order of priests who had been in Chicago far longer than the Cardinal, a mere native of Saint Louis, and the order's provincial superior not only ignored the Cardinal's furious commands, but issued Mr Mahoney a raise of two dollars a week, one for each lawsuit filed, to try to reclaim misspent monies that ought to have been spent on the real and crucial work of the church, not burnt to feed one man's towering ego.

★

Near the end of April the White Sox beat the Detroit Tigers and moved into first place by half a game, and the city, which had been cautiously optimistic about the South Siders but all too familiar with vernal promise and autumnal dismay, began to take notice, and trickle into shaggy old Comiskey Park, and turn on radios to catch the games. For the first time I could follow a game simply by walking down a street and catching snippets from radios in shops and apartments, balconies and porches, cars and trucks. Children carried transistor radios with them on their bicycles; bus drivers set their dashboard radios to WMAQ, 670 on your dial; and one generous cop put the game on his loudspeaker as he cruised along Halsted Street one night, the excited voices of Harry Caray and Jimmy Piersall bouncing off buildings like strange gods speaking from above.

I went to a game on the first day of May, a Sunday, with the Trinidadian cricket player in 2E and the Armenian librettist in 4D; the Sox were playing the Texas Rangers, and I wanted to see the Rangers' legendary Gaylord Perry, who threw all sorts of spitballs and balls covered with oil and jelly and hair gel and even, it was rumored, dabs of peanut butter that he kept in his baseball cap. The cricket player, curious about the best bowler in the sport descended from his beloved cricket, had never taken the train to the South Side, and was delighted by the burbling crowd of people in Sox hats and jerseys; it made him nostalgic for the famous Queen's Park Oval in Port of Spain, where he had watched many a match, and played in two regional "Tests," as he said with quiet pride. The librettist I had found in the lobby that morning, as we retrieved our mail, and when I told him we were off to the game in the afternoon he asked if he could come along; he too had never been to a Sox game, in all his years in Chicago, and in fact had never crossed Madison Street, the dividing line between the north and south sides of the city.

The cricketer's name was Denesh, and though we lived in adjacent apartments we had never exchanged more than polite greetings and inquiries about health and weather. On the train, crowded together in a corner, he told me that he was actually from Tobago, the small island north of Trinidad, and that he had grown up on Turtle Beach there, playing cricket in the sand with his friends, using palm splits for bats. He had become so deft with the bat that he was chosen for his school's First Eleven, as he said, the equivalent of the varsity in American sport, and then for the national team. I was impressed at this, though he observed with a smile that his nation in toto comprised two islands which together were far smaller than our United State of Delaware. Still, though, he had played for his national team, and, as he explained, that team chose players not only from Trinidad and Tobago but from many other nearby islands. He had played only a few matches at the top level, he said, still smiling, but no one had worn the maroon kit of the West Indies cricket team with more pride, and also during his time he had the great fortune of seeing the future not only of his team but of the very sport itself—a boy from Antigua named Isaac Vivian Alexander Richards.

"I first saw him when he was fifteen or so," said Denesh. "We played an exhibition match on Antigua, really a glorified training session, and several young Antiguans were invited to play. The atmosphere was loose and friendly, with players chatting with fans even during play. Then this boy came to bat. He was smiling but you could see that he was quite serious in attitude. He walked very slowly, stretching as he came, and our bowler said something teasing to him about wasting time. Instead of settling in to bat, the boy walked a few steps toward our bowler, just staring at him, not saying anything, but fixing him with something very like a glare. I had never seen a young player so self-possessed and sure of himself as this boy. And then his batting was superb, of course. But what I remember still is the joyous swagger of the boy that afternoon; he was completely at home in the game, already a master of its pleasures and intricacies, already confident enough to intimidate an older player just with a stern look. Most amazing. I have had many rich and memorable hours in cricket, but the immediate realization that day that here, in the flesh, just beginning his career, was one of the greatest players who would ever play the game I loved, growing into his manhood right before our eyes—that was wonderful."

★

At the Sox game itself the librettist sat between the cricketer and myself, and as I enjoyed the Sox absolutely hammering Gaylord Perry right from the start (they had eight hits and eight runs in the first inning, including two homers and a triple), I chatted with the librettist, another man I had not really spoken to in my eight months in the apartment building. He was a most dapper man, dressed in a suit and tie and even a vest, though it was a warm afternoon. His mustache was neatly trimmed, he carried his spectacles in a beautiful leather case, and even the pencil he used to write notes during the game was a lovely thing made of some sort of burnished wood, as far as I could tell. He had a small leather-bound notebook, in which he wrote occasionally in a meticulous hand; and it was this notebook that opened the conversational gates between us, for when I asked him what he was writing he explained that he was fascinated by the life and work of the Chicago novelist Harry Mark Petrakis, and that he was at last at work on a libretto about the South Side of Chicago where Harry was raised—a project he had dreamed about for many years, and in which he now found himself utterly absorbed.

"Much of what I need now," he explained, "is actual sensory data, as it were—the sounds and smells and *feeling* of things, from Sunday-morning light on brick walls in his old neighborhood, to the cadence and rhythm of Greek slang, to the angle of sheen from mahogany tables in the library he haunted as a boy; I have many times been in the Blackstone branch of the public library, and handled for myself the same books he read as a child, to feel for myself the heft and zest of them in the hand. Thus the baseball game; Harry was here as a boy, and I do not think much has changed. This week I will be visiting steel mills like the ones where he worked, and Greek Orthodox churches like the one he attended as a boy, and tasting such savories as *koulouria,* which are pastries, and *koufeta,* which are almonds. You must absorb so many smells and tastes and sounds and hints and intimations if you wish to tell a story properly, because words can only catch some of the story, and you must also write the spaces between the words. It is the same with music. The two composers with whom I work agree with me and we soak up as much as we can both before and as we work. In this case we envision an oratorio in which there is such a braid and weave and web and mingle of voices and music and tones that he or she who listens attentively will hear *more* than the words and the music; if we have done our work well, you will hear pain and grace and courage and snow and fistfights and foods and bullets and prayers and laughter and love-making in the dark upstairs. You will hear the neighborhood in which Harry grew up, you will hear his yearning and dreaming, you will hear the fear and rage and joy of the immigrant in Chicago particularly but also to a degree in every city in the world ever since we began to wander into the dark beyond the fire."

Something about his prim eloquence struck me forcibly, and by the fourth inning, by which time the Sox were up 12–2 and Chet Lemon had homered deep to center field, I had talked at length to him about Miss Elminides' travails. He was shocked and alarmed; he had for years admired Miss Elminides for her unfailing kindness during the awkward times when he and others in the building were facing financial difficulties. He sat silent for several innings, writing occasionally in his notebook, while I watched the Sox run out the game, but then just before we stood to leave he closed his notebook and turned to me and said quietly, "Something must be done. We must address this problem collectively. I have some ideas. I will visit Mr Pawlowsky tomorrow. Thank you for telling me about this." On the way home on the train the librettist was again silent, but the Trinidadian cricketer was burbling and verbose about the many juncture points he saw between your American baseball, as he said, and the great and ancient game of cricket. At one stop two young men tried to make fun of him for saying the word *cricket* so often, but he paid no attention to them, and we walked back to the building talking of great cricket bowlers of the past who also used various substances to assist their delivery of the ball, among them chewing gum, mustache wax, lip balm, honey, beeswax, and lard. There was a recurrent story, he said, of an Australian bowler who had mastered the art of using rendered animal fats on his deliveries, but he personally believed this to be airy nonsense, and just the sort of wry tale that the Australians loved to have other cricketers believe, perhaps because it was distracting to their opponents, but perhaps simply because the Australians were a people given to humor and the tall tale, not unlike you Americans.

★

It was that May, when Bucket pointed out an oriole's nest near the basketball court, that I grew interested in the wildlife of Chicago, and I spent many hours and many miles that month wandering the city and paying attention to residents of species other than mine. First I accounted birds, for this was the season of love and birth, and once you have begun noticing nests, I discovered, it is a habit hard to break. Even in my neighborhood, which was about as thoroughly urban as you could get, there were nests everywhere, from the tiny deftly hidden cups of hummingbirds to the big messy leafy condominium-size nests of crows in parks and in the huge old elm trees along the lakefront. I found the sculpted mud nests of swallows, the bedraggled nests of jays and starlings, the artfully camouflaged nests of sparrows in bushes and hedges; I began to notice the nests and bole-holes of woodpeckers; I began to notice hawks and herons and egrets by the lake; twice I saw what I was fairly sure was a falcon of some sort, whirring past so fast all I could clearly identify was speed and intent and a slate-blue color like a line of watercolor paint slashed on the sky.

I noticed rabbit tracks in muddy places after rain, and once found deer tracks near the lake; more than once I saw raccoons and opossums in alleys late at night, on my way home from the blues bars; and once spring was fully sprung the number of blackbirds and warblers and ducks and geese along the lake swelled past all accounting.

It was the ducks that led to my meeting our local beat cop, a burly young guy named Matthew, who turned out to be a wonderfully sharp-eyed observer of all sorts of life along the lake, from salmon and sturgeon, to osprey and owls, from the deer he had twice seen marooned on ice floes to the coyotes he was sure lived in a den somewhere near Dog Beach, to the endless number of riveting human beings with whom he had dealings in a "professional capacity," as he said politely. I was sitting on a bench by the lake one afternoon, drawing flotillas of ducks so I could go to the library and pore over their markings, when Matthew, walking by, stopped to see what I was sketching.

"Those are pintails," he said cheerfully. "See the extended tail feather? That's where the name comes from. Sometimes you can see a tiny bit of green on the back of the necks of the males, just a spot, not *all* green like the mallards. We have widgeon, teal, shovelers, black ducks, and, best of all, wood ducks. You got to keep your eyes peeled for the wood ducks. They are the most beautiful animals in the world. Fact. Also we have canvasbacks, redheads, goldeneyes, and buffleheads. Usually those are a little further out than the others. Also there are snowy owls along the lake if you look carefully. I saw one this winter up at Montrose Beach. Amazing bird. Came floating out of a snowstorm like the snow had made an animal and set it to fly."

Matthew was maybe thirty and had been a street officer, as he said, for two years, mostly in our neighborhood, roughly from Belmont to Addison streets and from the lake to Halsted Street, and while he had ambitions to rise to detective or perhaps gang specialist, when that time came he would miss the intimacy of the street, where he had come to know very nearly all the residents in his area, both human and not, and heard some amazing stories. Some were legends, like the recurrent but debatable sightings of a sturgeon twenty feet long near Belmont Harbor ("there's a lot of people down there who see what they want to see," he said, mysteriously), or the ghostly horse that was said to occasionally appear near the old Majestic Hotel, but others were stories of quiet courage or miracles that he would savor all the rest of his life. In the next few months, as summer simmered and I spent nearly all my time outside, I saw a lot of Matthew (summers were his busy season, he said, and he much preferred to cover his beat on foot rather than in the car), and one story of his above all others stays with me still.

There was a woman, he said, who lost her son when he was five months old. She lived near the Majestic, right by the lakefront. Everyone knew and liked her—she was one of those gentle engaging people with a great honest smile who when you saw her smile *you* couldn't help but smile, that sort of person. Everyone was thrilled when she had her baby, and everyone was crushed when the baby died in his crib. After he died she didn't emerge for a while, and then when she did emerge and walk slowly along the lake again, she was silent and dark, and no one could cut through to who she used to be, not Matthew or her friends or even Edward, for whom Matthew had the greatest respect.

One morning, though, said Matthew, as the woman was walking along the lake, she saw something struggling in the shallows, and she ran down to the beach, and found a baby wriggling and thrashing in the water. She wrapped it in her jacket and carried it back up to the seawall path, and luckily Matthew was driving by, so he drove her and the baby to the hospital. The baby was healthy, no one could find any trace of parents or identification, and the local alderman interceded quietly to allow the woman to adopt the child. During the process of adoption the child, a boy, was cared for by the woman, on the single condition that she check in with Matthew every day about problems, forms, insurance, and other stuff like that. By the time the adoption was officially approved and all forms filed, the boy was a year old, and the neighborhood celebrated his birthday with a picnic on the beach where he had been found. Matthew found a priest to baptize the child, using water from the lake. His mother named the boy Muirin, which means "born of the sea" in Gaelic, and Matthew told me that the boy, suitably enough, was totally absorbed by the lake, and was already a fine fisherman, young as he was.

"I see that kid every other day, I bet," said Matthew, "and you will too, if you keep your eyes peeled. Next time I see him I will point him out."

15.

MR MCGINTY, IN 2C BY THE BACK alley door, was a horse-racing fan of the first order, and he went around the building the week before the Kentucky Derby collecting bets. There were fifteen horses in the race and each apartment could choose any horse except the great Seattle Slew, who was reserved for Miss Elminides. The race was as always on the first Saturday of May and all bets and side bets had to be in to Mr McGinty by noon of the day of the race. The minimum bet to get into the pool was ten dollars, and doubling and tripling your bet was "heartily encouraged," as Mr McGinty said politely but sternly.

I knew nothing of racing and betting, and as usual I went to Edward for elucidation on the matter, and as usual I learned a great deal about a great many matters. It turned out that Mr McGinty was from Kentucky and knew horses and racing and betting intimately and thoroughly. It turned out that Mr McGinty had for many years made a rich living simply from betting on horse races at Arlington Park, on the northwest outskirts of the city. It turned out that Mr McGinty had been investigated unsuccessfully by various legal entities interested in the stunning consistency of his winnings over many years; he had never had a losing week, in more than forty years, and for nearly half of those years he was the single most successful single bettor at the track. The secret to his system, as he had explained again and again in depositions and to friends like Edward, was careful reinvestment of initial winnings; he would win the first race, and then happily play parlays, quinellas, exactas, and trifectas the rest of the day. He rather enjoyed the complicated mathematics of betting, considered himself conservative in tenor (for example he hardly ever picked a horse to win, and most often placed bets on horses to show, which is to say to finish among the top three in a race), and was of an arithmetical cast of mind and could calculate odds and probabilities with startling speed, a skill he proved to one detective with such amazing results that the detective later wrote a scholarly article about the experiment for a professional journal.

His increasing age, however, had eventually made it impossible for him to get to the track every day, and while he read a plethora of racing periodicals, he now reserved serious betting only for big races, for which he would prepare for weeks, and then use Edward as a runner to a friend who called in bets for him at the track. In this way Edward too had become interested in and astute at handicapping, and he and Mr McGinty had even discussed maybe going into business together on a racehorse, although nothing had been decided as yet.

What with Eugenia the actress's death, Miss Elminides unaware of Seattle Slew being reserved for her, and Ovious and his mother abstaining from betting for reasons of their own, the fifteen horses in the race were assigned by Wednesday night, and Mr Pawlowsky posted the chart in the lobby, complete with colored silks and a brief racing and genealogical history of each horse. I was away from the building Thursday and Friday, on magazine business, but Denesh the cricket player told me both nights had been busy with additional bets, and people stopping in to consult Mr McGinty about complicated parlays, and even an enticing offer by the apartments on the third floor to buy out the horses of the second floor, which was overruled by Mr McGinty after spirited discussion.

I got back to the apartment building on Saturday afternoon, just in time for the race, and I found almost everyone in the building crowded into Mr McGinty's apartment, staring at the television, laughing and chaffing and making last-minute bets, with Edward and one of the hermits on the third floor serving as bookmakers. I was startled to see one of the hermits but it seemed to me that people were carefully not saying anything so I didn't say anything. Mr McGinty hushed the assemblage as the horses went to the post, and there was a fraught silence as the gates opened and the horses burst into the sunlight.

Seattle Slew, the favorite, got off to a slow start, but quickly slid up the rail into second place, and for what seemed like forever ran neck-and-neck with another black horse called For the Moment, ridden by the famous jockey Angel Cordero; I remembered Mr McGinty saying that the one jockey who worried him in this race was Cordero, who was a magician and could get any horse to do whatever he wanted at any time. For the Moment was the librettist's horse, and I noticed him in the corner, leaning over the shoulder of little Azad, who was standing on Mr McGinty's night table. No one spoke but there was a sort of low nervous hum as everyone leaned in toward the little black-and-white television. For the Moment stayed in front by a hair until the final turn, when Seattle Slew eased powerfully away and held off a knot of late-charging horses; at the finish it was Seattle Slew by two lengths, with Run Dusty Run in second and Sanhedrin third.

There was a great burst of exultation and laughter, and I stood by the door watching with pleasure, for this was the first time I had seen almost all of the building's residents together, and it was entertaining to watch everyone congratulating Azad, who was beaming with joy at his winnings (he had earned thirty dollars, which he said he and his sister Eren were going to present to their mother). One of the dapper businessmen in 3B had won with Sanhedrin, and as soon as he was presented with his winnings—nearly three hundred dollars, the result of a complicated parlay—he turned and ceremoniously handed it to Mr Pawlowsky, saying that every one of us felt the same way, that we would do whatever we could to assist Miss Elminides in her time of trouble, and here was the first of what he hoped would be many votes of confidence and gestures of gratitude from the residents, who collectively considered Miss Elminides not only a friend but a grace and a gift in this world. There was the briefest of pauses, as I remember, and Mr Pawlowsky stood still for an instant before accepting the money; and then there was a round of applause, and everyone shook hands and clapped Azad on the shoulder as he ran for the stairs clutching his money, and then we went back to our apartments.

Not until two days later did I learn from Edward that half the building had not only laid bets on their own horses but quietly contributed hundreds of dollars more to the bets Mr McGinty had made on Seattle Slew on Miss Elminides' behalf—bets which had earned many thousands of dollars, which also had gone to Mr Pawlowsky for the cause. According to Edward, Mr McGinty had studied this race more closely than any other single race of his career, and had concluded that not only would Seattle Slew win, but that Run Dusty Run would finish at least third, and a horse called Get the Axe would finish fourth; he had laid his bets accordingly, investing every dollar in the building, and the payout was, in short, incredible. About a week later I encountered Mr McGinty at the mailboxes and thanked him for his astonishing work, and he laughed and said if he was really any kind of a good horseplayer he would have guessed that Sanhedrin would finish higher, given that Jorge Velásquez was aboard, and that he had learned his lesson, and would never underestimate Jorge Velásquez again, and in fact would lay serious coin on Jorge next year, if the Lord saw fit to allow him, Daniel Paul McGinty, to remain on earth for one more year, which he surely hoped He would, for there were two extraordinary horses coming of age next year, by the names of Affirmed and Alydar, and in his estimation they were exactly equal in every respect, and their races would be remembered as long as horses raced and people cared about the results.

*

May was an excellent time to observe constellations in the Chicago sky at night, what with the snow gone and the spring rain receding a bit, and I went up on the roof one clear night about the middle of the month with Edward and Mr Pawlowsky, and savored a conversation I remember to this day, especially when I hear inane chatter about cities and their disparate characters.

It was a cold night and we were all bundled up, Edward in a Navy blanket, and for a while we charted what we could see easily in the sky: Hercules, Scorpius, Lupus, and Serpens, the snake, "in which the brightest star is Unukalhai, the heart of the serpent—isn't that a great name?" said Mr Pawlowsky, who also observed that he had a special affection for Serpens because there had been a Navy cargo ship in the war called the *Serpens,* and it had done good work before being blown to bits in the Solomon Islands, with everyone aboard, sad to say, including a boy with whom he had gone to school, a reed of a boy whose dream was to be a priest.

"This reminds me," said Mr Pawlowsky, "that you and I might go by the convent this Saturday and help out the sisters. There's a good deal of basic repair work that needs doing and Edward and I thought we might recruit you as stevedore and young muscle. The reward is lunch from the gyro shop. A few of the neighbors are chipping in quietly to be of some assistance to the sisters. Their numbers are declining and there's no young muscle and you never met a kinder gentler bunch of women in your life. I am not religious but if I was *going* to join a religion I would go Catholic just because of those sisters. If they are examples of religious principles in action then the Catholic church is going in the right direction. Edward believes that all religions are cousins at heart and begin in the right spirit but then they are corrupted by the desire for power. This is a shorthand view of religious history but he certainly has a point. Name me one religion that stays true to its founding principles and doesn't get distracted by real estate and money and political or military adventures. You cannot; and no one can, which is ultimately sad, not to mention damning as regards the integrity of religions."

This line of talk led to discussion of cities like Jerusalem and Mecca and Dharamsala and Rome, in which religions played a huge part in the life of the place, either as keystones of founding tales or destinations for hejira or as administrative headquarters, and Mr Pawlowsky said along these lines he was proud of Chicago for two reasons, one being that Chicago was home to the world's oldest temple of the Bahá'í religion, which was on the far north side of the city and was a lovely place altogether, right on the lake; and also that in Chicago all sorts of religions existed together relatively peacefully, without the usual brawls among faiths, and bloody arguments about who knew God better than whom. "You could not get a better example of irony than religions in general," said Mr Pawlowsky, "as each one makes some claim to understand and interpret a Force that no one understands at all, which is why I do not belong to a religion, although Edward attends services regularly, all different flavors. The fact is that he has more of a questing intelligence than I do, and I give him a lot of credit for being open-minded. At the moment he is Presbyterian, I believe, because Lincoln attended Presbyterian services while president. This reminds me of the story of Lincoln at a revival meeting, when the preacher asked those who expected to go to heaven to stand, and then those who expected to go to hell. Lincoln stood for neither option, and when asked about it, said politely that he intended to go to Congress."

I laughed at this, and I could hear Edward snickering, but Mr Pawlowsky was now well and truly launched, and off he went deeper into the nature of cities. "What is it that sets cities apart, that gives them their particular flavors and idiosyncratic characters?" he asked. "Well, there is weather, landscape, topography, geology—the accident of location, so to speak, although no city arises by accident. Almost always a city grows up where trade and commerce can navigate and flow; so most cities are on rivers and lakes and seas and shores. Chicago, for example, where rivers flow into the lake, and the lake thankfully having access eventually to the ocean. But then also there are foods, music, languages, sports, and common myths. Cities are places of concentrated myth, it seems to me. And the myths that develop often have to do with the industries and styles of commerce by which the city earned its bread. So that Chicago, with shipping and steel and livestock, came to think of itself as a burly city, tough and muscular, with rough-and-tumble football and politics and literature. Today of course we are a city of offices and whirring computers and financial shenanigans, but our founding myths remain. I would guess not one in ten Chicagoans has ever seen a real fight where the antagonists are trying to slice each other's throats, but we airily say we are a tough city, nor have they seen a pig or a soybean plant, but we proudly say we characterize and epitomize the rural values of middle America."

Sometimes Mr Pawlowsky had a tendency to soar a bit, when he was in full oratorical mode, and Edward had taught me how to arrest the flight with a direct question, so I asked him four direct questions: What is Chicagoness? What is the city made of? Why is it different from any other city? What are the things that are here and only here and compose the here of here?

He leaned back in his lawn chair and thought a bit and then he said, "The prevalence of the lake. The way the lake is a sea and not a lake. The way the lake shoulders the city. The cutting of wind off the lake and the whirl of snow. Electrified blues developed by men and women who came up here from the Deep South and knew much about patience and endurance and hope. Our alleys which are another sort of road or path unlike in other cities where they are garbage dumps. South Side jazz. Gyros—we have perfected the gyro, and not even Greece has better gyros than we do. A certain blunt amused attitude. . . ." He paused a minute and looked at Edward. "Think of Chicago as a piece of music, perhaps," he continued. "In it you can hear the thousands of years of people living here and fishing and hunting, and then bullets and axes, and the whine of machinery, and the bellowing of cattle, and the shriek of railroads, and the thud of fists and staves and crowbars, and a hundred languages, a thousand dialects. And the murmur of the lake like a basso undertone. Ships and storms, snow and fire. To the north the vast dark forests, and everywhere else around the city rolling fields of farms, and all roads leading to Chicago, which rises from the plains like Oz, glowing with light and fire at night, drawing people to it from around the world. A roaring city, gunfire and applause and thunder. Gleaming but made of bone and stone. Bitter cold and melting hot and clotheslines hung in the alleys and porches like the webbing of countless spiders. A city without illusions but with vaulting imaginations and expectations. A city of burning energies on the shore of a huge northern sea. An *American* city, with all the violence and humor and grace and greed of this particular powerful adolescent country. Perhaps *the* American city—no other city in the nation is as big and central and grown up from the very soil. Chicago was never ruled by Spain or England or France or Russia or Texas, it shares no ocean with other countries, it is no mere regional captain, like Cincinnati or Nashville; it is *itself,* all brawn and greed and song, brilliant and venal, almost a small nation, sprawling and vulgar and foul and beautiful, cold and cruel and wonderful. Its music is the blues, of course. Sad and uplifting at once, elevating and haunting at the same time. You sing so that you do not weep. You have no choice but to sing. So you raise up your voice and sing of love and woe, and soon another voice joins in, and you sing together, for a while, for a time, perhaps a brief time, but perhaps not. . . ."

His voice trailed off and again he sat silently. Edward got up and ambled over to him, bringing the blanket, and they sat together for a while. I offered to go get some tea but they declined and I got the hint and went downstairs and went to bed.

*

All through May the White Sox battled to stay near the top of the American League West, and slowly the attendance rose as wary fans, long inured to early-season fireworks followed by mid-season collapses, began to cautiously trust the South Side Hit Men, as they were now being called, for their unearthly slugging—Jim Spencer drove in eight runs in one game, and Richie Zisk hit a ball deep into the center-field bleachers on May 22, the longest home run anyone could remember at Comiskey. I was at that game with Denesh and little Azad, who had never seen a baseball game before, and who was intimidated by the press of the crowd until the boy next to him, a boy of nine or ten who had come all the way up from southern Illinois for the game, made a concerted effort to be friendly and explain things. I was much impressed with this child's empathy, and for some reason remember his name: Jeffrey Tweedy, who later became a musician, I understand. Azad was crushed when the Sox lost to the Tigers, although Denesh was thrilled at watching Sox pitcher Wilbur Wood, who threw soft knuckleballs that Denesh said would be called "googlies" in cricket—a word Azad and I repeated with high glee all the way home.

The apartment building was also curiously filled with energy and anticipation that month, and Edward and I began to chart the various projects and ideas and conspiracies being hatched to assist Miss Elminides with finishing off the Third Awkwardness once and for all. Mrs Manfredi continued to inch up her production of empanadas, and expand her distribution network, helped greatly by a glowing review in the *Chicago Reader* newspaper. The dapper businessmen in 3A and 3B, predicting a tremendous rise in the neighborhood's gay and lesbian population in the years to come, opened a curious

store that sold clothing, scents and spices, lovely tiny silver earrings, tasteful tattoos done by a slender man
from Liberia, and dashing shoes and boots. The Scottish
tailor who lived across the hall from me with the detective donated every Wednesday's profits from his work to
Mr Pawlowsky, "*Adhbhar,* for the cause," as he said. The
hermit brother in 3D, delighted by his winnings on Kentucky Derby day, began to play the horses steadily and
successfully, with Mr McGinty's guidance, and even once
went out to Arlington Park with his brother in 3E,
although they took separate trains there and back. The
two young women from Arkansas in 4E arranged and
conducted a ten-kilometer charity run along the lake,
advertising it in support of Greek independence from
tyranny, which was technically accurate, said the former
sailor in the basement, who worked the event as security. The man who once had raised cheetahs, about whom
I never discovered anything else, despite the fact that
he lived two doors down from me in 2D for more than
a year, walked into Mr Pawlowsky's apartment one evening, and handed him a roll of hundred-dollar bills—
two thousand dollars in all. According to Edward the
money had come from the sale of "assets," the cheetah
man had said, which Edward found fascinating—did
that mean he owned cheetahs elsewhere, or had percent-
ages in racing cheetahs, or leased cheetahs to zoos, or
had some relationship with cheetahs in the wild such
that he could draw on a standing account? That which
we do not know will always outweigh that which we

do know or think we know, as Mr Pawlowsky once said, while discussing religions.

It was inconceivable that Miss Elminides was unaware of the burble of activity in the building, but if anything she became even more remote, and I saw her only once in the month of May—a meeting I remember vividly to this day, for it was the first time we spoke at some length, and the first time I got a sense of her past and personality. Curiously our conversation was not in the building but out by the lake, where I found her sitting on the seawall staring out at the darkening water late one afternoon. I ran right past her, dribbling my basketball, intent on working on my weak (left) hand, and it was another minute or so before I registered that the quiet dark-haired woman with her knees drawn up under her chin was my landlady.

Most of me instantly wanted to keep going, and dribble faster, and avoid the moment, for I was shy and uncertain with women in general, and not at all confident that I could be discreet and not mention the seethe of projects among the building's residents, but I was also as curious then as I am now about people—my greatest virtue, I suppose, except when it is a vice. Anyway I spun around and walked back to her, not dribbling, and asked if I might sit a moment and chat, and she said yes of course please do, and I joined her on the wall.

She said that she liked to watch the lake especially in the evening, as it reminded her powerfully of the sea. Even when she was young, she said, she was convinced that what people called the Aegean and Ionian and Mediterranean seas were all fingers of the great ocean, and that there was in the end one vast ocean that was the true earth, with islands small and huge as its guests, or passengers, or interlopers; maybe landforms are merely suffered temporarily by the ocean, which will eventually whelm them, she said. Even the lake before us, she thought, was in truth an extended finger of this great ocean, which is why it had tides, as it rose and fell in rhythms originating with the ocean, which itself yearned for the moon.

Even then, in my first year as a journalist, I had already learned the cardinal rules of my profession, which are to ask questions and then listen intently without interrupting; people will talk freely and surprisingly honestly if you give them a chance, an opening, a window, a genuinely interested ear, and I was *very* interested, partly because Miss Elminides was such a mystery to us all, and partly because I had such respect for Mr Pawlowsky, and admired him and wished him well, and knew of his feelings for Miss Elminides; and I suppose I thought that perhaps, if I listened carefully, I might glean something that would somehow inch them closer together. Not that I was any kind of matchmaker, but I was even then beginning to sense that stories were the true seeds of relationships, and that romance and friendship were as much a matter of shared stories as pheromones, or overlapping interests.

So she talked, and I listened, and here and there when

she paused overlong I asked a question, and she relaxed, and talked about growing up on a beach in Greece, with her grandparents (she never did mention her parents), and the foods she loved as a child, and the pet fox she had for years, and her grandmother's stories of spirits and angels everywhere around them, and her grandfather's stories of Chicago, the greatest city in the greatest country in the world, the city where someday she could live if all went well and she did well in school, and the little fishing boat her grandfather used, and the songs the neighbors sang every Thursday, a holy day for them (she did not know their religion, but it had something to do with Thursday being a holy day, on which they fasted until dark, and then feasted). She talked about the school she attended, and the other children of all sorts and shapes and predilections, including one boy who thought he was an owl, and was later institutionalized; and her first suitor, a boy who taught her to read maps and charts; and a girl who fell in love with her, and on finding her love unreciprocated, shaved off all her hair and locked herself in a church for two days. She talked a lot about her grandfather, who had sheaves of poems given to him by his friend the poet Konstantinos Kavafis, and her grandmother, whose death, when Miss Elminides had just turned twenty, was the proximate cause of her granddaughter coming to America.

I think I will remember that story all the rest of my life, in part because night had fallen and I could hardly see

Miss Elminides' face, so that her voice came gently out of the dark, disembodied; and because I think she had almost forgotten that I was there, and was telling the story to herself, in a sense, perhaps to better understand it.

The grandmother had failed slowly, eaten by some secret interior disease, so that she shrank day by day; she never seemed in any pain, said Miss Elminides, but she did seem mournful, for there was never anyone who loved being alive and talking to spirits and angels and laughing and cooking and eating and singing more than Grandmother did. When she died I was on one side of the bed and Grandfather was on the other. We each held a hand. When she died you could see the spirit go out of her body. My grandfather left a window open so her spirit could go home to the ocean. A few days later we packed up my things and he took me to the ship and I came to America. He said it would be wrong to fly in an airplane and I had to come by sea. He said that Grandmother's death was the end of the first part of my life and now it was time for me to begin the second part, in Chicago, and that once I knew what the second part would be, I would also know the third and final part. He said that all lives are lived in three parts like that. He said that the best part of his life, the second part, was his twenty years with me and Grandmother in the little house on the beach, and that now he had to go live his own third part. He said that he personally would love to live the third part of his life with me, as I lived my second part, but that this would be wrong, and he and Grandmother had talked about it and come to an agreement, and he would honor that agreement, although his sadness at our parting was greater than the great ocean itself. He said that he and Grandmother had provided for me such that I would be able to live safely in Chicago, and that once I was established there, in lodgings he had arranged and secured, I would be able to find the work I was to do, and grow into the woman I was to be, and he knew in his heart, as he and Grandmother had discussed, that I would be an extraordinary person, famous not for the things of small accomplishment like money or beauty, but for generosity of spirit, which would be as a sun to those around me, and provide light and hope to those who were in darkness, and lift many hearts that were heavy.

I remember the lapping of small waves in the lake, and the whistle and boom of nighthawks diving for insects, and the swirl and splash of a large fish in the shallows, as we sat there silent for a while, after she finished; I knew enough not to ask any more questions, and finally she said that she must be getting back to the building, as she had to be up quite early the next morning; I mumbled something like thanks and she said thank you for listening, heaven alone knows why all *that* came tumbling out, and she walked back home. I waited a couple of minutes to give her some privacy and then followed, not dribbling; somehow it didn't seem right to dribble in the street at night, even under the dim streetlamps. When I got home I thought about going up to see Edward and Mr Pawlowsky but somehow I didn't feel like talking, and later when I went to bed I remember dreaming about beaches and owls and rustling sheaves of poems.

16

LATE THAT MAY I WENT OUT on the lake for the first time, and it happened like this. It turned out that Mr Pawlowsky and the former sailor in the basement had long talked about going into business together as a salvage concern, to locate and reclaim various treasures at the bottom of the lake; what with Mr Pawlowsky's naval experience and connections, and the sailor's knowledge of the lake's weathers and currents, they were convinced they could choose a few wrecks, locate and raise them without fanfare, and sell what was recoverable to collectors and museums and historical societies. The law allowed any licensed concern to salvage and sell what it could of long-lost shipping, and while the sailor, a student of lost Lake Michigan ferryboats and steamers, had a couple of legendary vessels in mind, Mr Pawlowsky was set on recovering an airplane that the Navy had lost in the lake in 1943—a Wildcat, a fighter jet that had crashed on a training flight and sunk without a trace. The pilot had escaped, but the location of the plane had never been recorded, and the Navy, desperately trying to win two wars abroad, had never taken the time to find or recover the craft. Mr Pawlowsky, however, had known both the pilot and the men who fished him out of the lake, and he had never forgotten their estimates of where the plane went down, and where it might yet be found.

He explained all this to me one glorious sunny morning as we walked down to Belmont Harbor, a little south along the lakefront, where the sailor was waiting in what looked exactly like a whaleboat, "because it *is* a whaleboat," explained the sailor, who had borrowed it from a friend who ran a school for building wooden boats. I had never been farther into the lake than my knees before, and as we slid out of the little hooked harbor and into the lake proper I saw that Miss Elminides was right to be reminded of the sea; the lake stretched away endlessly in every direction, and the city shrank so quickly behind us that in minutes it looked like a tiny tourist's postcard, and then it vanished altogether, and we were alone on an immensity of deep blue-gray water.

All that morning, as the sailor fished for whitefish, which he called humpbacks and which he said were absolutely the best eating especially if you caught a big one of five pounds or so, Mr Pawlowsky explained about ships and shipwrecks in the lake, craft of every kind from huge freighters to tiny sloops, and those were just the ships that were *known* to be at the bottom of the lake, which was almost three hundred feet deep on average and almost a thousand feet down at its deepest point, at the northern end of the lake; up there was where he thought the truly huge lake sturgeon lived, beyond the reach of any fishery, and as no one knew how long sturgeon lived, there might well be sturgeon there who were old when Lincoln was alive, and who might well have heard him speak in Chicago, in 1858, when he said that the Declaration of Independence "will link patriotic hearts as long as the love of freedom exists in the minds of men throughout the world." It was just possible, said Mr Pawlowsky, that one of these sturgeon who were now ancient among their species, respected elders probably, were young bucks then, and adventurous, and had come down to Chicago to see the town, and sport in the shallows with their Illinois counterparts, committing foolery and horseplay, but perhaps also catching a voice ringing in the city, a voice they remembered to this day, and perhaps discussed in their mysterious councils in the murky depths of the lake.

Mr Pawlowsky went on in this vein for a while, while the sailor caught a remarkable number of trout and perch along with two large whitefish, and I kept mental notes on the wonderful array of birds overhead and in the water—mostly loons, grebes, and cormorants, although here and there I saw little troops of scoter ducks—until we reached the area of the lake where Mr Pawlowsky thought they might begin prospecting for the Wildcat. Here I was put to work cleaning and icing the fish that the sailor caught while they consulted maps and charts and laid plans for winching and grappling; they also spent nearly an hour lowering plumb lines, measuring wind and current, and jotting copious notes. After a while Mr

Pawlowsky opened the ice chest and brought forth sandwiches and beer, while the sailor again fished for a while; but this time he returned the three small whitefish he caught to the lake.

On the way back to Belmont Harbor I asked the sailor why he had not kept the little whitefish, and he said well, first, they were really too little to eat, and second, he wanted to be respectful to the life that had grown up around the airplane down there, as the airplane was serving as a sort of reef, and if he and Mr Pawlowsky could successfully salvage the Wildcat, then the fish down there would be losing their apartment building, so to speak, and he agreed with Mr Pawlowsky that a courteous gesture to those fish now would not be out of place, considering the magnitude of the changes that were imminent; and third, the lake had given us plenty of food today, and greed was never good. When we got back to the building he divvied up the fish, giving me two trout, dividing the two large humpbacks between himself and Mr Pawlowsky, and giving all the perch to Edward, who was delighted and had an oily sheen about his coat for the next week.

*

As June began there was a roaring hot spell and I played a lot of basketball at the park with Bucket and Monster—there's nothing quite so pleasant as playing intense basketball outdoors, with good players, when it's so hot you can sweat off a pound in an hour, if you play hard enough—and one afternoon I got into a weird fight with the leader of their gang, a guy named Luis. He was almost thirty years old, I would guess, and he was a gifted athlete, although not actually a great ballplayer—although he thought he was, which turned out to be the reason for the fight.

I had never seen him at the park before, and I have no idea why he was there that day, but he and I took an instant dislike to each other, and in the way of young men and ballplayers we immediately jockeyed to cover each other in the game. It was a Saturday, and we were playing games to fifteen, best of five, you have to win by two baskets. There were eight guys, so we played four on four, full-court. It was unbelievably hot, so hot that halfway through the afternoon, when a sudden brief Midwestern epic rainstorm drenched the court, the rain steamed and dried by the time we came back from getting water at the fountain behind the school.

Full-court games to fifteen baskets are tough enough, but with such evenly matched teams (I had Bucket on my team, with Monster and Luis on the other side) overtimes are almost inevitable, and all of the first four games spiraled up into the twenties or even late twenties by the time they were done. After four games we were tied, and everyone was tired and chippy; even Monster, who never spoke, said something curt after one rebounding melee, and I got cracked so hard by Luis on a baseline drive that I thought he broke my finger. That set me off—like many middling players I played best when I was annoyed—and after that I hammered him every chance

I got, setting picks with grim pleasure, grappling for position with elbows high, and cracking him back once deliberately when I went for a steal and got all hands and no ball. He grew infuriated too, and by the end of the fifth game we were no longer playing ball as much as we were fighting without fists.

He was older and much more muscular, but I was quicker and, I think, angrier. Part of it for me was that I had felt established in the park, I felt that I *belonged* there, it was a part of Chicago where I was known and even respected, a little; and to me this was huge, for I was still relatively new in the city, far from home and school and friends and brothers. And the park was not the magazine office, where I was paid to work, or the apartment building, where I paid to live, but a place I had *earned,* so to speak, by being myself. And here was an interloper, hammering me on my turf!

I was a fool, of course, and it was his turf, really, not mine; and I think that made me angry too, for in my mind I had glossed over the nature of the Latin Kings, what they actually were and what they actually did. I was young, I was sentimental, I was a fool, and to me Bucket and Monster were essentially cool guys, ruffians who admired my game and chose me quickly when they chose teammates; but here was their king, and maybe part of what made me so angry was that looking at him I realized what a fool I had been to gloss over the reality of the Kings, who were collectively murderers, rapists, thieves, drug lords, pushers of evil and death to children, human vermin who didn't think twice about smashing families and neighborhoods. It was Bucket himself who had once told me that the Kings had started right, as defenders of poor Spanish-speaking kids against white gangs, but soon they had gone the way of all gangs.

And here, not two inches away, for a solid hour, was the perfect encapsulation of the real Kings, an arrogant blunt instrument pounding my stupidity right into my face; and I got angrier and angrier, at my own illusions, at his infuriating ego, at some lost thing that he was somehow responsible for, and then it boiled over.

The fifth game went into overtime too, of course, and Bucket won it with a quicksilver pair of stunning baskets that I do not think any defender on earth could have stopped. There was a second of exhausted silence and then Luis swung at me with all his might, but Monster, who had seen this coming, pulled me out of the way. I lost my temper and said foul and vulgar things and Luis came at me again but now Monster was joined by the rest of the players, ostensibly protecting their leader. Luis was shouting incoherently and I was still so angry that it did not occur to me that I was standing on gang turf with seven members of a gang that had murdered more people than anyone will ever know.

Bucket said quietly, "He think you disrespect him," and I said angrily, "How the hell did I do that?" and Bucket said, "You play him even, man, and you skinny whitey and dork glasses." This last was true—when I played basketball I wore a pair of ugly old thick-rimmed spectacles, to keep my good glasses safe from damage.

Monster said firmly, "Man to man, best two of three buckets, then magazine man be leaving, Kings ball first," and Luis and I stepped in. I knew full well there would be no fouls. Luis drove right at me, head down like a football fullback, and I jumped out of the way, poked the ball away as he went past, and then picked it up and scored.

He who scores gets the ball again. Usually you "check" the ball with the opponent, a sort of polite gesture to be sure he's ready, but I knew if I gave Luis the ball it would come back at a hundred miles an hour, so I bounced it to Monster, who bounced it back, expressionless. Luis was fuming. I drove as hard as I could to his left for one huge step, and then spun back away as fast as I could, evading the forearm I knew he would throw at my head, and put up a little fallaway jump shot from about ten feet out. Not a shot I was very good at, but this one dropped through the net. Game.

Now Luis was apoplectic, and I had calmed down enough to realize there was real danger in the air; this could well end with me losing an ear, or worse. For a moment my mind grappled with the oddity of such rage in such a bucolic spot; you never saw a more typical beautiful summer Saturday city schoolyard playground, with the slightly bent rims, and the battered backboards tattooed by thousands of dusty balls, and the worn endlines and sidelines, and the scraggly tufts of grass along the fences, and the beginning-to-rust poles holding up the backboards, and the baking brick school walls, sprayed with graffiti of every sort of color, especially the black-and-yellow spoor of the Latin Kings. There was even, I had time to notice, a little spray-painted strike zone, where little kids played stickball.

Monster, to his eternal credit, made a judgment call then that I have thought about ever since; it must have been a remarkably brave act on his part, to essentially challenge the leader of his tribe in public, though he did it with a subtle brilliance that took me a while to appreciate.

"One shot and be done," he said to Luis, and there arose a howl of appreciation and shrill debate, and then Bucket said to me, "He going to hit you hard, man, be ready, better give me them glasses." I started to object and Bucket said "No, man, he get one shot, be ready. When you go down stay down." I gave him my glasses and dimly I saw Luis lunge at me and then my nose exploded, is as close as I can get to explaining it. I went down and stayed down. A few minutes later Bucket helped me up. Everybody else was gone. Bucket said, "You nose is broken, man, better get that fix right away. He have to win, you see. Way it is. Maybe wait a week before you ball up here again, okay?"

Bucket walked with me through the schoolyard and down two blocks—later I realized he must have escorted me to the boundary of his territory—and then he left and I walked home holding my bloody shirt against my nose. At the apartment building Mr Pawlowsky led me into the alley and washed off the blood with a hose—I remember there was a lot of blood, and the water in the hose was so hot I gasped—and then set the two pieces of my nose back together with a quick wrench of his wrists, saying he had set many a man's nose in the Navy. It was possible and indeed probable that most men who had ever served in the United States Navy had broken their noses while in service, although probably most of those breaks were not incurred in *direct* service, you understand, but in extracurricular activity.

So it is that even all these years later I can look in the mirror and see Chicago; there's a hook or bend in my nose that looks exactly how Broadway bends between Roscoe and Aldine streets, near Belmont Harbor. I don't notice it much anymore, but little kids see it right away, and ask about it forthrightly, in their relentlessly curious way. I tell them a sailor in Shanghai did it, or a plummeting falcon in Ireland, depending on whim, but sometimes then I think of that blazing day.

Years later a detective friend of mine in Chicago told me that he heard Luis and Monster were dead but Bucket became some kind of social worker in the projects on the west side of the city, which could be true. I would like it to be true; he was a gentle soul underneath his rough veneer, I thought, and I bet he would be a superb social worker, all too knowledgeable about darkness and light.

17

ONE DAY ABOUT A WEEK later I was home sick when I saw a most amazing thing. This was on a Thursday. I had staggered down the street to the grocery store for orange juice, the only thing that would stay in my stomach, and when I dragged myself back into the building I remembered to check my mailbox; but as I shuffled down the hall I noticed the back alley filled with animals of all sorts, from dogs to squirrels to what appeared to be a black-crowned night heron perched on the fence by Mr McGinty's bathroom window.

Not for the first time in my life I doubted my eyes, and thought I was hallucinating, and decided that the shadowline between this world and the dream world had been breached without my knowledge, and concluded that I was a lot sicker than I thought I was, and had better shuffle upstairs and go back to bed until Monday, but just then Mr McGinty came out of his apartment to get his mail. He saw me staring into the alley and laughed.

"You think you're hallucinating, don't you? So did I, the first time I saw it. But this is Thursday morning, and on Thursday morning Edward holds what you might call office hours in the alley. It used to be on the front steps but it got too crowded there and people stared. The alley's private and there's a lot more room. He sits at my chess table and they come up to him one by one for some sort of consultation. I think it's probably more spiritual than medical but I have never asked. Not my place. The first couple times I saw it I stared too. I mean, who wouldn't? But I think it makes everyone uncomfortable if you stand and stare and I wouldn't want to be disrespectful to Edward. You might take a good long look and then wander away, is what I would suggest. Not that I am telling you what to do. But we wouldn't want to be disrespectful to Edward."

I got the message and stood at the back door for a moment and looked out at the line. You wouldn't believe the number and shape and size and variety of animals there were. I saw dogs of every sort, and all sorts of birds from sparrows to the heron (it was a night heron, I confirmed later in a bird identification guide), including what surely was a red-tailed hawk, standing patiently about halfway down the line. There were two raccoons, and an opossum, and rabbits, and three rodents of some sort, and what looked like an otter, although I had not known that there were otters in our neighborhood. In all I estimated that there were more than twenty animals on the line. As I watched a boxer dog turned away from Edward and walked quietly down the line and around the corner, and everyone on line moved up a space without jostling. At that point I thought I had been there long enough and the last thing I wanted was for someone on line to see me gaping, so I got my mail and went back upstairs to bed.

★

It turned out that Eugenia, the woman in 3C who had been an actress in the Broncho Billy films, had left a startling sum of money in her will to Miss Elminides, and a lesser but still very substantive sum to Mr Pawlowsky—the first for "kindness and generosity," and the second for "generosity and kindness," according to the letter from her lawyers. There was no explanation of how she had come by such sums—investments from her earnings? her husband's estate? some inheritance?—but the money was real, as Miss Elminides and Mr Pawlowsky discovered when they went to the bank and were handed bits of paper proving that the slip of a woman with the brightest orange hair you ever saw, the tiny old lady who loved to wear her costumes from the movies, the slight cheerful old lady who left the enormous stuffed horse in the basement, had indeed left a lot of money to her landlord and to the building manager.

She had also, according to the provisions of her will, left gifts and mementos to several other residents: all her costumes from the Broncho Billy films to her hallmates, the dapper businessmen in 3A and 3B; a beautiful engraved King James Bible to the hermit brother in 3E, and a lovely old Book of Common Prayer to the hermit brother in 3D; a complete set of the works of Willa Cather to the two young women from Arkansas in 4E;

and a hundred dollars in twenty-dollar bills to Ovious and his mother in 4F, and to Eren and her parents in 4A. She had also left the stuffed horse in the basement to Azad, in 4A, with instructions that he could either keep it or sell it to a collector or museum, but the choice must be his, not his parents'; and should he wish to keep it, it would remain in her storage stall in the basement, subject to supervision by Mr Pawlowsky. Azad, after much consultation with his parents and with Edward, elected to keep the horse for at least as long as it took for his father to carefully research and weigh offers for its purchase from collectors and museums; and the dapper businessmen, to their credit, offered to handle this project, inasmuch as they were already researching the market value of Eugenia's Broncho Billy costumes. They were careful and thorough men, the dapper businessmen, and it was September before they felt prepared to present suitable offers to Azad and his parents; which is why one of my sweetest memories from that summer is shuffling down to the basement on Saturdays for Mrs Manfredi's empanadas, and seeing Azad and his sister proudly astride their own tremendous horse. In the years since then I have seen many a child atop many a horse, but I have never seen children happier about it than those two.

★

At work Mr Mahoney pressed his attack on Cardinal Cody, and while the Cardinal responded with the usual strong-arm tactics of astute city politicians, Mr Mahoney was unmoved, knowing he had the unswerving support of the magazine's publisher (a priest of towering height who was seen in our offices once a year, on the feast day of the saint who had founded his order) and the order's superior, who had grappled with bishops and cardinals beyond counting, said Mr Mahoney.

"Tin-pot dictators who think that the color of their robes confers authority over the mind and hearts and allegiances of the faithful, whereas the first principle of canon law is that an informed conscience is the first and last moral arbiter," he said. "Why exactly it is the case that generally the higher a man rises in the hierarchy of the church the bigger a pompous idiot he becomes is a mystery to me and many others. This is not always so, and we celebrate the few who understand that humility is the final frontier, like the late Angelo Giuseppe Roncalli for example, but the current Cardinal Archbishop of Chicago is not among those men, I am sad to say. I have lived in Chicago all my life, and the city's civic and religious life has often been overseen by men of almost unimaginable pomposity, men who believe that money or weaponry affords them authority over the lives of their fellow citizens. Sometimes I veer dangerously close to despair about the predilection to pomposity in this great city but then I remember that despair is technically a sin, although here too you can only too easily picture the poor pompous ass who decreed that a state all too normal and well-known among human beings would be categorized as sinful. It is nothing of the sort, of course. It is sad, unfortunate, wearisome, an affliction, something to be endured, something you endeavor to lift from the shoulders of your fellow travelers. Speaking of travelers, you are one day late in turning in your piece about parish life on the high plains of these United States, and I will hope to receive your sterling copy by the end of business today so that I can take it home and read it tonight. I am sure your sentences will be clean and orderly so that I do not have to make editorial comments by the light of the elderly lamps Mrs Mahoney and I have procured over the years."

Mrs Mahoney, I should note, was a legend of surpassing proportions in the office, for not one of us had ever laid eyes on her, although she telephoned for Mr Mahoney fairly often, late in the afternoon; I had spoken with her many times, and she had the most lovely soothing voice, slightly deeper than you would expect in a woman. She always asked for "John," and he would answer his office phone every time with the same courtly line: "Do I have the pleasure of addressing Miss Halloran, of Schaumburg?" Schaumburg was a town north and west of Chicago, and Mr Mahoney liked to say that he had been there once, to carry away the few hereditary possessions of his beloved in a rickety old truck, along with his beloved herself, and he did not see that there would ever be an occasion for him to be there again, if God was merciful.

I realize now that I have never properly accounted the rest of the men and women in the magazine offices, beyond Mr Mahoney, and our ruddy-faced Irish executive editor Mr Burns, and the towering publisher whom we saw once a year, and Maria in the mail room and Clarice in circulation, over whom I swooned but said nary a word all year long. There was Ms Cahill, who was small and hilarious and freckled and brilliant, and who was not taken seriously for a while until she wrote a series of searing articles about prisons that made readers weep. There was Ms Tuohy, a lean stern knife of a woman who had briefly been a nun and then left her order and married a man who had once been a priest; their young son was appointed an altar boy during my first months with the magazine, a scenario that somehow seemed circular and funny to me, although I could not find the words to explain why it seemed so suitable and sweet that a nun and a priest would be the parents of an altar boy. There was Eudora the receptionist, whose swooping rising soaring voice as she answered the phone was so attractive to callers that often they would call back again just to hear her cheerful operatic aria as she announced the magazine and inquired as to how she might be of service. There were several small intense people in Circulation and Accounting whose names I never did catch; they were mostly male and always wearing suits and ties, although the colors of their suits in summer were sometimes colors I had never imagined cloth would be—teal and puce and lime, for example. There was My Man George, as he called himself and everyone called him, who was technically the janitor, I think, but was actually one of those invaluable souls who did carpentry, electrical work, plumbing, and general repair, all with deft easy grace and speed, and all without hardly a word. I admired My Man George a great deal, having no repair skills of my own whatsoever, and I spent a lot of time asking him questions to draw him out, but about all I ever got out of him was that he had been a pig farmer in the South at one point, an oc- cupation he had enjoyed, and that he had very much enjoyed hosting epic pig roasts at harvest time. He was the most cheerful courteous man I had ever met, I think, but he was also a past master at listening to questions, and murmuring such things as *well now* and *that is a fine ques- tion,* while focusing on his work and not actually answer- ing the question, and then saying, as soon as he was done with his task, "Now I must be back to work, this has been a pleasure to talk," and he would vanish, smiling. The first few times he vanished like this, leaving his smile hanging behind him, I was nagged by a feeling I had seen this before somehow; finally I remembered Lewis Carroll's Cheshire Cat, who vanished quite slowly, beginning with the end of the tail, and ending with the grin, which re- mained some time after the rest of it had gone.

*

Beginning on June 16, when they beat the Red Sox and their magical pitcher Luis Tiant, the White Sox went on an epic tear, winning eighteen of their next twenty-three games, including eight in a row at one point, defeating some of the best pitchers in baseball along the way: Oakland's Vida Blue, the Angels' Nolan Ryan, and Mark Fidrych of the Detroit Tigers, who was famous for talking to the ball before he threw it, and for kneeling down and grooming the pitchers' mound by hand to get it just right. The Sox beat Fidrych on July 8, a Friday night, before a standing-room-only crowd of 45,993 fans, among them Edward and me and Ronald Donald, the Scottish tailor who lived across the hall from me in 2B, with the detective.

Ronald Donald, like Denesh the cricket player, had never seen a baseball game, and much like Denesh he watched silently and intently for the first few innings, trying to get the pace and rhythm and "geometry" of the game, as he said, before asking questions about rules and specifics of play. He did ask, early on, why the tall young man with the long hair who was throwing to the Chicago players seemed to be murmuring to the ball before he let it out of his possession, and he laughed loud and long when Edward came back from McCuddy's Tavern across the street balancing a pitcher of beer on his back, but otherwise he sat transfixed as the Sox racked up ten runs and won the game 10–7, putting them in first by three games over the Kansas City Royals.

On the way home on the train Edward got Ronald Donald talking about how he got to America, and how he came to Chicago, and how he learned to be a tailor, and what he thought of baseball, and how he came to live with the detective, and about fish. It turned out that Ronald Donald had grown up thirty feet from the sea on an island in far northern Scotland, and his father and grandfather were fishermen, and he was a fisherman too for his first twenty years, after which he fled fishing and Scotland and went as far away as he could go; he got a job as a crewman on a freighter that went all the way from Dumbarton to Nova Scotia, and then crewed on a boat all the way to Chicago, where he liked the look of the city, "mostly because it was July when I got off the boat, and there was fireworks over the lake, and your wee American flags everywhere, so I stayed. It seemed a *delighted* place, you know? Not stern. I think now I stayed because it was a ferocious hot day and I was cold to my bones after twenty years in Scotland. A sensible man would have continued on to Brazil, but not me."

I asked him how he managed the icy winters since, and he answered that by the time his first winter rolled around he had met Vincent, which was the first time any of us had heard the name of the detective.

The train was delayed at Clark Street for a while and most people got off to catch buses or walk up to the next stop but we stayed on the train, because the tailor was now well and truly launched in telling stories. Part of his openness, I thought later, was that he was slightly beered up, but more of it was that he liked and trusted Edward, as everyone did, and I think now too that maybe he was one of those men who seem staid and private and closed but who are actually shy, and live behind walls of their own making, walls which they would do anything some-times to breach, but hardly ever do they get the chance.

He talked about his family, his father the fisherman ("a hard man, a cold man, a frigid man, a man I hated when I left, but now I feel bad for not seeing how unhappy he was, what pretense he lived by"), and his mother, who was always sick, and died when he was sixteen ("only the forty years old, poor girl, worked herself to the bone every day since she was four years old, she was from Glasgow and grew up in hell"), and his two sisters, whom he corresponded with steadily and had twice been back to visit, the one now in Belfast and the other on the coast of Spain. He talked about their neighbors, in a village too small to have a post box or a policeman, and about the weather ("cold and wet, with spells of wet and cold"), and about his grandfather, who lost his mind in his last months of his life and went through the motions of his life without any of the substance: "Eating soup without any soup in the bowl, and pulling on boots that weren't there, and fishing without any lines, and combing the hair he used to have, and talking to his wife, who was long dead and buried, and calling in his dogs at night that were long gone too, poor old fella. He was good to me, and he knew I would be going long before I did. He told me when I was twelve years old that I could leave when I was twenty and the sisters were in school. Which is what happened. He was a grand old man, the old man. He had fought her brothers for his wife, one by one, with his fists alone, just for the right to ask her to tea. They were set against him for some reason and he challenged them one by one like the old warrior days. Four brothers there were too. He told me once he used his left hand mostly in the fights because he knew one hand or the other would be damaged permanent and he preferred to keep his strong hand for the fishing and the children he was sure they would have."

Finally the train began moving again, but because there had been no warning for the sudden resumption of service it was nearly empty, and the tailor took advantage of the acoustics to sing an old island song his grandfather had taught him. I didn't catch the title of the song but I still remember a couple of lines: *May the hills lie low, may the sloughs fill up, may all evil sleep, may the good awake.* As we walked home to the building the tailor tried to teach us to sing but I sing like a frog and Edward could not stay in the right key no matter how hard he tried.

18.

SOMETIMES I THINK I have been so fixated on the apartment building and its residents that I have not given a full enough account of the amazing things that happened to me as I wandered footloose around the city. In those days I was young and fit and tireless and penniless and relentlessly curious, and I had neither kith nor kin in Chicago, and was not yet wholly absorbed by romance, and was adamantly dedicated only to basketball, so I walked endlessly, for to be pedestrian cost not a penny, and I was untrammeled by routes or fares, and did not have to worry about where to park a car or stash a bicycle. So I walked; and there were days when I thought it likely that I had walked farther and deeper in Chicago that day than anyone else in the whole city, and this was a city of three million souls.

Many of whom I met: some briefly, with only a word of greeting, like the enormous center for the Chicago Bulls basketball team, Artis Gilmore, who was not only seven feet tall but had an Afro easily another ten inches high; he and I passed each other on Madison Street one day, and I said hello, and he said hello, and he had the most wonderfully resonant voice, like a bass drum or a cello in its lowest register. I met a roan horse walking down Lincoln Avenue, a moment I remember vividly not only for the unusual sighting (usually the only horses I saw were wearing helmeted policemen) but for the fact that the horse nodded hello as he or she walked by. I met buskers by the score, a hundred street basketball players, dozens of people fishing the lake (one of my habits was to stop and ask what they were fishing for, to get a sense of what lived in the lake). I met librarians and bookshop owners and probably every gyro vendor north and west of the Loop. I met train conductors and bus drivers and taxi drivers; another of my habits, that summer, was to walk along a line of lounging taxi drivers outside a theater or the ballpark and, explaining that I was a journalist, ask them about themselves. I met teachers and policemen (curiously never a policewoman) and many mayoral candidates—it seemed like every other person in the city that year was running for mayor—and bartenders.

It was a bartender, come to think of it, who made me realize that the dapper businessmen in 3A and 3B were right about the future of the neighborhood. A man named Raymond tended bar at the Closet, around the corner on Broadway, which was set up in such a way that the bar was immediately accessible from the door; you could take a single step into the bar and signal to Raymond, who would pull you a beer as you stared up at the television by the door, which was always set to sports. I had popped by for a beer a few times without ever stepping more than three feet into the bar, being a man even then easily distracted by sports and their intense theatrical grace; I would step in off the street, signal Raymond for a beer, and then get so absorbed in the game that I didn't pay any attention to the other patrons at all.

One Saturday in June I ran along the lake dribbling my ball left-handed for an hour, and then ran back down Broadway cross-dribbling and dribbling behind my back and conducting spinning reverse pivots around startled dog-walkers, and when I got back to my street I popped into the Closet for a beer. Just as I signaled to Raymond, a friendly man next to me asked me to dance. I declined politely, and when Raymond came over with my beer I asked him what's with the guy asking people to dance?

"Listen," says Raymond, "do you know what kind of bar this is?"

"It's a very friendly bar," I said, "and you have cable, too, bless your soul."

"That's not what I mean," said Raymond.

"What do you mean? And can you see if the Sox are on? They play the Twins today."

"Let's try another tack," said Raymond patiently. "Do you know what your nickname is in the neighborhood?"

"I have a nickname?" I said, feeling cool and local.

"Yes. You didn't know that?"

"No."

"You do have a nickname. People call you Het."

"Heck?"

"Het. Which is short for . . . ?"

"Hector?"

"No," said Raymond, patiently. "Let's try another tack. You're a heterosexual guy, right?"

"Yes," I said, "but that's kind of a personal question, isn't it?"

"Well," said Raymond, "we are not."

"Not what?"

"Heterosexual. Everyone calls you Het because you are and we are not."

At which point I finally got the picture, which I have to say instantly changed my view of the Closet, which I suddenly saw was filled with people dancing with people of their own personal gender. I finished my beer, which Raymond gave me on the house, and the Sox won that day, with eight runs on sixteen hits, two of them homers.

The very next day I was walking along Broadway, marveling at my new knowledge of the neighborhood, and noticing things I had not noticed before, like two men walking along bound by a very thin silver chain at their belts, and a woman on the bus dressed completely in cellophane except for a huge red belt, and a lot of women with meticulous short haircuts, which I had vaguely assumed had something to do with summer, when in the distance I heard the faint approach of trumpets and drums. It sounded exactly like a parade approaching, which indeed it proved to be, but it was not a parade like any I had known in the past, for this was, bless my soul, the Chicago

Gay Pride Parade, which wound north to south through the city, and apparently reached its apotheosis in my neighborhood, for everyone near me politely went bonkers, with people dancing in the street, and wearing feathers and masks, and laughing and cheering at the wild motley of the marchers, and roaring with applause at a tableau of what I later discovered were the 1969 Stonewall riots in New York, a sort of independence day.

People were so packed along the parade route on our street that we really were crammed in shoulder-to-shoulder, like at a baseball game you really care about, for example the White Sox that year, and by chance I found that I was shoulder-to-shoulder with Raymond the bartender, right in front of the gyro shop. You could hardly hear a voice in the tumult, but I shouted into his ear that I was grateful to him for setting me straight, as it were, and he shouted back no problem, that's what neighbors are for, man, and we both grinned, and we all stayed pressed together on the curb for another few minutes, cheering and laughing, until the parade finally wandered away and little kids and dogs ran out to grab feathers and coins. I love that part of parades, when the main business has left the scene and there's still laughter in the air and glitter in the puddles and kids and dogs are whirling around for no reason and even though everyone probably has to go places and do things, they don't, quite, yet.

★

July was the month when apartments in our building turned over the most, Mr Pawlowsky had explained, because people who were moving wanted to be set in their new places before school started, while it was still warm and dry enough to move couches and tables easily, and while they could borrow friends' pickup trucks and not have to tarp the load; and also people moving *to* Chicago from elsewhere, like college graduates getting their first real jobs, wanted to get into their places and settle down and get to know the neighborhood and the grocery store and the garbage collection schedule and the bus schedules before they got sucked into work. And as July proceeded, the building saw its first changes in a year.

First Ovious and his mother, in apartment 4F, left. Ovious's mother's boyfriend had formally extended the invitation to come live with him in his house on Cermak Road, on the west side, in an old Czech neighborhood, and Ovious's mother had accepted the offer. According to Edward, Ovious himself was not thrilled about this for a number of reasons, but he and his mother moved out on a Saturday, Mr Pawlowsky and the sailor in the basement doing most of the heavy lifting. I had been away all afternoon playing ball and caught just the tail end of the move when I came back up the street, dribbling with my left hand; Ovious, sitting glumly atop a piano in the bed of a truck. I waved and called his name and he looked up but didn't wave as the truck pulled away, although weirdly the piano suddenly groaned a low chord—C, I think.

Next to leave were the two young women from Arkansas in 4E; they were moving closer to downtown with two of their friends from college, and they were gone in an hour, assisted by a sudden efficient crew of tall muscular young men whom I took to be suitors. That left 4E open as well, and the librettist joked that it must have been his Harry Mark Petrakis oratorio that drove away residents on his side of the hall, this did not bode well for its success, etc.

Finally there came a serious blow—the four dapper businessmen in 3A and 3B moved out. Financially prescient as they were, they had foreseen not only the changing demographics of the neighborhood, but its incipient rise in property values, and they had joined forces to buy not one but two narrow buildings on Cornelia Avenue, a couple of blocks away. The good news was that they would not be far away, and that we were all welcome to stop by at any time; the bad news was that they would be very much missed, as they were generous and cheerful men, always quick to help any resident, and to provide just the smile or wry quip you needed when you slogged home feeling weary and bedraggled, only to find one or two of the businessmen, beautifully dressed and beaming, on their way out to dinner or a show. Something about them always cheered you up; as the librettist said once, they always made you feel vaguely as if you were in a movie somehow with Cary Grant and Fred Astaire, a lovely feeling. They left in the evening, just as the Corona Borealis constellation was becoming visible to the north, and Miss Elminides shook hands silently with each of them on the front steps of the building, as many of the rest of us watched from the lobby. Mrs Manfredi cried.

So now, what with Eugenia's apartment 3C also empty, five of the apartments were without tenants; but by the end of that month they were all filled again, and this is how that happened.

It turned out that the dapper businessmen, in exploring property values in the neighborhood, had taken a thorough and meticulous look at the convent around the corner, and concluded that the best approach financially was for the nuns to sell it to a developer, who would tear it down and put up condominiums. The nuns, who could not afford repair and upkeep on the old wooden building (and there was a stunning amount of repair necessary, after a century of benign neglect), would realize a serious amount of money, enough to either make a deposit on another residence or use as an endowment from which to pay living expenses; the dapper businessmen, knowing how developers would drool over such a location near the lake and minutes from downtown, could easily require the establishment of a whopping health care fund as part of the negotiations.

By now the nuns were down to ten members, from a high of fifty at their apex, thirty years before. They had so few members that they no longer bothered to elect a Mother Superior, but instead took turns "being sentenced to being the nominal authority," as Sister Maureen said,

smiling. Sister Maureen was the grinning nun who had
sold me my bed and table and chair for fifty dollars when
I had moved into the apartment building, and since then
I had been over to the convent several times with Edward
and Mr Pawlowsky for small repair jobs for which we
were paid in laughter. You never met a happier band of
survivors than those nuns, who were not at all bitter that
they were in ostensible decline, but rather energized that
the archdiocese seemed to have forgotten about them,
which allowed them to do whatever they thought most
necessary to do. Three of them still taught in schools; one
was a roving nurse; one wrote sermons and homilies for
a company that provided texts for priests and ministers
of all denominations; one worked in sales and repair at a
bicycle shop on Belmont Avenue; three were aged and
frail, and did not often leave the convent, but did still
offer spiritual consultations and direction to former students; and there was Sister Maureen, who had discovered at age thirty that she was a gifted plumber, so good
that she gave Mr Pawlowsky pointers about equipment
and trends in the industry.

It was Sister Maureen, as nominal authority that year,
who made the decision to sell. For all that she loved the
old boat of a building, she said, and for all that she and
her sisters loved the stories and legends and love and joy
in the place over the years, and for all they loved the angles of light and the idiosyncrasies of a home in which
they had lived most of their lives, they could see the writing on the wall; the future, financially, could only grow

dimmer as the building fell ever more into decline, and the sisters too. The decision was clear, and made far easier than it might have been, she told Mr Pawlowsky, because they trusted the dapper businessmen implicitly, and indeed had left all financial details to them. Thus the convent was sold on the last day of July, on a complicated contract that entailed a tax-exempt fund for their health care costs, money set aside for moving expenses, a bonus payment designed to ease transition costs, the promise of a historical exhibit about the sisters and their legacy in the new buildings, and lifetime use of the rooftop sundeck. The sisters had the whole month of August to pack up their possessions and find other living arrangements.

But just as Sister Maureen and the dapper businessmen were set to begin site visits for possible apartments, Miss Elminides offered the ten sisters the five vacant apartments, at ten percent below market rate. The sisters met at breakfast to consider the offer, prayed over it in their tiny upstairs chapel, and then accepted the offer unanimously that afternoon.

★

In the last days of July Edward and I went on a terrific burst of historical sightseeing, covering a remarkable amount of the city at an incredible pace. Years later, remembering how many places we went in so few days, I wondered at what seemed almost manic behavior; but I think now that Edward had some intuition of my leaving, and he wanted to be sure to soak me in Chicagoness through and through, to the very bone—although it was more like to the very soles of my feet, as I actually wore a hole in my right sneaker during those days, and had to borrow a pair of sneakers from Denesh the cricket player for a while.

We went to Daley's Restaurant, on the far south side, where we had whitefish from the lake. We had enormous hamburgers at Lou Mitchell's on the west side and the Green Door Tavern on the north side. We went to the glorious old dark wooden Berghoff restaurant on Adams Street in the Loop, where Edward pretended to be a guide dog and I had a beer at the vast curving bar. We tried to find the house where Phil Everly of the Everly Brothers was born in 1939. We went to the Wise Fools Pub to hear Koko Taylor, and to Kingston Mines to hear Eddy Clearwater and Miss Lavelle White, and to a club called John's to hear John Littlejohn. We went to an outdoor concert (the great jazz pianist Dave Brubeck) at Ravinia Park, way up north by the Chicago Botanic Garden. We went to jazz clubs on the south side to hear a very young Mulgrew Miller and a masterful McCoy Tyner, who slipped into the club at midnight to play a set on the harpsichord, an instrument I had never heard played so hauntingly before.

Again we studiously avoided any site having anything to do with crime, as Edward felt strongly that crime ought not to be encouraged by tourism. We went back to the Billy Goat Tavern on Michigan Avenue by the river, Edward not pretending to be a guide dog this time but getting his own bowl of beer. We went to the site of the old Chicago Beach Hotel, which used to be on the lakefront on the deep South Side, until the city filled in the lakefront there to build Lake Shore Drive, which meant that the Beach Hotel no longer had a beach, which meant that it went out of business.

Lovely old theaters like the Congress and the Portage, on the north side, and the Ramova and the Music Box, on the South Side. Raceway Park, on the South Side, where we stood outside the old walls and felt the roar of stock cars circling and thundering inside. Wrigley Field, which was only about a twenty-minute walk from the apartment building, but which we would not enter for superstitious reasons having to do with hexing the White Sox if we stepped inside a National League park, beautiful though it was—although we did happily have a beer across the street at Ray's Bleachers bar, where Edward spotted none other than Bill Veeck, owner of the White Sox, holding court at a table covered with Schlitz beer cans and his wooden leg; he had lost the original leg while in the Marines in the war. Lovely old castles of hotels downtown like the Drake and the Palmer House, through which we wandered gaping at the ornate details, Edward again posing as a guide dog.

We walked along the river as far as we could, on both banks; we made a game of sprinting through every park we could find; we cut through every alley that looked promising and mysterious, secure in the knowledge that I could outrun trouble and Edward could, if necessary, defeat it physically; we made a pact to walk atop any stone or brick wall with enough purchase for our feet. Edward got into the habit of checking with local dogs in neighborhoods he did not know, and their advice often led us to odd fascinating corners and sights—obscure fountains, remarkable trees, once a hidden aviary with more than a hundred parrots and parakeets of every color and species, tended by a tiny old man who could not have been more than four feet high.

There were many other riveting things like that, and the only reason we finally stopped is because it was becoming evident that Mr Pawlowsky needed Edward to help him court Miss Elminides. Still, though, even all these years later, I will suddenly remember something like the aviary, or the time a policeman let Edward ride his horse in Union Park, or the time a man selling drugs on a corner near Humboldt Park made a disparaging remark and Edward knocked him down and nosed his bag into a sewer. It seems to me that we did so many things at such a comic and headlong pace that if I tried to record every one of them there would be no room in this book for anything else to happen.

*

The young woman I had met on the train had given me her mailing address at college, after I confessed I did not own a phone, and used the telephone booth in the gyro shop to call my family for holidays and birthdays; and I had stayed in touch, writing a letter or a postcard here and there, intrigued by her for reasons I couldn't quite articulate, reasons that seemed deeper than her being at-

tractive and witty. She wrote back, long handwritten
letters, thoughtful and funny, and twice we had chatted
on the phone (calls that cost me mountains of quarters,
I remember), and once I had coffee with her briefly at
her college cafeteria, and once we had gone for a walk
downtown when she paused in the city between trains;
that time she was on her way home to Wyoming for
spring break, but took the latest train west so that we
could wander around Chicago together for four hours—
four hours that changed everything.

Her train from college arrived at Union Station, on
Canal Street, and I immediately walked her over to the
Picasso Something or Other, between Dearborn and
Clark. We sat there contemplating it for a while as I explained how Mr Pawlowsky thought it was a horse, and
Edward thought it was a comment on dogness, and other
people thought it was a woman, or a cricket, or a huge
steel joke. She leaned toward the joke explanation, being a student of Picasso's work, and we talked for a while
about how mysterious it was that unbelievable idiots like
Picasso, who beat up women and cheated and lied to
everyone he knew, could make astonishing and deeply
moving art. This line of talk led to a tremendous braided
conversation about art, artists, idiots, money, grace,
mercy, literature, dogs (she loved dogs, and very much
wanted to meet Edward), cricket, the nature of value,
basketball, the value of education, magazine journalism,
finance (her dream was to work for an international bank
or investment firm, and so travel the world, whereas my

soaring dream was to be able to dribble and shoot better with my left hand, and write novels), the energy of cities, the stark beauty of wild country (like, for example, Wyoming), and much else—all conducted as we walked east to Grant Park, and then south along the lakefront, and then back up Michigan Avenue over the Chicago River (stopping in the Billy Goat for awful coffee), and then back west along the river to the train station.

I calculated later that we had walked about five miles, during which something happened that I still do not have words for, after thirty years as a journalist. We came to some understanding; we arrived at some mutual decision; we committed to an enterprise; we plighted a troth; we signed on for an adventure; we embarked on a voyage; we agreed to agree. We also kissed for the first time, as she boarded the train to Wyoming. I walked all the way home that night, up LaSalle to Lincoln Park and then north along the lake, probably four miles in all, and by the time I got to my apartment I was so weary I fell asleep instantly. The next morning when I woke I thought I had dreamed the whole thing, but then I saw, tumbled on the floor, pebbles from the lake she had given me as talismans by which to remember the first day of our voyage.

19

ON THE LAST DAY of July, a Sunday, the White Sox won the first game of a doubleheader against the Kansas City Royals to go into first place by five games. Chet Lemon homered twice for the Sox; the Royals' George Brett, the best hitter in baseball, went hitless; and Comiskey Park was crammed to the rafters—more than fifty thousand fans, according to the newspaper the next day. I caught the first game with Denesh and Ronald Donald, but missed the nightcap, which the Sox lost, as I had promised Edward to help with a certain project.

It had become painfully clear both to Edward and me, and to most of the rest of the building, that Mr Pawlowsky entertained feelings for Miss Elminides, and that Miss Elminides had feelings for Mr Pawlowsky, but the two of them were shy, and dignified, and reserved, and private, and cautious, and not given to sentimental gesture or unsupported speculation. Yet you could tell that there was some common feeling between them, a grave affection, an amused pleasure, almost a reverence—each very much admired and trusted the other, and turned to the other in moments of duress or strain, and each wore a certain small smile or used a certain tone when speaking of the other.

I think now that each of them was afraid that a romance might ruin their friendship; that if, for any number of good reasons, their romance did not flower or flourish, their deep affection and respect and attraction would be permanently injured or even lost—a thought neither could bear, even while both of them surely dreamed in private what it might be like to be lovers, partners, maybe even spouses. Certainly Mr Pawlowsky dreamed those dreams, as Edward had occasion to know; and perhaps Miss Elminides thought of Mr Pawlowsky's eyes and hands when she sat and played her instruments quietly in the blue hours of the night.

Finally it was Edward who decided, much against his usual predilection to discretion, to shove the situation gently toward a deeper possibility. His idea was a night repast on the roof, to which Miss Elminides and Mr Pawlowsky would be invited separately, and encounter each other with pleasant surprise, at which point the escorts would withdraw, leaving the two of them to contemplate the stars, and share an excellent bottle of wine, and enjoy some local savories provided by anonymous friends. I was recruited for this, to escort Miss Elminides to the roof; Denesh, resplendent in his cricket whites, was to serve briefly as wine steward; Mrs Manfredi provided the fare; and surprisingly Edward chose Eren, Azad's little sister, who was four years old, to escort Mr Pawlowsky to the roof, on the excuse that she wished to see the legendary Ring Nebula, and also maybe Sagittarius, the Archer, who invented the bow and arrow.

So it was that on a hot night in early August I knocked at Miss Elminides' door, and when she opened it (I smelled honey, and could hear what sounded like a cello) I asked if she would do me a favor and come up on the roof for a moment, that there was something Edward and I wanted to point out. I went up the roof stairs first and extended a hand for her as she stepped out, and I remember watching as four or five thoughts, or sensations, or emotions played across her face as she saw the table and chairs, and tall candles (donated by the librettist), and Denesh smiling as he held out the wine for inspection, and Mr Pawlowsky standing shyly, holding Eren's hand. Miss Elminides was startled, pleased, displeased, nervous, annoyed, thrilled, and discombobulated, all in the space of three seconds; but you never saw a more graceful and elegant soul under duress than Miss Elminides, and she smiled graciously and shook Eren's hand and accepted a glass of wine from Denesh, and that's the last I saw, for Eren and Denesh and I all went back downstairs, leaving them alone at the table. Edward delivered a basket filled with Mrs Manfredi's savories, and then he retired also, and he and I listened to the Sox play the Texas Rangers on the radio. Oscar Gamble hit a triple to the deepest part of center field, which hardly ever happens in baseball, and the Sox won 5–4.

★

Looking over what I have written so far, I think perhaps I have not spoken enough of the quiet hard difficult painful things I saw in Chicago. I saw scattered broken teeth in an alley. I saw plenty of men and more than one child sprawled out in battered old clothes huddled in sleeping bags wrapped in newspapers shoeless on heating grates and park benches. I saw a dead dog on the beach and a dead dog by the door of Saint Michael's Church in Old Town on the northwest side. I saw a policeman arrest a boy who could not have been more than ten years old; he was so short, this boy, that all you could see of him in the backseat of the police cruiser was the top of his head. I heard people crying as I walked along residential streets at night in summer when people leave their windows open. I saw a man punch a woman on Randolph Street, and when she staggered backward from the blow she slipped on the curb and fell into the street and her left shoe came off and sat there by itself for a moment while several men passing by grabbed the guy who punched her and a cabdriver helped the woman sit up; I went to get her shoe for her but a man got there first and held it politely for a moment until she was ready to stand up again. I saw a bar brawl, in a blues bar, on a Sunday night, when you would think the odds would be against a sudden crash of glass and a table overturning and guys picking up pool cues and the bartender punching a guy and one man swinging a pool cue and hitting another man in the head with the awful sound of a pumpkin smashing against cement.

I spoke to a policeman one night who told me he was weary weary weary of his profession, weary of the pain and sadness and brokenness, weary of the greed and violence, weary of the poor idiots he would arrest and book and testify against and then arrest again months later, weary of being weary, weary of the poor women and children who had to depend on thugs and snakes, or try to survive on their own when the snake was killed or incarcerated, weary of the sheer stupidity of criminals, their foolish schemes that came to nothing and caused wreckage along the way, weary of the ease of drugs, weary of the complicit authorities and enablers of the drug trade, weary of the arrogance of petty chieftains crowing that they owned a single block on which they strutted and preened like king rats, weary of the clogged elephantine lugubrious legal system with its endless cheating and cynicism and beautifully dressed liars, weary of the fear he saw in the eyes of children when his squad car turned a corner, weary of the way they scattered and ran like cockroaches into the dark alcoves of their project housing, weary of the screams and gunshots he heard every single night he ever cruised among those awful monumental jails where hope was incarcerated and despair was always on the menu.

"Weary weary weary," he said. "Weary. That's the right word. It has the right sound, you know? Tired doesn't do it. Exhausted is normal. 'Weary' has the right ragged sound to it, though. I am eighteen years in, and if I can make it two more I can quit. I'll be forty-one years old.

Be a teacher maybe. Though God knows what I would teach. Criminal economics, maybe. Illegal entrepreneurship. I should be a lawyer. That would be a good joke on the suits at the court house who defend guys who sell cocaine to kids in grade school. Did I tell you about the one time I got suspended? I arrested a guy who was pimping his own niece. Age thirteen. Every weekend. He was the responsible uncle who took the niece on weekends while his sister worked long shifts as a nurse. This went on for almost a year. We caught the guy, but a bright young kid fresh out of law school finds a hole and the guy gets off with probation. Goes right back to pimping the niece. I couldn't take it. A friend of mine bumped into him on the street, and things got heated, and my friend made it clear that there was going to be a change of professions immediately or the guy would have a few accidents. I got suspended a week for that. No one ever said anything to me but they knew. I still think of the poor sister, you know, working her ass off every weekend, and her own brother a total snake. That kind of thing makes you weary, man. You fight the good fight but sometimes you just get weary. All you can do is figure you cut one snake at a time from the snake team, so that's good. You don't think about how many new snakes are coming up from the minor leagues. Two more years, man, two more years. Listen, I have to go. Pleasure to chat. Fight the good fight."

★

The librettist had finished his oratorio about Harry Mark Petrakis in July, shepherded it through rehearsals, and enjoyed a moderately successful opening night, with brief but laudatory reviews in the newspapers; but the production did not pack in theatergoers until the city's beloved legendary *Sun-Times* columnist, of all people, wrote a glowing adulatory piece for the Sunday edition, which had a circulation of almost a million readers.

I still remember that review, partly because it was posted prominently by the mailboxes in our lobby for weeks, and partly because I loved that man's brusque honesty and rough humor and spitting fury at arrogance; many times I had bought a *Sun-Times* from a kiosk, read his column on page two, laughed out loud at how deftly and lewdly he had skewered some pompous ass like Jesse Jackson or the mayor, and then put the paper back in the kiosk, satisfied that I had gotten my thirty-five cents' worth of journalistic pleasure.

"I am not much for oratorios, as a general rule," he wrote. "Me personally I thought oratorios were probably the expensive Italian version of Oreos, which upscale Polacks like my friend Slats Grobnik would buy when he was trying to impress a new girl at the Friday night bingo-and-polka soiree down at Saint Stanislaus. But I got lured into an oratorio last night, for reasons having to do with love and beer, and I am typing these words at four in the morning, absolutely amazed. Here's a sentence I never thought I would write in this lifetime: I have never been so proud of my city and its literature, and I have never been so startled and moved by the kind of music I have passionately hated all my life, as I was last night at the Ivanhoe Theater, listening to a new oratorio about the life of our great Chicago writer Harry Mark Petrakis; and if you love Chicago, and love hearing music that somehow makes you happy and gives you chills and makes you weep with sadness all at the same time, you will get your raggedy butt to the Ivanhoe as fast as your flat feet will carry you, and buy as many ridiculously expensive ducats as you can afford, and go every night until the singers lose their voices and have to go into ward politics as local muscle. It's that good. Trust me. Have I ever led you astray?"

After that the deluge: the *Sun-Times* film critic Roger Ebert went, and wrote a soaring review; music and drama journalists rushed to cover a production hardly any had bothered to attend initially; the oratorio became a popular date destination not only for Chicagoans but for visitors from other states (especially, for some reason, Minnesota); three colleges made it required for coursework; the Chicago public television station WTTW not only taped a performance but aired a documentary about its creation, starring the librettist as witty talking head; the run was extended once, twice, thrice; there was talk of taking the production on the road, and licensing independent productions; and the librettist remembers getting a letter from a Harvard freshman named Peter Sellars inquiring if he could mount a production on a boat in Boston.

In short, the oratorio was a smash hit, and by the middle of August the librettist was, if not a rich man, a man quite sure of his financial security for years to come. A careful soul, he had taken the precaution of preserving both his copyrights and the right to approve and profit from subsequent productions by any other entity, "in any media heretofore known or henceforth invented," as he said with a smile, quoting from the contract.

He told me this in the stands at Comiskey Park; on a whim he and I had caught a Monday-night game against the hated New York Yankees, who weirdly had hit three home runs but only scored three runs, and lost 5–3, because good old Oscar Gamble had singled in the winning run against the Yankees' terrific relief pitcher Sparky Lyle, who had the biggest mustache I had ever seen on a human being. It was so big it looked like he was wearing otters on either side of his face, as the librettist said. The librettist was in a particularly cheerful mood, which I took to be a result of his professional success until I found out the next day that he too, like the late actress Eugenia in 3C, had given Miss Elminides a check for a great deal of money, with a note saying he was most grateful for her kindness and patience and faith in his work, and she would be doing him a further kindness if she would accept what he viewed as an investment in *her* gift for communal warmth and trust, without which no culture or people can long abide or persist.

20.

I DID GO BACK UP TO THE BASKETBALL court where my nose was broken, a couple of weeks later— partly from stupid defiance, and partly because I had genuinely liked the quality of play there; some of the runs I'd had with Bucket and Monster had been basket- ball at just about the best I could play it, the sort of games where your skills mesh with the skills of other guys and everyone gets lifted up a level. I loved games like that, when you and your teammates are playing better than you usually are. Games like that are fun, and exhausting, and creative, but there's some deeper thing in them that I don't have words for, quite—some kind of joy, I guess. Games like that get bigger than the score, and you are awfully glad you got to play in them, and you feel a sort of half-conscious vestigial tiny sadness when you play in games that are not at that level. Not *too* much—I mean, ball is ball, and there's never a bad game of hoop, unless guys are preeners or thugs, or "flexers," as my sons say— but after playing in games at the deepest level you always unconsciously measure the game you're in against the great games, and you never forget the great ones either.

But it wasn't the same, that August. Bucket showed up occasionally, but Monster never returned, and after a while I grew weary of having to endure Not My Fault, whose manic chatter and overweening ego, without the slight cause or reason or excuse for such ego, increasingly got on my nerves. Plus the play seemed chippier, and there were new guys who seemed to be more interested in making statements about manhood than playing the sort of loose fast generous games that I loved. For a while I kept going there because I liked the forgiving rims, and playing with Bucket was so much fun that it was worth dribbling up Broadway on the chance he was at the park, but after one evening when three fights broke out in one game and Not My Fault shot every single blessed time he got the ball, I walked home knowing I wouldn't be back.

Before I left I picked up a pebble from the edge of the court, where the asphalt was crumbling into what looked like cake crumbs, and tucked it in my sneaker. I still have it, too, in a little bowl of talismans from courts where I had been lucky enough to be inside the deeper game—a court in Boston, in a park under elm trees; a court in Brooklyn, where we swept broken glass off the court with huge push brooms before we played; a court in Harlem, where the unspoken rule was all weapons were left with a silent burly man by the gate; and that court in Chicago, where Bucket slid through tangles of guys like he was a shadow and Monster set picks like sudden walls. I played on many other outdoor courts—meticulous new courts, and battered old courts, and courts with grass sprouting from cracks, and courts enclosed in wire mesh, and courts perched along beaches, even once a court composed entirely of close-cropped grass; but I only have prayer beads from a few courts in that bowl, and only the ones from Chicago are black, so when I see them from across the room, or pick them up and smell them like a truffle hunter, I am immediately transported back to that hot crumbling schoolyard court, where I am trailing Bucket on a fast break, knowing as well as I ever knew anything that he will drive right to the basket, and flip the ball back over his shoulder at the last possible second, even as he pretends to follow through on his layup, so that the defender will be taken completely out of the picture, and I will catch the ball and lay it in all in one smooth unconscious motion, and turn to hustle back on defense, and point to Bucket to say thanks, and he will grin that slight small smile, and we will not say a word, and that will be glorious and perfect and unforgettable, and somehow somewhere it will always be a hot evening in Chicago, almost dusk but not quite.

★

It was back in February when I had gotten into the habit of rising very early to catch the first bus downtown along the lake, the Sound Asleep Bus, driven by the dignified and gracious and eloquent Donald B. Morris, and by August he knew me well, and let me sit behind him in the first seat on the lake side, and I would ask him questions, and he would tell me stories. During the winter and through the spring he told stories mostly about his time in the war, and about religion and the Chicago Bears, his two favorite topics in life. When summer came, though, he began telling me stories about passengers he'd had on the bus, and how he came to be driving the bus, and how driving the bus was like being the mayor of a small town for a little while, with all the conundrums and pleasures of mayoring, such as "One time a *baby* was born on the bus, lady was quite overdue, and foolish me, I hit the curb pulling away by Melrose Street, and she have the baby right in her seat. Gentleman comes up to me *as the bus is moving,* which is against bus rules, and tells me lady having the baby, so we pull over and get some blankets I keep for emergencies and we take care of that. She name the baby Justus. Also a lady died on the bus one time, a *very* cold winter day, two feet of snow, she die somewhere between Belmont and Dearborn, everyone else get off the bus except her. I thought she was asleep but no. I have been asked to marry passengers, which I did not do, but I was honored at the request, which was heartfelt and genuine. We have never had an accident, no. We *have* had flat tires. We have never had fisticuffs, no. We *have* had altercations. Some drivers *very* worried about gunplay and theft and such but not me. I trust in the Lord to care for us. Plus it is *very* early and people not violent before sunrise. I have been driving for twelve years come winter which this year begins on a Wednesday. There *was* a time early on when I was first driving this route when I thought about assign seats, because *some* people very annoyed when someone sit in the seat they think *their* seat, but assign seats is too much trying to be in *control* of things, you cannot *control* all things, you must let things happen, within bounds. So one morning after my regulars are all on the bus I stand up and say we do *not* have assign seats on the Sound Asleep Bus, and we will *not* have them in the furthermore, so do not ask me about this again, but we *will* get along, and we *will* be civil, and we will *not* put bags and parcels on open seats to reserve them, but treat each passenger as you would wish to be treated, which is to say with civil behavior, and this is scripture also of course. I did not say that, because religion is a private matter, of course, but people *know* that, and abide by it, for the most part. This is Dearborn Street. Watch your step. God bless. Go Bears."

★

Late that August I had the urge to climb and see the sights again, and I spent many hours sprinting up stairs in apartment buildings and towers, and surreptitiously climbing fire escapes on old hotels and tenements, and taking elevators to the tops of office buildings and trying to figure ways to get out on the roof. I climbed out onto the roof of the old convent around the corner, on what must have been its last days in that form in this world, and while you could indeed see for about a mile in every direction from up there, you could also see some serious holes and worn places, and twice I found tremendous nests, which I hoped were hawks or crows rather than members of the order Rodentia.

I think now that what absorbed me, up on the heights

in Chicago, was the sheer geometry of the city—the tumble and jumble of buildings splayed up against each other, at all different heights and volumes, so that sometimes the city looked like a vast array of children's blocks of different manufacture and color and ingredient, arranged by many hands over many years. And each section of the city had a different geometric feel—the near north, where I lived, was mostly buildings of two and three storeys, with the occasional vaulting cluster of condominiums or hotels, all interspersed by the spire of a church or the dome of a temple; the south and west sides were houses and bungalows and cottages and brownstones and sagging wooden flats of two or three floors where large families had lived for a century, succeeding each other every twenty years, the porches and tiny yards and back stoops filled with one language after another, the clotheslines in the alley filled with washing of one culture after another—greens from Ireland, reds from Italy, blues from Poland, orange from the Dominican Republic.

I also climbed trees, where I could find purchase and avoid law enforcement. I surfed tall old elms in Lincoln Park, and sweetgums and basswoods in Grant Park, and oaks in Skinner Park, on the west side—I remember tree-surfing in Skinner Park in particular because it was a day of incredible gusts of wind, and I was at the very top of a tremendous oak, and I was thrilled beyond measure because the tree was whipping back and forth with something like a sapling's silly glee, and I was terrified because it was an old tree and the chance was not infinitesimal that it would snap altogether and I would end up in several pieces in Iowa and Nebraska and points farther west.

It was easy to gain serious height in the Loop downtown, where height was a calling card and a marketing niche, but the vista there was mostly of other tall buildings, so mostly when I was atop roofs downtown I stared out at the sea of the lake, which went on forever east and north, and only dimly suggested a southern shore in Indiana. There was always shipping of some sort on the lake, day or night, and often there was weather out there wholly different than that of the city; more than once I saw a storm on the lake while the sky was clear and calm in Chicago, and once I saw a black wall of weather approaching so noticeably fast that I got down off the roof as fast as I could. That was the old Chicago Board of Trade Building on Jackson Boulevard, a lovely old limestone structure with a roof statue of Ceres, the Roman goddess of farming, holding wheat in one hand and corn in the other. The Board of Trade Building was probably my favorite in the city to climb, not only because of its height (it was something like six hundred feet tall), and because it had hosted a famous hundredth birthday party for Abraham Lincoln in 1909, but because it had all sorts of corners and shelving, and very few security guards, and all sorts of odd beautiful sudden sculptures; I would wander out on one of the decks on the upper floors and encounter a statue of an American Indian holding a shock of corn, or notice suddenly, while approaching the building from the north, that there were enormous bulls carved right into the stone, twenty feet over my head.

*

It was also late in August that for no reason I could tell I was suddenly weary of the city, weary of the dense huddle of buildings, of stone and brick, of jostling pedestrians, of bus exhaust and tangled traffic, of the ubiquitous strut and splat of pigeons, of broken glass and puddles gleaming with oil, of the stench of trash bins and the arrogance of skyscrapers, of broken men slumped on steam grates, of the screech of trains and the grainy dust drifting down from the elevated tracks; and I wanted to be away, to escape just for a day, to sprawl and breathe someplace green and vigorous and silent except for birds and crickets; weirdly I suddenly wanted to hear a grasshopper startle from a tangle of brush along a back road. An odd desire, for I have never been a rural man, let alone an adventurer in the wilderness, but that one day I found myself starving for something not glass and metal and concrete.

By chance Sister Maureen, the leader of the nuns who were moving into the building over Labor Day weekend, was driving to Iowa, to visit her order's motherhouse in Dubuque and explain what was happening with the nuns in Chicago, and she offered to give me a ride out into the country, leave me anywhere I wanted, and pick me up on the way back; it was about three hours to the land of the Meshkwahkihaki, the people of the red clay, she said, and she thought she would leave at dawn and drive back at night, if I didn't mind spending the day on foot somewhere in the country along the way. I told her this was exactly what I wanted, for reasons that were murky, and so the next morning we left the city just before dawn, with a thermos of coffee and a pear each, gifts from the other sisters for the road.

For an hour or so we didn't speak much, and just enjoyed the hum of tires on the highway, and the world brightening slowly behind us, and the occasional deer or hawk, and once a coyote with the tail of something hanging from its mouth. Sister Maureen talked a little about Iowa, and the motherhouse, and the nuns there who were mostly great but two had illusions of grandeur, and how she was a student of the First Peoples in Iowa, and much enjoyed collecting and recording their stories, on the theory that, as she said, the best way to celebrate a people is to share their stories, because the best way to kill a people is to kill their stories, for example look at what the English tried to do to the Irish, although it didn't take, because we are too damned stubborn, as my grandfather said, and all too familiar with duress. He was from County Mayo, you see.

As we crossed the Rock River Sister Maureen said I think this is perhaps where you want to be, and she pulled over and let me out. We agreed to meet at this exact spot at sunset, and she drove off, leaving me her pear, and I spent the day wandering along the river, and climbing into the craggy rocky hills, and noticing deer tracks, and twice a thrash of wild turkeys, and what I thought might have been a fox or a bobcat, although it vanished as soon as it saw me, and left no prints on the rocks. I ate the pears slowly, savoring every bite. I lay in the grass watching hawks and swallows and swifts. I climbed a massive old maple and found a flying-squirrel nest. I found the biggest cottonwood tree I ever saw. I sat in the river and watched dragonflies and damselflies quarter the surface for insects. I found a pool under the bank that looked like it would be a great place for otters and catfish and I dove under and held on to rocks at the bottom of the pool as long as I could and twice fish nosed past curiously. I looked for turtles and frogs and toads and mussels and snails. I found the bones of a perch. I found the feathers and bones of a robin where a small hawk had torn it apart. I saw two different kinds of crayfish, brown and red, the red ones testy and argumentative. I did a lot of nothing. I napped in a honeysuckle thicket for a while and when I awoke I sat there slowly pulling the nectar-laden threads from the flowers and tasting a honey I had not eaten since I was a child on a gleaming summer morning long ago and far away. I heard a train somewhere in the distance. In more than ten hours in that forest by the Rock River I saw two members of my species, a man and a boy in a pickup truck in farmland to the west. Late in the afternoon the wind picked up and I sat on a hill and watched the cornfields sway and dust devils swirl in the soybean fields. Just before sunset, as I was walking back to the highway bridge, I saw a kestrel hover over a field like a tiny bronze helicopter, and suddenly drop like a bright stone into the dirt, and rise up again into the air with a snake.

★

September proved to be a tumultuous month. The nuns moved in, taking the whole west side of the third floor and 4E and 4F, next to the librettist. Azad, in 4A, began school, which reduced his little sister Eren to tears for weeks. The man who had invented propeller hats, in 2A, delivered an enormous check to Mr Pawlowsky to give to Miss Elminides; he did not want to hand it to her in person, being shy, and all he would say about where the money came from, according to Edward, was that it had something to do with where computing would eventually inevitably have to go. Miss Elminides received a letter from the authorities in Greece explaining that a Greek citizen named Giannis had been arrested in the Turkish city of Çanakkale, and that Greek authorities were pursuing repatriation with an eye toward indictment, but that Turkish authorities were at present recalcitrant and unhelpful, to say the least, and that the case would apparently have to be pursued at higher political levels, which promised to be a slow process, to say he least, and that they, the Greek authorities, would keep Miss Elminides posted, and that they wished her well, and would pray for her estimable grandfather, God rest his soul.

It was a tumultuous month for me also. I was asked to play in a men's league in Evanston which featured more than a few college football players using the league to stay in shape for spring practice, so it was all I could do to hold my own and not get hammered by guys twice my size; twice I was so tired after intense games up there that I fell asleep on the train home and woke up deep on the South Side, discombobulated and sore from head to toe. At work the Cardinal Archbishop of Chicago tightened the screws grimly, so that the office grew tense, and even Mr Burns lost his temper one day and threw a roaring stomping fit that ended with a typewriter being flung out the window onto Madison Street, narrowly missing an unemployed plumber. The gyro shop where Leah worked was the target of an attempted shakedown by the city tax assessor, and had to be rescued by Mr McGinty, who somehow knew everyone who worked for the city, and called in a favor. The man in 2D who had once raised cheetahs burned his left hand so badly while cooking that he had to be hospitalized for four days, during which Edward and I tended his birds—his apartment was filled with parakeets of every conceivable color, so many that we never did arrive at a final count, no matter how many times we tried. One elevated train crashed into another at rush hour in the Loop, tossing people like bread crumbs from the platform. Denesh lost his absolute favorite cricket bat, the one with which he had played his final match; it had been mounted over his couch, and had perhaps been stolen somehow, although none of us could figure how it had been done. Four horses were murdered one night at Arlington as part of an elaborate insurance

scam, which unraveled because one of the stable boys at-
tending the horses was so angry at the killings that he
led investigators to the money trail. The White Sox,
having fallen out of first place on August 19, lost two of
three to the Orioles as September began, and fell five
games behind the Kansas City Royals. Four inches of
rain fell one day, a windstorm howled through the city
another day with gusts of fifty miles an hour (small boats
on the lake were overturned, and a baby carriage was
blown clear across Lake Shore Drive, although the child
in it reportedly held on with both hands, and was un-
harmed), and lightning on still another day hit the Board
of Trade Building and partially melted the corn in the
goddess Ceres' right hand.

Also I received a letter from the young woman I had
met on the train. She had accepted a job with a bank in
Boston, and she was moving there from Wyoming immediately, in fact flying to Boston an hour after she posted
this letter, a flight which precluded a long train trip during which she should happily have paused in Chicago
for a while. But, she wrote, she would be delighted if
I thought I could find a way to live in Boston also. What
with a year's experience on a renowned magazine, and
the gleam of my diploma from Notre Dame, I would be,
she thought, an excellent candidate for jobs in Boston,
and if indeed I did move to Boston, perhaps we could
pursue our mutual interest in each other, and see what
fate had in store.

"Consider this an invitation," she wrote, "and not

pressure in any way or form, for I cannot make promises, nor can you, and perhaps I am being more forward than I should be. But it seems to me that there is certainly something between us, and I would very much like to see what that something can be. However I do not want to have a relationship with a thousand miles between us. As you know I did that twice already during my college years and it didn't work either time. Probably it didn't work because neither of the guys turned out to be such good guys, but I know myself well enough to know I don't want to try that with you. I will understand one hundred percent if you feel that this isn't the time for whatever reason for you to leave Chicago, and I know how much you love the city and your life there, but I have to be honest and say that I hope you *will* come to Boston. I hope that very much. Write me after you read this letter?"

21.

THE WHITE SOX WERE ON THE ROAD through much
of early September, out west against the Oakland Athletics and the California Angels, and I was terrifically busy
at work anyway, trying to finish a series of articles about
differences among religious practices in parishes around
the city, and there were many days when I was hardly
in the apartment building at all, rising before dawn to
catch the Sound Asleep Bus and coming home around
midnight. I looked at my notes from that time recently
and counted more than fifty parishes I had visited, from
Saint Adalbert to Saint Wenceslaus; and at each parish
I made an effort to talk not only to the pastor and assis-
tants, if any, but to teachers, janitors, parents, children,
neighbors, detractors, and the local police and firemen,
who I had discovered usually knew far more about the
actual intricacies of community life than any official or
activist. I also had learned to visit taverns, to chat with
bartenders and the old guys at the end of the bar at two in
the afternoon, and restaurants, to chat with the older wait-
resses; those professions were in the listening business, and

often I found gifted storytellers with tremendous memories for local lore. For professional reasons I also stopped into the offices of whatever small neighborhood newspaper I could find, but in general those were not productive visits, as the editors and reporters I spoke to either wanted to sell me an idea or make me buy information of unverifiable accuracy and doubtful provenance.

I had thought, when I got the assignment from Mr Mahoney, that my series of articles would be somewhat pro forma, reporting on infinitesimal differences among parishes probably by cultural heritage—the Lithuanians at Saints Peter and Paul on the South Side would approach Easter in ways that the Poles at Holy Trinity on the north side would not easily recognize, something like that—but I was quickly and thoroughly disabused of this notion, and found myself entranced by the rich and colorful and myriad differences. Each parish, it seemed to me, was its own village of a sort, with its own cast of characters and its own welter of common myths and traditions and theatrical flourishes, some of which would have given the Cardinal Archbishop of Chicago a heart attack, had he known of them. Officially, for example, women were banned from the altar, and officially subservient to the pastor and assistant pastors if any, but in fact most parishes were cheerfully run by women, either under titles like religious education director or school principal, or sans title as members of the parish council, fund-raising coordinator, or parish secretary. At three parishes the women who ran the Altar Society essentially

ran the whole business of the parish, from church maintenance funds to admission marketing for the school and
even insurance coverage for the pastor's Chevy Impala;
at another parish it was the Mothers' Club that quietly
made sure the operation hummed smoothly, and at one
parish I was sure a group of women called the Sodality
of the Madonna had arranged things such that all orders
and commands and instructions from the pastor, an arrogant buffoon, were quietly run past the Sodality for
editing before issuance.

Like many other Catholics at that time, I was annoyed
at what seemed the inarguable patriarchal mania of the
church—a tendency with no validation except the weak
excuse of hoary age and the fact that the founder was
male; the latter also a silly excuse, as He was a Jewish
man, and if we were to adhere to His example closely,
we would all be Jewish and skinny and live in Judea and
speak Aramaic and Hebrew and take up carpentry for
spiritual reasons. So it was startling, and rather pleasant,
to discover that in many parishes women quietly skip-
pered the ship, sometimes amusing themselves and their
fellow lay travelers by a certain ironically obsequious respect for the hierarchy. The many nuns who worked in
the parishes in various capacities were most artful at this,
and I saw some hilarious exchanges between wry and
witty nuns and pastors who hadn't the faintest idea that
they were being shepherded as easily as you might steer
a turkey toward a scatter of corn.

It was also pleasant to discover that there were very

few arrogant bloviators among the hierarchy, as far as I could tell—most of them were decent and hardworking men who understood full well that their work was to serve not only their congregations, but an idea at once so preposterous that it could never be proven or validated, yet so relentless that two millennia of evidence against had not yet managed to quash it. A difficult profession, theirs; and I came to much more respect and admiration, as I researched and wrote that series of articles, for the many men who by their own sworn vow led lives of sometimes terrible loneliness, even as they were incredibly busy and surrounded by hundreds of people who needed their help and attention and patience and open ear and open heart. I had never had even the tickle of an urge to be a priest, but after I finished that assignment my estimation of their general grace and courage went up several thousand percentage points.

*

All these years later, I think I was too young, when I was living in Chicago, for any number of things. I was too young to realize how cool and funny Azad and Eren were, and how much fun it would have been to hang around with two tiny fascinating people and laugh my head off. I was too young to pay much attention to the byzantine and incredible and revelatory machinations of politics and commerce and crime and punishment. I was too young to think at all in the least about the primacy of education and the incredible potential depth of family life. I was too young to pay attention to the unmistakably

foul fingerprints of epic and criminal pollution and en-
vironmental degradation in the lake. I was too young to
pay attention to the fact that of the three million people
in the city maybe a million did not have quite enough to
eat or lived in dangerous conditions or endured constant
assault and battery or had no real hope or possibility of
ever elevating their standards of living. I was too young
to begin to discern the prevalence of rape in our culture,
in every aspect of our lives, from families to churches to
schools to clubs to the military, and too young to see the
dense curtain of lies and shame and fear that muffles the
screams of the women and boys and girls who suffer such
insidious predation. I was too young to pay attention to
the remarkable virtues and vices of religions, and the
ways they elevated their adherents, and stole from them
too. I was too young to understand the constant cheating
and turning of blind eyes and bribery and deft corporate
theft and eloquent complicated lies that in many ways
defined business and politics and civic administration in
Chicago then and probably now. I was too young to see
how the city acted as a vast cold magnet for the young of
the surrounding country, who were drawn to Oz with
wide eyes and covetous impulse, leaving behind their
small towns and villages and cities to wither by the year.
I was too young to see the cold calculus of economics, by
which the rural areas labored mightily to provide product, which was then shipped at small profit to the city,
where great profit was made upon it by those who had
nothing to do with it but take it with one hand and sell

it with the other. I was too young to see the white gangs attack black ones attack brown ones attack white ones, and all colors of gangs attack children from Korea and Japan and China and Malaysia and Vietnam and Cambodia as their families also, just like the white and black and brown ones, flooded into the city looking for work and school and peace. I was too young to notice but a few of the thousand broken sodden homeless souls on steam grates and under bridges, and wonder why so many of them had been soldiers in our wars, or members of tribes and clans here many thousands of years before agriculture and settlements arrived. I was too young to realize what a time machine Mr McGinty was at age ninety-nine, and how a thousand hours of listening to his stories would have not only been a most amazing education in American history but would have easily afforded me stories enough for ten novels. I was too young to realize that Mr Pawlowsky was not merely shy about opening his heart to Miss Elminides, and not just leery of being bruised by possible rejection, but that he had also, at age fifty-three, built a life he loved, a life in which he was stimulated and comfortable and rich in his way, and perhaps it was frightening for him to contemplate a different sort of life, even with the undeniable attraction of having Miss Elminides at the center of it. I was too young to see that Miss Elminides too, for all her grace and ease and calm and dignity and aura of elegance, was also shy and lonely and perhaps bereft and adrift in a city and country she had not chosen for herself. I was too young to be utterly astounded and absorbed by Edward, whose intelligence and depth of character I took a little for granted; I could not know then that I would never meet another being like him, let alone a *dog* like him, and I have met many excellent beings, and dogs, since then.

★

The White Sox, having after going 62–38 from April through July, and leading the league by five games at one point, went 27–32 the rest of the way, and slid to third behind the Kansas City Royals and the Texas Rangers. They finished the season at home with three games against the Seattle Mariners, first with a Saturday doubleheader at which the announced attendance was something like five thousand (although the librettist, who was there, told me later that the actual attendance was half that, and there were so few fans in the park you could clearly hear the players chatting on the field), and then with a final Sunday afternoon game, on October 2.

Five of us from the building went to the game, feeling that we ought to salute the great season, and the end of summer: me, Edward, Denesh, the librettist, and Azad, who was allowed to accompany us if he finished his chores beforehand, which he did. We took the train down to the park, expecting to find another sparse crowd, but to our pleased surprise there were a lot of people streaming through the gates, smiling and laughing; even the beer vendors, usually taciturn and suspicious, were smiling and chatty, and Edward pointed out to me that the ticket-takers and security guards were deliberately ignoring small boys hopping the stiles and teenagers crowding in suddenly behind ticketholders before the gate could click shut. You had the distinct feeling that no one there that day particularly cared if the Sox beat the Mariners, or even felt bad about how the season had slipped away in August and September; certainly I didn't hear anyone say *swoon* or *slump* or *choke* that day, or afterward, come to think of it. Maybe it says something about the low expectations of seasoned White Sox fans, but the overall mood among the fans (and the players too, it seemed) was delight in a terrific year, and in a colorful and engaging team that for most of the season had been the best in the west—an alluring phrase that certainly had not been spoken much by Sox fans over the years.

I'd guess there were twenty thousand fans there that day, and the Sox lost 3–2, and Richie Zisk and Oscar Gamble both went hitless, and Chet Lemon didn't even get to bat, entering the game only as a pinch runner, but still it was one of the best games ever. The ushers let you sit anywhere you wanted, on this last day, and we went all the way down to the third-base box seats, using Azad's wide-eyed joy as an excuse to claim great seats right on the railing. It was clear and cold and the Sox third-baseman Eric Soderholm hit a home run (his twenty-fifth of the year) and everyone had a ball. When the game ended there was a sweet moment when everyone in the park stood up and applauded for what seemed like ten minutes but probably was two or three. Usually when a game ends the players trot off the field briskly with their heads down, probably thinking of girls or beer, but this time the Sox players all came back out of the dugout and applauded the fans, and then a dozen or so walked around the edges of the field shaking hands with fans and chatting and signing autographs. Oscar Gamble signed an autograph for Azad, which I would bet he still has, probably carefully framed, and Richie Zisk shook hands with the librettist, who said something to him that made Richie laugh.

I watched all this with pleasure, feeling some swirl of affection for my friends and the fans and the players and the team and the park and the city and the terrific fading summer; and then I noticed that Edward was missing. Before I could even mention it to my companions, though, Edward jumped the railing from the field, holding, of all things, a baseball bat, which he presented to Denesh as a replacement for his beloved cricket bat. On the way home on the train I asked Edward how exactly he obtained the bat, but he pretended that the crowd of happy fans in the car was making too much noise for him to hear properly, which made me grin and stop asking questions. All the way home little kids on the train came over to Denesh and asked if they could touch the bat, just like kids ask if they can pet your dog. He said yes of course and almost every kid touched it like it was holy or loaded with sunlight or something like that.

★

After that terrific unforgettable White Sox season ended on October 2, the papers were immediately filled with stories about the Bears; one day I measured the coverage in the *Sun-Times* alone and counted six full pages about the Bears, one page total about the hockey Blackhawks and the basketball Bulls, one page total about horse racing at Arlington, half a page about other sports in toto, and a guest column by the legendary sportswriter Irv Kupcinet, buried in the opinion pages, about the White Sox, who had drawn more than a million fans to the South Side for the first time in many years—a feat that Irv, a veteran conspiracist, thought had been overlooked because of the fascist nature of "the professional gladiatorial assault and battery now miscalled 'football,' as if a word coined to describe the autumnal American version of rugby, traditionally played by boys on chilly oak-lined fields until they achieve the age of reason, could be applied to the deliberate and premeditated acts of militaristic ferocity, without even the excuse of national defense or international policing," and indeed "the only excuse for 'pro football,' the sole motivating force for such untrammeled violence and mayhem, the be-all-and-end-all, is money, cold and impersonal and hauled to the bank through the sea of mud and blood on the gridiron, regardless of the damaged bodies and minds of the men who years from now will not even be able to remember that once they played a boys' game gone terribly bad."

I was vaguely curious about the Bears, and interested to see their great running back Walter Payton, the best player in the game that year, and I thought it might be a classic Chicago experience to attend a game at Soldier Field, but Edward refused point-blank to accompany me, no one else in our building or at work seemed interested, and I found that going alone was not an appetizing prospect—somehow it seemed that you could go alone to a baseball game, and fit in, but going alone to a football game seemed odd—football games were for going in packs and gangs, and apparently heavy drinking was required. Finally I even asked Mr Pawlowsky if he wanted to go.

"I do not," he said, "and I can tell you, if you have not already asked, that Edward almost certainly will not go. We are not much for football, at any level, and you have seen him laughing over hockey. Both of those sports entail much armor and smashing, although there is of course grace and creativity evident occasionally. I suppose that is what interests some of their fans, the ones who are not watching to see if indeed there will be blood or possibly someone losing an arm. Did I tell you that Miss Elminides received letters from the bank and the city that all is well? The Third Awkwardness is over, I think. The point of sport is grace and creativity, isn't it? Against obstacles—opponents playing defense, weather, weariness. Much of what is said about the value of sport is nonsense but some things are deeply true. Probably being on a team teaches you something about humility and camaraderie. At least you hope so. Being in the Navy taught me about camaraderie, among other things, like organized foolishness. But also a sort of grim courage. I never saw a Nazi but I understood why we took up arms against them. Someone has to stand up when the time comes. Edward teaches me that also. You remember the incident with the Gaylords. There are many more stories like that. I think I should ask Miss Elminides on a date. Perhaps to dinner at a restaurant. We cannot always dine on the roof. Myself I was never much for sports but I understand people enjoying them as theater—the *narrative* of a game, the moments of tension and release, the communal energy. My brother Paul loved sports for that reason. He never cared about the score but only how well the game was played. Edward believes there are moments in life when you must take chances that seem mad and that one of those moments is approaching for me with Miss Elminides. He suggests sooner than later. Yet I am old and she is young. What if she says no? Then we would never be friends again the same way. What if she says yes because she feels indebted or sorry for me? Where would we live? What about Edward? I am more than fifty years old and set in my ways and have nearly nothing in the way of bank accounts and pension funds. What would we live on? A man cannot ask a woman to share his life if there is nothing to live on. That would be selfish. That sort of thing is for the movies and not for Miss Elminides. And what if she says no? What then? Would I have to leave the building so as not to make her uncomfortable? God forbid she would be uncomfortable. I would never in a million years make her uncomfortable. The very question would make her uncomfortable, wouldn't it? So then why would I ask such a question? The last thing I wish to do is make her uncomfortable. She has had enough discomfort this year to last a lifetime. I have the utmost faith in Edward's judgment, but for the first time in our relationship I am moved to question it. Or is it the case that he is right and I am cutting things too fine? You cannot be a clerk all your life, as my commanding officer in the Navy said to me once. I think he meant that I was too careful, too cautious, too meticulous. But how can you be too meticulous? Things break down and need to be repaired. Things are always declining toward decay and someone has to be sensible and fix them. Who will fix things if I don't? You have no advice for me whatsoever? I have come to trust your judgment also, you know, young as you are. But you have not leapt into love either, have you? Not that I know about. Haven't you wanted to? Have you not had the opportunity? The subject hasn't come up in our conversations but you are young and strong, your whole career opening as we watch with pleasure—haven't you thought about asking a question for which you have no idea of her answer? Haven't you?"

★

I spent a lot of time on the roof *that* night, I can tell you. Edward came up at one point to see if I was okay but after a while he went back down, as he saw that I was wrestling with a private matter. He must have communicated my unrest to Mr Pawlowsky, for he came up at about midnight, draped in his Navy blanket, and set up a lawn chair next to where I was sprawled out staring at the sky.

"Note the constellation Horologium," he said after a while. "The pendulum clock. Like many constellations, hard to discern and puzzlingly named, in this case by a Frenchman named Nicolas Louis de Lacaille, who identified some ten thousand stars and named fourteen constellations. I think he did not see so well and often I am at a bit of a loss to see the shapes he saw. Still and all, a remarkable man. Traveled all the way from France to southern Africa to see stars better. You have to admire the courage to do something that everyone else would think silly. He spent one solid year there charting what he saw every night, including what he called nebulous objects. You and I are both charting nebulous subjects, are we not?"

At which point I told him about the girl from Wyoming, and how she had moved to Boston to take a job, and she had invited me to move to Boston also, without any promises but with promise, so to speak. I told him that I had dated various girls briefly in the past few years, and much enjoyed their company, although in all cases their company did not last more than a few months, as the problem seemed to be that I could not get as fully and intricately interested in them as they wished a young man would, which they discovered slowly, and which annoyed them, and which led to seething dissolution. I told him that I was intrigued by the Wyoming girl, but that I could not honestly say that I was in love with her, or entranced, or overwhelmed, or anything like that, and that while one part of me wanted to be cool and adventurous and sail away to Boston to see what might happen, the rest of me thought that was crazy talk, because here I had a job I found increasingly absorbing, and a city I had come to love, and all I could say honestly of this girl was that she was intriguing in a way no other girls had been for me, but what sort of basis was that for uprooting a life? And most of all, more important than the job or the city, I had *friends* here, unexpected friends, friends of two species, friends I would miss terribly, friends who had been so gentle and generous to me from the moment I had walked up the stone steps of the building, friends who had shown me endless subtle aspects of the city and its denizens, friends whom I admired immensely for their grace and dignity and intellect and tenderness . . .

At which point I couldn't talk anymore because I couldn't get any words past the sudden rhinoceros in my chest and throat.

Neither of us said anything for a while. Over on Halsted Street I heard police sirens for a couple of minutes, fading away to the north. Somewhere out on the lake a tanker blew its foghorn, although there wasn't any fog; maybe it was warning another ship of its presence. I saw one nighthawk, and then two, and then four. Nighthawks have a sort of buzzing sharp whistle that once you identify it you can pick it out of a welter of sounds at night even if you can't see them whizzing after insects in the dark. People mistake them for bats but once you see their slicing loopy flight (not the zigzag flutter of bats) and hear their brief piercing whistle you know them and like them and look for them when you are sprawled on the roof too filled with feelings to speak.

"I am going to ask Miss Elminides to dinner at a restaurant," Mr Pawlowsky said quietly, "during which I am going to ask her to come to an understanding."

This caught me by surprise and I said *what?*

"I have been too cautious and careful in life, perhaps," he continued. "I don't know why. Not timid, exactly, but careful. Judicious. In many ways this has been a good thing. I have not hurt anyone with reckless and careless and selfish behavior, that I know of. But I have perhaps been too . . . careful. For a long time I thought this was a virtue in a careless world but maybe it was more like a polite vice. Edward has indicated his feelings about this and I believe he is correct. The fact is that I have deep feelings for Miss Elminides. I do not know how to express them articulately. I am no journalist. But I want to *be* with her all the time. I want to wake up next to her and fall asleep next to her and cook for her and negotiate decisions where we don't see eye to eye at *all*. I want to walk with her and maybe even travel. Yes, travel. I don't want to live on different floors anymore. I want to be standing next to her when bad news or good news comes. I don't want to analyze things constantly anymore and weigh my reactions thoughtfully. I want to laugh and cry and argue and watch movies and leave notes under her coffee cup and pinned to the bathroom mirror. I don't want to lay out pros and cons on pieces of paper and tabulate the results. I want to come to an understanding that we will be confused together. Perhaps she will not *want* to come to an understanding, which would be awful, but I am going to ask. I am going to ask tomorrow. Or tonight, given that today is now tomorrow."

Again we sat silently, listening. For some reason I couldn't explain then or now I believe we were both thinking of Edward for a while. It must have been one in the morning by this time but you could still hear a remarkable number of things in the city. I heard a bus sighing to a stop somewhere within a couple of blocks, and cars whirring singly along Lake Shore Drive, and someone laughing, and somewhere far away the thump of music from a door propped open in an alley. I thought I could hear the lake muttering, and once an airplane far overhead, and then again the nighthawks, although only two this time. Did nighthawks have regular rounds like nurses or doctors on the night shift?

And then I said aloud that I was going to Boston. I still wonder sometimes how that popped out of my mouth; what was the proximate cause of *that*? But some things you just decide inside, I suppose. Some things you decide without deciding. If I was being cool and literary I could say something mysterious like the two nighthawks were the cause, and if there had been only one I would still be living in Chicago and probably still going up to the roof on summer nights to gawp at the stars and listen for nighthawks and tankers on the lake and laughter in the streets below, but I am not cool and literary, and I have no idea, even now, why I suddenly knew that I had to go, had to take the unreasonable chance, and said so. A few minutes later we went downstairs and shook hands and went to bed.

22.

EVEN THE *NAME* "CHICAGO" seemed cool to me as a child—it was *itself,* it was idiosyncratic, hatched in its own place, not a colonial name like New York or New Orleans, or a paean to a particular religion's heroes like San Francisco or San Antonio, but a name grown from the land and water of that place; although it was while I lived there that I discovered from Mr Mahoney that the word *Chicago* was an abbreviation of the Potawatomi name for the place where the river entered the lake, roughly *chicagouate,* referring to a species of garlic that grew particularly well there.

"So it is," said Mr Mahoney in his wry tone, "that every day many thousands of people around the world use a word meaning 'garlic' for the city in which we live; we might as well call ourselves Garlic City, or Garlicville, or Garlicton, or Garlicsburg, any of which would be not only historically accurate but redolent, in a manner of speaking. A visionary man such as yourself might see to it that a proposition for a name change make it onto the Cook County ballot. I would do it myself but at the moment I am seriously discommoded by His Eminence the

Cardinal, who is threatening to have me excommunicated from Mother Church. I have replied with evidence that his financial wheeling and dealing has lost some five million dollars from the coffers of the archdiocese—coffers filled by donations from most of the two million Catholics here, many of whom are poor as mice. An honest man, a man who adheres to his vows as a priest, would admit chicanery, apologize, ask for forgiveness, and amend his ways. That is not the way of the Cardinal Archbishop. Some observers of all this find it entertaining, in the same way they found the heavy-handed blundering exploits of our former mayor Richard Daley amusing. Neither man is amusing. Both use their offices as gathering points for money and power, and both ignore and demean and insult the very citizens they are sworn to represent. There is nothing entertaining about criminal activity, despite the evidence of popular culture, which insists on celebrating thieves and assassins. For us to be famous as the city of Al Capone and John Dillinger, for civic corruption and strong-arm politics, is a shameful thing. It is especially shameful when the man sworn to lead two million of his companions in an effort with the most blunt and direct mission statement of all time—feed the hungry, clothe the naked, house the homeless, succor those in despair—instead leverages personal profit from business transactions, lies and dissembles, stashes money in slush funds and shady real estate investments, lives as floridly as an ancient emperor, flaunts his power with supercilious glee, and attacks those who would call him to account for the breaking of his vows and the shattering of trust among his fellow congregants."

Thus Mr Mahoney, in the full flower of his considerable oratorical skills. His suggestion about the ballot measure appealed to me, though, and for a week or so I pursued the possibility, until I discovered that there was no such provision in Illinois law for a general plebiscite of that sort; there was only the possibility of "initiatives," which were so complex and difficult to file that essentially it was impossible. Edward was of the opinion that Abraham Lincoln would have eventually suggested an amendment to state law, allowing voters more direct influence occasionally than merely through their elected representatives, but he himself was suddenly elected president in 1860, and had to generally abandon what had been close attention to the peculiarities of Illinois legislation prior to that time.

★

I have not said enough about Edward's friends, I think. He had an inordinate number of friends, of many species, but let me concentrate on the dogs for a moment. There was Basher, a young boxer dog, and Wendell, who was some amalgam of wolfhound and husky, and so tremendously powerful but graced with the most gentle temperament. There was Maximus, who had been a racing greyhound before being adopted by the cantor at the temple, and there was Beatrix, of indeterminate species, and the blue-tick brothers, two hunting hounds with voices like faraway church bells. There were several black Scottish terriers I could never tell apart (although Mr Pawlowsky said he could tell them apart easily by their idiosyncratic gaits), and a Newfoundland named Grahame who reportedly had lost her left ear in a battle at sea. There were free-range dogs, many of them of mixed ancestry, who ranged as they chose along the lake, and there was one small lean gray dog that looked awfully like a slumming coyote to me, although Edward had made it clear that I was not to mention coyotes in this dog's hearing, for reasons that were not explained. Mr Pawlowsky told me once that one of the many things he had learned from Edward was that most dogs were exquisitely sensitive about parentage and heritage, and that a lot of scuffles and disagreements started with scurrilous remarks and muttered caustic comments that were ostensibly offered as jokes but were neither meant nor received as such. "Not unlike human culture," as Mr Pawlowsky observed, "where a great deal of what passes as social discourse is more verbal jockeying and snide commentary; you have to admire canine culture at least for the fact that you can respond to what clearly is a sneering dig by biting the speaker in the ass. We don't get to do that so much, and maybe we would be a better society if we did."

October that year stayed warm and clear and crisp all the way through Halloween, and something about the nights being so pleasant and starry sent people out to clubs and cafes in remarkable numbers; I wouldn't be at all surprised if that was the most profitable October ever in Chicago, at least judging by the crowds of people I saw crammed into blues bars, jazz clubs, gyro shops, pizza joints, party boats on the lake, street fairs and festivals, school barbecues and picnics, church carnivals, block parties, and impromptu parades and processions of every conceivable shape and size. I saw a Catholic priest cradling a silver box (called a pyx, I discovered later) reverently in his hands as he walked along Clark Street, followed by perhaps a hundred people, many of them singing a song I did not know. I saw a line of eighteen firemen walking slowly down Roscoe Street, for reasons I never discovered. I saw a dancing line of more than a hundred people in Portage Park, on the west side, all of them dressed in amazing bright colors and dancing with absolute abandon while dozens of men and boys hammered steel drums in a dozen different rhythms at once, a mesmerizing sight and sound.

The epic event for me that October, however, was the Greek Festival at Saint Demetrios Greek Orthodox Church on the west side, just past Lincoln Avenue. This was an epic event for the whole west side of Chicago, a famous street party that people for miles around began talking about and preparing for months, but I will always remember that year's festival for a single infinitesimal moment—not even a whole moment, but a slight gesture that I realized even then wasn't slight. Sometimes even now I watch it unfold slowly again in memory, almost lost in hoopla and bustle and tumult, almost obscured by throngs of laughing people and wriggles of smoke and tides of shouts and music and the billowing of tents breathing in and out with the evening breezes; but not lost.

According to Edward it was Miss Elminides who had suggested to Mr Pawlowsky that he and Edward come to the festival; the way Edward remembered this was that there had been a discussion of the best Greek food, and Mr Pawlowsky had opined that the greatest achievement of Greek cuisine was the gyro, the perfect marriage of flavors and edible packaging, and Miss Elminides smiled and said that while the gyro was an excellent version of the sandwich it could not be mentioned in the same reverent tones as many other savories traditional to her ancient culture, savories she had many times marveled over during her lifetime, and Mr Pawlowsky demurred politely, and said something about other Greek foods in his experience being like Greek music in that a little went a long way, and Miss Elminides at that point proposed that Edward and Mr Pawlowsky attend the Saint Demetrios Greek Orthodox Festival, which she knew for an inarguable fact to be a remarkable and thorough and entertaining celebration of Greek food and music.

In Edward's opinion the next few seconds were some of the most enjoyable seconds he ever spent in this life, because Mr Pawlowsky was so evidently torn by warring impulses, and of two contradictory minds, and wholly flummoxed, and trying to entertain two conflicting ideas in his head at once, that you almost expected his ears to spin, or smoke to issue from his eyeballs, or what hair he had left to twirl itself madly in the manner of a desert dervish. He wanted to instantly accept a direct and alluring invitation from Miss Elminides, but also instantly realized it would entail a serious voyage for him away from the apartment building. Saint Demetrios was easily three miles away—maybe forty blocks!

But to his credit Mr Pawlowsky said yes before you could count to ten, and Miss Elminides said that would be lovely, and she would check the schedule of events and choose the best of the music being performed, and then she took her leave, and Edward noted with high glee that Mr Pawlowsky then went into something of a brown study, from which he was only resurrected by having to fix a leaking faucet in 2A.

So they did all go to the Saint Demetrios Festival, and somehow I was roped into it too, because I was coming back from playing basketball at Northwestern University and would pass right by and might as well pop in if only to make a heroic effort to sample the wide array of gyros being sold, and so I was there at about ten o'clock, eating gyros happily with Edward, when we saw the slight but not slight thing. Miss Elminides had seen the musicians opening their instrument cases, and said something to Mr Pawlowsky, who realized that he ought to go claim two good seats in front of the bandstand. I think now that he didn't think about what he did next, but just did it out of the love and tumult in his heart. He bowed ever so slightly and held out his right arm for Miss Elminides, and without hesitation she put her left arm into the crook of his elbow, and they walked down the aisle of the little bandshell toward seats in the first few rows.

Edward and I were behind them as they walked toward the stage, so we didn't see their faces, but the way they held each other's arms so gently and naturally, as if they had always walked that way, with Mr Pawlowsky leading by a hair so he could gently use his shoulder to part the crowd and Miss Elminides sailing just slightly in his lee, was as eloquent and articulate as any facial expression I ever saw. We make too much of faces, I think, and often miss the supple expressiveness of the rest of the countries of our bodies; and not just human beings, either, but all beings; we all shiver and leap and shuffle and drag and skip and scuff and wriggle and wave and wag and flitter and flag in so many ways that language can't keep up, and we are always having to invent words for the ways we move to say how we feel.

Edward and I looked at each other, but we didn't say anything, because it wasn't like any words were necessary, but each of us knew that the other one was delighted at what he had just seen, and we went to try the spanakopita, which was extraordinary. I have looked in vain for spanakopita as good as that spanakopita at the Saint Demetrios Festival for years now, and have not come anywhere close. Perhaps, as a friend of mine says, you have to be actually at a Greek festival, in a city, on a wild Saturday night, just before the band starts, surrounded by people who are laughing and jostling and talking and eating, to savor great spanakopita properly. I'd like to say that he's wrong about this, because I dearly love spanakopita, but more often than not I suspect he is right, and there are even times I think maybe the very best spanakopita has to be eaten while marveling with pleasure that you just saw a slight thing that isn't slight at all.

*

You would think after my decision was made I would be happy, or anticipatory, or thrilled to contemplate prospective romantic and geographical and occupational adventures, and certainly I felt something of this, but mostly I found that I was melancholic. Indeed, to coin a phrase, I had the blues, and there was and probably still is no better place in America to have the blues than Chicago, all due respect to the Mississippi Delta where the form was invented, but where blues clubs do not have delicious steaks from Kansas and Nebraska and vibrant cheeses from Wisconsin, paradise of cheeses. Also Chicago had been where the acoustic blues of the country became the electric blues of the city, and I was partial to the electric blues, which had verve and snarl and punch in it, like the rock music I loved, while retaining the old dark weird of the blues as it had squirmed to life in the slave lands of the South.

So it was that October that I haunted the blues bars along Lincoln Avenue, mostly Kingston Mines and Wise Fools and John's, and night after night sat in corners and *felt* the music more than heard it—does that make sense? Part of this was sitting close to the stage, which was easy to do in those old rattletrap clubs in the years before they became tourist destinations; Kingston Mines was such a hovel that part of the roof fell in one night when Eddy Clearwater's band was playing, and famously the band never missed a beat, even as water poured down in torrents near the pinball machines. But part of it too was the way with the blues you can safely ignore the lyrics and feel the tidal pull of the music, its thunderous chant and chorus, its moan and shriek, the way its repetitive nature, in good hands, becomes a sort of roaring meditative thing, lit up and sharpened and electrified by the piercing brazen needling ringing guitar.

I found, after many hours in dark corners nursing my whiskey and swimming inside the music, that I didn't care much about the singer or the song—it was all the same to me whether the singer was male or female, mumbling or shouting, whispering or roaring, charismatic or wooden, and it was all the same to me what song was being played, old standard or gleaming new original, updated classic or obscure nugget unearthed from a scratchy record or handed down from guru to apprentice. It was the music that I liked, and sometimes loved; the way you always knew the form, but were always surprised and sometimes delighted by the delivery and the passion and the skill, and even, occasionally, moved by something—the sharp sneer of a guitar commenting acidly on the tumult of the other instruments, the bar extended twice or three times by a band delighted by its flow that night, the rare haunting saxophone (saxes are uncommon in blues trios and quartets), the way a singer sometimes would stop singing words altogether and just hum or growl what was in his or her heart, beneath the words.

I know it sounds fanciful to speculate how a city's music might reflect something deep and true and real about the place; and also Chicago, of course, is filled with all sorts of other music, much of it certainly characteristic of some of the city—I mean, there's a lot of polka music in Chicago, understandably so, with such large Polish and Czech and Slovenian and Latvian and Slovakian populations. But with total respect for jazz and polka and rap and opera and rock and pop, I still think Chicago sounds like the electric blues, and the electric blues sounds like Chicago, and even if you hear a good blues band in Dublin or Dunedin, as I have, you are immediately in Chicago, in a dark corner, nursing a whiskey, hoping that the roof will not fall in, and being amazed by the mastery of the bass player, who is somehow playing chugging lines that sound eerily exactly like a night train through rustling fields of corn.

You might not also hear, in that electric blues, wherever it is being played, poorly or well, the faintest hints and intimations of traffic along the lake, and jackhammers and piledrivers pummeling the Loop early in the afternoon, and the thrum and rattle of elevated trains, and the bellow of tankers and barges far out on the lake, and the grim clang of descending winter, and the jungled sound of millions of people in one particular place in America arguing and laughing and singing; but you might. I do.

23.

SOMETIME THAT MONTH I remember taking my worn shiny basketball and crossing Lake Shore Drive at rush hour, to do my hour of dribbling up and down the lakefront, when I realized with a start that I had not driven a car in months—a whole *year*, come to think of it. This was an amazing thing. It wasn't that I was a gearhead, particularly—unlike many of my friends and peers I had no interest in tinkering with cars, and racing them along the beach highway where I grew up, and puttering around in their innards, and proudly changing the oil myself with great ceremony and leakage, and knowledgeably discussing fan belts and gear ratios—but I had driven a good deal in college, back and forth across much of America to campus and back, and to realize that I had not been behind the wheel, whirring down highways and byways, stuck in traffic cursing gently and praying for something glorious on the radio, was . . . startling.

Thereafter for a while I found myself yearning to drive a car again, and I finally got the chance when a friend at work lent me her battered Pinto for a weekend; she was going away on a romantic adventure with her boyfriend, to a remote cabin in Wisconsin, to see once and for all if they could make it as a couple, which it turned out they couldn't, for all sorts of reasons, she told me later, some of them having to do with *someone* preferring to hunt deer rather than make love to his girlfriend, and *someone* preferring to drink copious shots of whiskey rather than discuss serious matters with his girlfriend, and *someone* blubbering about a hangover instead of snuggling with his girlfriend, who by the time they got back to Chicago was most definitely his former girlfriend.

All this was not my concern, however; I spent the weekend with the Pinto, which cured me thoroughly of my yearning for cars. The Pinto was a tinny rattling moist smoking roaring garish lurid rusting foul-tempered wreck which started only when it wanted to and lurched from one gear to another with an audible moan. It yawed terribly to the left, so much so that my arms were sore after driving it for ten minutes; the left rear tire was congenitally flat, and had to be refilled every hour or so; the license plates hung by a whim, and rattled ferociously in the wind when the car, coughing desperately, achieved twenty miles an hour; the right taillight was long gone, the hole covered by years of layers of duct tape; something had clearly expired in the trunk, possibly a horse, from the persistence and volume of the stench; there were something like a thousand sandwich wrappers and paper coffee cups and cigarette butts and tampon boxes strewn around the interior; there was a crack the size of Venezuela across the front windshield, and a hole as big as my fist in a side window; the only music was a cassette of a woman being stung by a thousand hornets, and shrieking about the experience; the gear shift was missing its knob altogether, so that when you shifted gears you lost skin on the palm of your hand; and there was a huge bumper sticker reading HONK IF YOU ARE HORNY TOO! on the rear fender, which caused no end of cacophony and gestures from other drivers. Also it was, no kidding, painted in orange and white stripes, apparently in a tiger motif, perhaps by the boyfriend as some kind of unconscious scream of passive protest about their affair.

I drove it anyway, of course, wincing as I shifted gears, and returning lewd gestures here and there to other drivers. For the first hour or so the experience was not unpleasant—I drove north along the lake all the way to Zion, almost the Wisconsin border, and it was a gentle afternoon, cloudy but warm, with ducks and geese whizzing past, and vast armadas of cloudbanks over the lake, and pretty girls bicycling and running along the shore, their lithe loveliness not yet completely hidden by parkas and hats. But then the car started sputtering and cursing, and I had to buy gas, and refill the declining tire, which entailed rooting in the trunk for a valve cap (missing from the tire, of course), which entailed breathing in the toxic fumes from the dead horse, which caused my eyes to water terribly. By the time I got the car back to Chicago it was amazingly out of gas again, and the tire was, of course, flat. I put another twenty dollars in the tank, filled the tire, parked it in the church lot with a note on the dashboard pleading a spiritual emergency (as per instructions from my friend, who used this dodge to park in church and temple lots all over the west side), and walked home. I don't think I was ever quite so happy to be on foot as I was that day. It was twilight and I saw an owl, too, near Clark Street, which made it, all in all, a good day.

*

By pure chance one day late in October I discovered where Miss Elminides went all day and what she did for work; she was a second-grade teacher at, unbelievably, Saint Demetrios Greek Orthodox School, where the festival had been held. I had spent the morning at Saint Matthias Catholic Church on Claremont and at the Catholic Worker House on Kenwood, working on my series of articles about spiritual practice, and at lunchtime I was strolling past the schoolyard at Saint Demetrios, looking for a gyro shop, when a fusillade of small bright children poured out of the school doors into the playground, followed by, to my astonishment, Miss Elminides, looking as calm and elegant as always.

For an instant I thought about not calling out to her, and respecting her privacy—she never had actually told me or anyone else what she did all day, and I suspect only Edward and maybe Mr Pawlowsky knew she was a teacher—but she saw me first, and smiled, and gestured for me to come through the gate. We shook hands gravely and she introduced me to the four or five children leaping around her eagerly like brilliant birds; clearly they worshipped her, and they regarded me with fascination, as someone who knew Miss Elminides well enough to be welcomed with a smile, and invited into The Presence!

She told me she had been a teacher there for nine years, and that her first day as a teacher was her thirtieth birthday, and that the very first poem she read aloud to her students was a poet's lovely poem about *his* thirtieth birthday:

> *The day that I turned thirty was a wintry*
> *Day with summer and apples and hawks*
> *In it and I realized that every day was an*
> *Epic birthday if you think about it so I'm*
> *Thirty today and ten and ninety and love*
> *Finds me and there is a mink in the creek*
> *And everything is happening all the time*
> *Including backwards and we had best be*
> *Attentive which I will try to be every hour*
> *Henceforth and you too and let us burble*
> *To each other about what we see, cousins*
> *And sisters and brothers as we all are yes*

I think I will always remember the way she essentially sang these lines, there in the jumbled schoolyard, with children bounding and leaping around her, two of them holding her hands and jealous of the others who wanted to touch her also; and the banks of vibrant green bushes and hedges behind her, against which her indescribably blue clothing also almost sang; and the way when the bell rang she said a word or two quietly and dozens of children instantly came to her as if summoned by a magician; and the way they walked before her, proud of their queen, and opened the door for her and her guest; for I was invited into the classroom also, to speak to the children for a moment about my work, Miss Elminides' conviction being that all manners of things and people were potentially lessons, and a brief visit from a working journalist might perhaps spark a child or two in directions unexpected and remarkable.

I did talk for a few minutes about stories, and why they were nutritious and even holy, and how we took them for granted, which we ought not to, because good stories were absolutely crucial to a good life and a good family and a good city and a good country, not to mention a good classroom. I talked about how my job was really to be a storycatcher, to wander around inviting people to tell me stories that mattered, whether they were funny or sad or sweet or confusing. My job, I said, was to catch and share as many good stories as I could, because stories are what we are, what we are made of, and if we don't share good stories, then we will drown in poor stories, thin and shallow ones, stories told by people who only want power or money, and there is so much more in life than power or money. The coolest most amazing people I have met in my life, I said, are the ones who are not very interested in power or money, but who are very interested in laughter and courage and grace under duress and holding hands against the darkness, and finding new ways to solve old problems, and being attentive and tender and kind to every sort of being, especially dogs and birds, and of course children, who are the coolest beings of all, and of course children in *second grade* are the coolest of the cool, especially if they have a teacher as cool as Miss Elminides, am I right?

In mid-sermon they had sat there staring politely at me (one boy gaping vacantly like a trout) but my last lines got them roaring, as I knew they would, and they shouted and danced between their desks for a moment until Miss Elminides gently said *all right* and back they flew into their tiny chairs, their feathers rustling and their faces glowing. Miss Elminides saw me out of the classroom and to the doors to the playground, and we shook hands gravely again, smiling, and she said one of her lesson plans in spring was to invite Edward into the classroom, to give her children a chance to meet an illuminated being. I said I thought that was a terrific idea and I would love to be there to watch what would surely be an amazing hour and she said she would consider it although it might be better to have the children encounter Edward wholly on their own, without the distraction of such an accomplished older man as myself. She said she would ponder this matter further, and meanwhile her most sincere thanks for sharing myself with the children, and what a fortuitous coincidence that I had happened by, and that indeed there was a wonderful gyro shop nearby, over on Washtenaw Avenue, I should ask for *keftethes,* which were tiny savory meatballs, the perfect thing for a light repast.

The *keftethes* there were nearly the best in the city, topped only by those made by a grandmother on Green Street. *Those* meatballs made you a better *person,* that's how good they were. Edward, of course, knew the shop, which had no name or address, but he would lead me there sometime before Christmas, if I asked.

★

I had written to the Wyoming girl, at her new address in Boston, to tell her of my decision, and she had written back thrilled, using many exclamation points!!, and I had also called her twice on the phone, once briefly from the booth at the gyro shop (with Leah smiling at me from the counter; somehow she knew I was calling a girl), and she said she hoped I would be able to get to Boston as soon as possible, and she was waiting anxiously, but that I should take my time, as she understood my attachments in Chicago, and would be loath to influence my timetable, given the depth of my friendships there, Edward in particular.

But I found that once the decision was made, I began to leave Chicago, piece by piece, somehow; and while I savored every hour of my last weeks, and felt a deeper appreciation of Mr Mahoney's sinewy courage against the blowhard Cardinal Archbishop, and Leah's alluring smile as she sliced roast lamb for gyros, and Donald B. Morris's abiding love for the Bears in the morning on the bus, and Mr Pawlowsky's calm wry wit, I could for the first time since my arrival see where I could *not* belong to this small unusual lively community; for community it was to me, and all these years later I think that *community* is the best word for all the riveting beings who remain somewhere inside me, and who prompted this account, and who come back to me sometimes, set in their places and stories in that riveting city, when I see a swirl of snow, or hear foghorns out on the water, or hear baseball games murmuring on the radio, or see a kid dribbling a basketball so shiny with wear that it seems to almost glow.

It was as if once I made the decision, then doors and windows opened to what was going to happen next; and it doesn't finally matter to this account that what *did* happen next was that the girl from Wyoming and I broke up a year later, though I came to love Boston, and spent ten years there, before eventually moving on again, this time west toward the sunset, toward the mother of all oceans, toward another girl who did entrance and overwhelm and utterly confuse me, and who said yes when I asked her to marry me one bright day by the sea, and who gave birth to our children, and who to this day rivets and puzzles and delights and astounds me in more ways than I could articulate in a dozen books. Sometimes now I think we will move one more time, even further west, out into the islands scattered deep in the bluest of oceans; but even if that comes to pass, and I end my days like Robert Louis Stevenson, bathed by sunlight through thickets of palm trees, under the eyes of albatrosses and frigatebirds, I will carry my Chicago with me, and think of Mr Pawlowsky when I see constellations, and of Miss

Elminides when I hear a mandolin, and of Edward when I encounter an illuminated being of any size and species; for there are many more of those than we know, and perhaps we brush past them all day long, and would be wise to look for them, and ask, here and there, for their quiet blessings.

24.

EDWARD'S *OBSERVED* BIRTHDAY, I discovered, was
in November; this year, said Mr Pawlowsky, it would be
November 19, the day that Abraham Lincoln delivered
the Gettysburg Address. Apparently not even Edward
knew his actual birthday, let alone his true age, and over
the years the tradition had grown up between Edward
and Mr Pawlowsky that Edward's birthday be celebrated
generally in November. In their first years as roommates
it had occasionally been celebrated on November 6 (Lincoln elected president for the first time), November 8
(re-elected president), but for the past few years it had
been celebrated on November 19, as Edward was lately
more interested in brief piercing speeches than in the
electoral process—thus his absorption in the speech Lincoln made from the train as he was leaving his beloved
Springfield, Illinois, to go to Washington to assume the
presidency in February of 1861: "My friends, no one, not
in my situation, can appreciate my feeling of sadness at
this parting. To this place, and the kindness of these
people, I owe everything. . . . I now leave, not knowing
when, or whether ever, I may return. . . ."

I had no idea what to give Edward as a present. For a while I thought of wheedling a bone from the butcher at the grocery store, or getting him a new blanket, or a radio of his own, or even a cassette player, perhaps, but none of these seemed quite dignified enough for Edward. Finally I settled on a beautiful sturdy copy of the collected poems of Walt Whitman, on the theory that anyone who so enjoyed Lincoln's writings would enjoy the sprawl and roar and tenderness of Whitman, the greatest of American poets, along with Emily Dickinson; but old Emily is a poet you have to pore over for years before you get the brilliance under the gnomic brevity and idiosyncratic capitalization; that poor woman never met a capital letter she didn't like, and threw them all over the page willy nilly, as if ink did not cost a penny.

Rather than a formal party for his birthday, Edward had something like a slow celebration all day long, with some visitors wandering into the apartment to convey their regards, and others making much of him on his social rambles through the neighborhood. It was a Saturday, and on Saturdays Edward ranged widely, as a rule, on errands for Mr Pawlowsky and on mysterious agendas of his own. Twice that day I saw him enter apartment buildings far from our own—once up on the north side, as I was dribbling up Broadway to play ball, and once on the west side, as I was coming back late that afternoon from a baptism at Our Lady of Good Counsel. When I popped in before dusk to convey my own regards and present the Walt Whitman, Mr Pawlowsky showed me the hilarious pile of gifts Edward had accumulated during the day—betting slips from Mr McGinty, honey from Miss Elminides, various bones of various hues and origins (including one from a cheetah), empanadas, a lovely winter vest from the dapper businessmen, a poster detailing all the edible fish found in the lake, two new brushes, and a set of four small waterproof boots, for ferocious days; these were from the two young women from Arkansas who had lived in 4E, who had much admired Edward. Also there was a bright new blanket with ROYAL SCOTS NAVY stenciled on it, and "In My Defence God Me Defend" printed in smaller letters below, a gift from the Scottish tailor and the detective in 2B.

There were also a startling number of postage stamps, both new and canceled, and Mr Pawlowsky explained, smiling, that Edward had a major serious yen for stamps, especially pink ones and those having to do with Lincoln; his single favorite of all was the pink Lincoln four-center, of which he had seven, so far, with negotiations in progress for an eighth, which was in the possession of a brilliant mathematics professor in Lisle, a town west of the city. For a while, in their early years together, Edward and Mr Pawlowsky had made an effort to organize the stamps into books and sheets, and there had been some talk of careful cataloguing, and the building of wooden bureaus with special sliding drawers for exhibits, but that talk had piddled away and now Edward just kept his stamps in a closet, "organized mostly by color, as far as I can tell," said Mr Pawlowsky—brighter ones down low where Edward could reach them easily, and the darker colors on shelves above, to be brought down occasionally on request.

Edward was delighted with the Whitman, which was gratifying—it's hard to choose the right gift for a dog you admire, and when you get it right it's a good feeling—and I read aloud from it for a few moments, trying to catch the swing and roar and mercy and energy of the man; I still think that Walt is as close to distilled Americanness as you can find in print, along with Mark Twain and Willa Cather; and there was a time there, sitting by the window in 4B, as the sun slid into Iowa, with Edward and Mr Pawlowsky sitting quietly listening to me read old Walt, that I still remember with a startle in the heart. The memory comes to me sometimes at dusk, usually in the autumn, and sometimes I find myself moved to pull old Walt down from the shelves, and read a little, quietly, thinking of my friends in their apartment by the lake.

I hear America singing, the varied carols I hear . . .
The carpenter singing his as he measures his plank or beam
The mason singing his as he makes ready for work, or leaves
off work,
The boatman singing what belongs to him in his boat, the
deckhand
Singing on the steamboat deck,
The shoemaker singing as he sits on his bench, the hatter
singing as he stands,

The wood-cutter's song, the ploughboy's on his way in the
  morning . . .
The delicious singing of the mother, or of the young wife at
  work . . .
Each singing what belongs to him or her and to none else,
The day what belongs to the day . . .

★

The thought occurs to me that I have gotten all this way in this account of my life in Chicago without ever saying much about my actual apartment, 2F, which had a big front window facing the street, which was always fascinating theater, although my window faced north, which meant that I never did see the sun, although quite often I could see the sun slide along the windows of the brownstones across the street, which caused window-shades to come down and go up in a pattern much like a wave breaking on the beach.

Although perhaps I have not said much because there is not much to report. There was a bed and a table and a chair from the convent, the bed ancient beyond reckoning and overstuffed with straw, so that occasionally a stalk would wriggle free and do its level best to puncture me. There was a rickety arrangement of bookshelves built with bricks and planks I had borrowed from a construction site on Addison Street (to which I actually did return the materials finally, piling them neatly on the front steps of the condominium complex that had arisen somehow without my bricks and planks). There was a large cardboard box covered with a blanket that I used as a table for bills and mail. There was a pot and a pan and a spatula, gifts from my mother on my graduation from college. There was a stereo set, my first big purchase in Chicago, on which I played the same ten or so records incessantly (which must have annoyed Denesh, my neighbor in 2E, although he never complained), and on which I listened nightly to jazz (WDCB) and rock (WXRT, with Terry Hemmert, who had a classic relaxed gravelly radio voice and adored the Beatles). I had two spoons and two forks and one knife and I was lonelier sometimes than I have admitted heretofore. I had two plates and a salt shaker shaped like a hawk that my brother Tommy gave me and whenever I felt particularly lonely I grabbed my worn shiny ball and went out to play or dribble along the lake, working on my left hand. I had two pairs of sneakers and one black suit for all occasions, as I am of Irish descent and know how to dress correctly for weddings and wakes. I had twenty books, mostly Robert Louis Stevenson and Jack London and a Bible in which my grandmother had written with a shaky hand *On my wedding day 1911 town of Kildare county of Kildare to John my iordaltha love, iordaltha* being Gaelic for certain and constant and trustworthy. I had a photograph of Abraham Lincoln that Mr Pawlowsky gave me, the last photograph ever taken of him alive, in which he is grinning. I had three pairs of pants and three shirts suitable for office wear. I had two pairs of black socks which both wore out over the course of the year so that after April I no longer wore socks, figuring that no one noticed socks anyway, which turned out to be true of men but not of women, interestingly; why would women be looking at men's ankles? I did have seven pairs of white basketball socks which I washed and rotated religiously and repaired meticulously whenever they seemed to be growing weary. These hung on a string pinned across the room and on the rare occasions when anyone else entered my apartment and asked about them I explained that they were an art installation by my sister who was an avant-garde artist in São Paolo, which was a whopping lie. I thought about buying a second basketball during the year but I could not abide the thought of not playing with my worn shiny ball which sometimes when in my doldrums I thought was my best and truest and most constant friend. In the first few weeks I was in Chicago, as it got darker and colder by the day, I was sometimes overcome by loneliness, and would dribble my ball as quietly as I could, close to the floor, working alternately with both hands; but even I knew that this was rude to my neighbors, and I stopped dribbling in the apartment, although once or twice I did have to go out to the lake quite early in the morning and dribble for a while until calm was restored.

*

And yet I sit here years and years after leaving Chicago and I still can hear the wind sliding off the lake, and the faint sound of grinding ice on the shore in the basement of winter, and piano music trickling out of the window of the man behind the temple (who was a composer who never titled his songs but only numbered them and was up to 332, the rabbi told me once), and the stories of the two sturgeon ten feet long and a thousand pounds each who once haunted Dog Beach and picked off cats and squirrels and once a poodle, and the boy who stole a motorboat from the marina and went out into the lake and for some reason having to do with ritual or madness cut off his pinkie fingers and nearly bled to death. So many stories that are now just scraps and tatters of fading stories to be forgotten unless I tell them now even in their truncated staccato versions. The old woman on Cornelia Street who reportedly rose into the sky from the roof of her apartment building and was not seen again by mortal eyes. The great war between rats and crows that raged up and down Pine Grove Avenue so savagely for weeks one summer that people were afraid to walk alone in the street and traveled only in tight armed phalanxes. The blue snow that fell all day one day in the years before there were such things as cameras. The healer who lived on Roscoe Street across from the convent and would never accept money for touching people and accepting their ills. The family with nineteen children whose habit was to adopt a new baby every time the oldest child left. The soldier who came back from secret service in the tunnels of Cambodia and never spoke another word the rest of his life although he was by all accounts the nicest most tender smiling man you ever met. The rabbi who ran off with both his director of

lifelong learning (female) and the cantor (male), supposedly to what was once called the Northwest Territories
in Canada and is now called Nunavut, which is Inukti-
tut for Our Land. The boy who was by many accounts
the best football player in the state of Illinois until he cut
so sharply one way in a game on a muddy field that his
defender's knee tore completely apart with a terrifying
ragged sound and the great football player walked off the
field and never played again, although in another version
of that story (told to me by the dairy manager at the grocery store on Broadway) he switched sports to tennis on
the theory that he would never be directly responsible
for an opponent's injury again.

And so many more stories—about the days before
there were any office buildings or large commercial con-
cerns at all in the neighborhood, and the north side of the
city along the lake was a sort of large village, where everything was tenements and shops and the streets were not
quite paved; about the man who claimed to be the last of
the original Potawatomi Indians who had lived in Chicago before white people came to build forts and take all
the fish and furs, and who gave erudite talks about his
people and their culture and history and legends, but
who turned out to be a man named Saul from Beaver
Crossing, Nebraska; about the nun who left her hour-old
infant in a shoebox at dawn at Our Lady of Mount Car-
mel on Belmont Avenue and a man bicycling past stole
the box and so found his son whom he named Samuel,

which means God has heard me. And so many more stories that, if they should be written every one, I suppose that even the world itself could not contain the books that should be written. Amen.

25.

MR PAWLOWSKY TOLD ME enough stories about Edward to fill a dozen books, and while many of them have slipped my mind over the years, and slipped through my fingers too because I did not know enough then to jot notes to serve as spurs to memory, some of them remain adamant and resistant to erosion; the story of the boy left on second base, for example, which would be a story sufficient in itself to say something piercing about Edward, if you could only tell one chapter of his character.

The boy was eight or nine years old, as Mr Pawlowsky told the tale. His family lived in a mossy old wooden tenement behind which there was one of those tiny neighborhood playing fields you often see in old cities— unnamed, not officially a city park, probably essentially an accident of motley development over the years, a sort of asymmetrical space that no one claimed to own and everyone used as playground, baseball and football field, dog run, picnic ground, and refuge for new or illicit romance. The grass grew in uneven patches, most of the field was dirt, and the backstop, which had been built by neighborhood dads years ago, sagged.

The boy was small for his age and no great athlete, and was picked only reluctantly for teams by the other boys, and even then only when they were so short-handed that they had no choice but to let him play. He had rarely caught the ball and never even been on base; he was such an easy out that he was never walked.

Mr Pawlowsky said that Edward just happened to be strolling past the field when the boy came up to bat, and something about the game, or the angle of light that evening, or the boy's strained face, made Edward stop and watch for a while—"he's like that, you know, alert to things, and patient enough to wait for them to arrive," said Mr Pawlowsky. The boy missed one pitch badly, waited out two pitches below his knees, and then gauged a slow pitch perfectly and lined it down the right-field line. The outfielder, shocked, got a terrible start on the ball, and by the time he got to the ball the boy was standing on second base.

"According to Edward there was the usual derision and shouting from the other boys, and overmuch congratulatory blather, so that everyone knew it was false in character and intent, but the boy at second base never said a word. The next batter popped up and that was the end of the inning, but then what Edward was waiting for happened: the boy wouldn't leave second base. The other kids yelled at him and ragged him and shoved him and all of that but he wouldn't budge, and after a lot more yelling the game broke up and the other boys went home, probably because it was by then too dark to see. The boy stayed at second base, though. Edward stayed where he was, sitting along the left-field line. The boy never sat down on the base or fidgeted or anything, according to Edward. He just stood there and Edward just sat quietly, waiting. It was a lovely late-summer night and there were a remarkable number of swifts and then nighthawks loose in the ocean of the air. Along about midnight Edward approached the boy and they came to an understanding and Edward walked the boy home. Edward did *not* give the boy a ride home, as some versions of the story have it. Now somehow that story says a great deal about Edward, although I am not sure it's easy to articulate just *what* it says about Edward. But it's one of those stories where the teller and the listener know what it's about, even if the words don't, quite."

★

One Saturday morning in November I woke early and went down to the basement for Mrs Manfredi's empanadas, and something about the line of grinning sleepy residents, and the patience and courtesy with which they waited on a line that went halfway up the stairs, struck me forcibly, and I was filled with regret and remorse about my decision to leave. This was made worse a moment later when Azad and his sister Eren showed up, holding hands; their parents had let them come downstairs alone for the first time to get their own empanadas, and some for their mom and dad. I was third from the front when word filtered down that the children had shyly joined the end of the line, and I knew what would happen: they would be passed up the line until they got to the front, each resident tousling their hair, and this is exactly what happened. A moment later I got my empanadas and went back to my room and ate them and then packed a small bag and took the bus down to Union Station and got on the Empire Builder train from Chicago west, rattled. I had no plan except just get on the train, and think for a while; something about trains then and now seemed to focus and sharpen my mind—maybe the sliding scenery, or the rhythmic regularity of the ride, in which you could lean back and dream rather than have to concentrate on the conduct of the car.

I watched the Illinois farmland roll by. I thought about the girl from Wyoming but everything that seemed so right and alluring about going to be with her now seemed foolish and callow. What if there were no jobs? What if none of the college friends I knew in Boston wanted to get a cheap apartment with me? What if what felt like a magical mutual attraction wasn't at all, as usual, and I was once again fooling myself? And most of all, waiting patiently at the end of the line of questions, was the one I had hesitated to ask myself forthrightly: Why was I leaving friends and a job and a city and a life I enjoyed immensely, for what seemed the airiest of pipe dreams? In the year since I had arrived I had met friends I savored, friends who were startling and generous and riveting; and foremost among those friends were the man and the dog in 4B.

It was two hours from Chicago to Milwaukee, and for

most of those two hours I thought of Edward. I had never known a dog as a child; our family beagle, Cleo, was banished to life on a farm before I was born, as penalty for serial romantic assaults on other dogs (including a neighboring wolfhound, which led my dad to speculate Cleo must have used a ladder), and the arrival of four small boys in five years after his banishment precluded the possibility of another dog in the house; as my father said, why get a dog when you had perfectly good badly behaved messy roaring beings already in hand? I had some casual acquaintances among the neighborhood dogs, but no real companion, and certainly no close friend, as Edward had proven to be. Indeed Edward had opened my eyes about the whole idea of relationships with beings of other species than mine; like many people I had casually assumed such relationships were matters mostly of property, affectionate at best, but Edward had made me see that the much deeper play had something to do with real admiration and genuine reverence, a lesson I have not forgotten in the years since I first met him on the steps of the building, the day I moved in with my basketball and my duffel bag. He and I had nodded gravely to each other that day, and I had thought that here was a fine example of a dog of indeterminate species; but he had turned out to be my closest friend in Chicago.

I got all the way to Red Wing, Minnesota, on the Mississippi River, some six hours from Chicago, before I turned around and took the train home again. There were a few hours to wait in Red Wing and I sat in the lovely old stone station and thought about how someday I would stay on that train all the way west, through North Dakota and Montana and Idaho and Oregon to Washington, finishing up by the vast Salish Sea, where I would wander Seattle and eat oysters and listen to the piercing screams of gulls; and I thought too about how sometimes in life you just take leaps and hope for the best, and don't hedge your bets and make sensible decisions based on what you know, but deliberately make decisions based on what you don't know, but might find out. On the way back to Chicago I slept so deeply that the conductor had to wake me up when we got to Union Station, and I was so groggy that I walked to my office, only realizing it was Sunday when I finally heard the absence of commuter trains overhead on the elevated tracks.

★

Just before Thanksgiving that year I deliberately took a sick day on a Thursday to watch Edward's office hours in the alley. This I did with Mr McGinty, the two of us standing by his kitchen sink in the morning and silently watching the line slowly shuffle forward. Again there was a remarkable variety of beings, and again there was apparently a sort of truce or détente between animals who would usually be predator and prey, or combatants; there was a sharp-shinned hawk behind two mice, and near the end of the line there were several crows standing patiently behind a red-tailed hawk, perhaps the same hawk I had seen last time. Mr McGinty declined to open the kitchen window, on account of the cold and from respect for Edward's privacy, so we didn't hear any snatches of conversation, but it was fascinating enough to watch the quiet advance of the line, and the way animals turned from their time with Edward and walked or flew thoughtfully back to their regular lives. Again there were a number of dogs of various kinds, including a wolfhound the size of a pony, though no cats. Just as we thought the line was drawing to an end a small deer trotted up and joined the queue, behind a gaggle of squirrels. Mr McGinty made a note about the deer; it turned out he kept a list of species, just from curiosity, and at this point, he said, he would not be totally surprised if a sturgeon appeared one day, or a brace of salmon, or a mountain lion. He *had* seen coyotes, eagles, geese, ducks, and once what sure looked like a lynx, although probably that was a large bobcat— the two cats are hard to tell apart unless you are fairly close to them, and he wasn't about to go out to get a better look, mostly from respect for Edward but also because a lynx could tear your face off in a second, and he liked his face where it was, personally.

By the time the line was finished and Edward had gone upstairs it was lunchtime, and Mr McGinty made sandwiches, and we talked about the Chicago of his youth for a while. Old saloons and straw-boater hats, and society ladies wearing long skirts that brushed the ground. Horse trams and cable cars. Wooden sidewalks and gas-lit lamps on the streets. Bicycles everywhere, and not the lean balanced machines of today, said Mr McGinty, but the frail tall old things of yesteryear, which could be ridden only by madmen and acrobats. The first cars and the last horses. Restaurants where the only thing on the menu was beefsteak and beer. Hot dogs sold from carts in alleys for two cents each. Candy made from molasses. Penny arcades and kinescopes and gramophones. The summer circus on Ashland Avenue. The old *Chicago American* newspaper, "which started publishing when I was eleven years old," he said. "Paddle-steamers on the lake. The time the Chicago River burst into flames because it was so foul and filled with flammable jetsam; that was in 1899, when I was young, and I remember my father telling me about it, for he had seen it happen as he was walking home from work.

"Magicians and vaudeville on theater stages all up and down Lincoln Avenue as far as you could see. . . . There might have been fifty theaters on that street alone, and sometimes when I was a teenager I would wait in the shadows to watch all the actors and magicians flood out onto the street at two in the morning after their last shows; it seemed to me sometimes they all stepped out of their doors at the exact same moment, laughing and greeting each other all cheerful and familiar and calling nicknames and insults; it seemed like the most wonderful thing in the world to me, to be an actor or a magician like them, and join their guild, but my life went in a different direction."

It was on the tip of my tongue to ask him about the shape of the rest of his life, for all I really knew of him was that he was a genius horseplayer, but by then it was early afternoon and as he said a man who is near one hundred years old had best take a nap every afternoon or else, so we shook hands and parted. Before I went upstairs to my apartment, though, I stepped out the back door into the alley, just to gaze for a moment at the place where Edward held office hours, and there was a big barred feather caught in the fence—a hawk or an owl feather, I think. I still have it here by my desk all these years later, and it gives me a deep pleasure to see it every morning.

26.

ONE OF THE LAST THINGS I had to do as I prepared to leave was to alert John the Mailman that I would be leaving, and ask him to file a forwarding address for me, and thank him for his quiet hard work, which had been a boon to me, for I loved letters and postcards and magazines and newspapers, and received gobs of such things, and sent more, all of which John had to carry to and from his truck. In my time in Chicago John had carried, by my estimate, thousands of pieces of my mail alone in and out of the building, as well as the rest of the residents' mail, and I much admired his steady work ethic. He appeared every afternoon just after three o'clock, and while he was cheery and friendly he never actually paused in his work; conversations with him were conducted on the move. The only time he was still was when you were rooting through his truck for a package (in my case mostly brownies from my mom, and packets of periodicals from my dad and brothers), and I had learned to seize those moments to ask him about his dragonfly studies. He was quite serious about this work and had made several notable discoveries about their predation patterns, about which he was apparently something of an expert.

I came home early one afternoon from work specifically to thank John for his work, and by happy chance I had not one but two packages waiting in his truck, so I rooted as slowly as I could and peppered him with questions about dragonflies. It was a cold afternoon, with the wind slicing in off the lake, and perhaps he wanted to warm up a little, for he came as close to relaxing and chatting as he ever did with me, and I remember his eloquent passion to this day.

"They are the most remarkable creatures," he said. "We take them utterly for granted and hardly notice them but they are astonishing beings. They can fly at forty or fifty miles an hour, you know—twice as fast as the fastest man can run. They can catch and eat anything they want. They can fly instantly in any direction whatsoever, including backwards. As larvae in water they are big and quick enough to eat small fish, and when mature in the air they eat any and all insects. I suspect they can and have eaten shrews and newts and lizards also but that is subject to further study. A perfectly designed flying and eating machine, with some six thousand known variations. Isn't that amazing? And we hardly notice them. And there may be thousands more that we have not identified as yet. It makes you humble. The legion of things we see but do not see. They can eat their weight in an hour and then do it again an hour later, you know. You see a lot as a mailman. The hermits in your building, the woman who had been a film actress. The hermits have never received a single package in seven years and Eugenia received a certified check every week. I try to pay attention. And their names are euphonic and melodious, you know—the Migrant Hawker, the Scarce Chaser, the Great Pondhawk, the Keeled Skimmer, the Green Darner, the Downy Emerald. Who could fail to be entranced by this? We hardly notice them at all though they are everywhere. Also Edward receives mail, you know. Generally packets of stamps, but also surfing literature. Someday perhaps I will travel to the southern hemisphere and study Thorntails and Yellowjacks and Perchers and Dropwings. That will be a pleasure. Did you find your packages? One was a set of books, and the other I believe contains brownies or cookies. You get so you have a sense of what's in a package. The wrapping style generally gives it away more than the shape. Now *that* would be a fascinating study—what you can ascertain about senders from the way they wrap packages. I must be going. Check by the wheel-well for the books and by the windows for the cookies. I put packages with food closer to the windows. I wish you the best in your travels. Massachusetts, eh? A land of many ponds and wetlands. Keep your eyes open. I am particularly interested in Hawkers and there are at least eight species there, but I have long suspected there is a Skimmer called the Striped Glider in Massachusetts; if by chance you see one, send me a note in care of the post office. Bright orange tail with a black needle on the end. You can't miss it.

Travel safely. Don't forget to send me a note if you see the Glider. I'm *sure* it's there. See you!"

★

I have wandered through and marveled at many cities since my years in Chicago—cities all over the world, from the ancient seethe of Rome to the glinting brio of Sydney; cities on the shoulders of mountains, cities by the lip of the sea; so very many cities astraddle rivers, or camped for centuries where two rivers meet; cities looming out of the flat plains like huge shards of light and glass, cities insisting on themselves amid inhospitable deserts, cities huddled defiant and disgruntled against endless ice and snow, cities wrapped like long urban shawls around the curving shores of bays; and each of these cities had a flavor and a character all its own, formed of more than merely locale and climate, and the accident of its original economic or military excuse. Each had been created, was constantly being created, by the people who lived there, the way they lived, their adamant dreams, the web and weave of their languages, the games their children played in streets and fields, the music issuing from their windows, the rustle of the trees, the burble of birds, even the way rain arose and swirled and flowed away; one way to savor a city, I have discovered, is to walk through it after a shower, and watch and listen as the water slips back to mother ocean, however far she is; you can almost hear the shape and skin of a city this way, its curves and rills and subtle hills.

Often I had to look hard for a city's particular smells

and stories, and wander around neighborhoods and alleys and parks, before I began to catch its deeper salt and song. Often, I found, this deeper sense of the city was not at all where the shepherds of tourists claim it to be; in New York City, for example, the thrum of it, the actual city in which people live and love and fight and die, is not on Fifth Avenue or perhaps even in lower Manhattan, but in brave shaggy Harlem, and cacophonous burly Queens, and along the gull-shrieked crab-scuttled shores of Staten Island, and in old dank redolent taverns in Bushwick, where the Mets are always losing by a run in the bottom of the seventh on the murmuring television above the bar.

Many of those cities I came to love, often to my surprise; as lovely and welcoming and gleaming and harbor-profligate as Sydney is, for example, I came to like the rough sprawl of Melbourne more, a brisk muscular city that welcomes penguins to its beaches at dusk. I liked old blunt ragged Tacoma more than officious Seattle, grinning Vancouver more than dowager Montreal, windy wet saltshot San Francisco more than preening sultry Los Angeles. I liked cold gruff Edinburgh more than imperial London, wild Jakarta more than prim Tokyo, tumultuous Montevideo more than vaunted Buenos Aires, wind-whipped Alexandria more than regal Cairo.

But never, among all the cities I have wandered over the years, cities all over the earth, did I feel and smell and sense anything quite like the verb that is Chicago; and always, no matter how many years passed, I could hear and see and touch something inside me that only Chicago has and is, some intricate combination of flat sharp light off the lake grappling with dense light from the plains to the west, the fields to the south, the forests to the north.

All cities are riven by the stutter of engines, all cities shine in the fitful sun and endure the whip of weather, all cities are filled with shouts and imprecations and the mosaic of music, the thunder of commerce, the clash of soldiery, the eternal war of feet against the earth; but sometimes I wonder if there is not one city for each of us, one city that is our own somehow, in ways having nothing to do with nativity or residence; indeed I suspect that for many people the city in which they were born and have lived their whole lives is not the city in their hearts, the city in which they would have lived most happily and comfortably, the city they probably will never know. I have lived in four cities, in my long lifetime, and I have savored them all, and very much liked three, and lived in them with pleasure, and happily explored their secret corners and subtle stories, but I loved the fourth, the one in which I lived the least, for five seasons, years ago when I was young.

∗

My last day of work at the magazine was a Friday in the middle of December. Mr Mahoney took me to lunch at the Berghoff Cafe, on Adams Street; the ladies in the circulation department gave me a baseball signed by Richie Zisk; my colleagues in the editorial department gave me a beautifully bound copy of Walt Whitman's *Leaves of Grass*; and Mr Burns called me into his office late in the afternoon for an "exeunt interview," as he said.

Again he was dressed in a glowing gray suit of the finest cut and cloth, and my attention was distracted by the way you could see a corner of the elevated train tracks in the window behind him; without warning there would be the roar of a train every twenty minutes or so. But once again, just as he had been on my first day, he was cheerful and blunt and memorable in his peroration. A most remarkable man; I can still close my eyes and see his round pink shining face blooming from his suit jacket like a rose.

For a moment I thought it actually was going to be an exit interview, for he asked me a few questions, which I tried to answer honestly and articulately—Had I enjoyed the work? Had I learned anything useful about professional journalism? Was there anything I could suggest about more effective operation of the office? Was I not a far better man for having worked with the fearless and sinewy Mr Mahoney? Did I need a reference for a journalism job in Boston, to which he understood I was headed, lovely old city, beware the Mafia, learn a smattering of Gaelic if you are living in South Boston, it will be helpful in the social ramble?—but then his natural ebullience and garrulity reasserted himself, and he delivered a soaring speech about journalism that I still recall with pleasure and awe. Over the years since I heard it, in his office on Madison Street, I have sometimes thought that perhaps those few moments marked the beginning of my life as a writer, for that was the first time I heard someone express, eloquently and passionately, what stories were actually for and about, at the deepest level.

"You think you have been working on a magazine," he said. "You think you have been apprenticing in the legendary guild of ink-stained wretches who collect and report fact and opinion. You think you have been training to be a journalist, a profession long in the tooth, if not in the esteem of the rich and respectable. And some of this is true, in the same way a man *is* playing professional baseball if he plays for the A-League Appleton Foxes in the wilds of Wisconsin. But he is in the shallowest waters of the professional game, the puddles at the edge of the sea, and so have you been pittering in the waves like a child at the shore. At this magazine I hope you have learned the rudiments of our craft, the way that you must balance ego and humility, the way that the profession is finally one of service, not of heroic gratification of your urge to be important. We are *not* important. We are *crucial,* yes; without us there is naught but lies and thievery and souls easily led to the altar of Mammon, thereupon to be sacrificed to serious profit, which is our first and foremost deity and principle; but we are not important in the eyes of the world, and will never be. I hope you learned that here. Those among us who expose and uncover the most chicanery and greed will be soon found to have feet of clay, and hands of the stickiest glue, and the sexual proclivities of maddened weasels; those among us who ferret out the true facts of imbroglio and crime will be soon enough banished and exiled, doomed to flog useless products of one kind or another for the rest of their days; those of us who write most beautifully and gracefully and eloquently and powerfully will be suspected of plagiarism, rumored to be dope fiends, assumed to be self-absorbed egomaniacs, and eventually doomed to be forgotten, our books and articles turned to mold and mulch. That is the fate of all journalism.

"But we *are* crucial. That is what I hope you have learned. We listen for and collect and share stories. Without stories there is no nation and no religion and no culture. Without stories of bone and substance and comedy there is only a river of lies, and sweet and delicious ones they are, too. We are the gatherers, the shepherds, the farmers of stories. We wander widely and look for them and gather them and harvest them and share them as food. It is a craft as necessary and nutritious as any other, and if you are going to be good at it you must double your humility and triple your curiosity and quadruple your ability to listen. Mr Mahoney has the highest opinion of your promise as a journalist but I will advise you to savor his compliment today and forget it tomorrow. Always assume you can do better. It is a safe assumption. Always search for the deeper story. At this magazine, being absorbed by spirituality not as a talisman but as an implement of daily labor, we have searched for stories of spiritual substance; I hope you have learned that the best stories are most often not found where you think to look, but where you didn't. The heart of the Cardinal Archbishop of Chicago, for example, is a crumbled house where honesty and humility once lived; to look there for more than motes of grace is to waste the hours granted you by a merciful creator. But to look everywhere else—that is the journey that we will continue to make as long as we are able. We will do so without your assistance, which was more than passable, and always, as far as I can tell from reports, honest in intent, if raw in the execution. Do you have any questions?"

"About my work?"

"About your future."

"No, sir."

"Better get to Boston, then."

"Yes, sir."

And so I did. I went around the office one last time, shaking hands, and then Mr Mahoney accompanied me down the stairs to the street. We shook hands for a long minute, and then he smiled and gave me a worn pencil. "A better man would give you a more notable gift," he said, "but I think a pencil is a glorious gift. Use it well. Drive safely. Be joyful. Be tender. Everything else is secondary to tenderness. Remember that."

27

I LEFT CHICAGO ON THE FIRST DAY of winter. I borrowed an old Impala from a college friend and loaded it with everything I owned, which was once again mostly my worn shiny ball and crammed duffel bag; I had given away everything else but my grandmother's Bible and Robert Louis Stevenson's *Kidnapped* and my new copy of *Leaves of Grass,* and stuffed all my clothes and backup sneakers into the duffel.

This was before dawn. I wanted to be away at first light, for murky reasons. Edward carried the ball and the Bible downstairs and I carried the duffel. The car was parked right in front of the three stone steps I had walked up with such hope and trepidation five seasons before. Miss Elminides had made me a thermos of coffee and Mr Pawlowsky had made me a packet of ten ham sandwiches, which he calculated would sustain me to the border of Massachusetts. Denesh had given me a cricket ball from his playing days, which I still keep on my bureau at home. Mrs Manfredi made me a bag of empanadas for the road and Mr McGinty had given me a betting ticket for Arlington as a keepsake; months later a horseplayer friend of mine in Boston checked on it and discovered it was worth a hundred dollars.

I had gone around the building the night before and knocked on every door, even the nuns', to say goodbye. The librettist and I shook hands for a long time and talked about the White Sox and he said maybe someday he would come to Boston and work on an oratorio about the famous mayor James Michael Curley and we could go to a Red Sox game although it wouldn't be the same as this wild sweet hilarious amazing season with the South Side Hit Men. The two hermit brothers didn't answer their doors when I knocked, although the television volume was turned up when I knocked on the door of 3E, which I think was the hermit who had served as bookmaker with Edward on Kentucky Derby Day.

Ronald Donald the Scottish tailor also shook hands with me for a long time and said how he and the detective really should have made more of an effort to be better neighbors, being right across the hall and all, and he regretted not making more time for that, but he had enjoyed what time we did spend together, and wished me well, and sometimes the way to be a good neighbor was to just be friendly in small doses. The detective came out of the kitchen and shook hands briefly and said he had a baking emergency for which he hoped I would excuse him, which I did.

Little Eren was asleep by the time I got to their apartment but Azad was allowed to get up from bed and come out and shake hands with me in the hallway, sleepily, in his pajamas. His pajamas were covered with horses in all different colors. He said he would send me a baseball card of Richie Zisk as a surprise sometime and that would be funny. About five months later, just as the baseball season opened, I did get a Richie Zisk card in the mail, with a note from Mr Pawlowsky that Azad wanted me to know that Richie had gone over to the Texas Rangers.

I knew Mr McGinty was asleep by the time I got to his door, so I left him a note saying that I had really enjoyed his company and his kindness to me, and that I hoped he would think of me on Kentucky Derby Day, because I certainly would be thinking of him, the greatest horseplayer ever, no other candidates need apply. The man who raised cheetahs was not in his apartment or perhaps was asleep when I knocked. Sister Maureen answered right away when I knocked on her door (she was in 3B, with sisters flanking her on either side and four more upstairs in 4E and 4F) and she took me around to the other nuns' doors to shake hands, and then they presented me with six pears, one for every state I would pass through on my way to Boston. For some reason this was the one thing that made me cry that night.

I even went down in the basement to say goodbye to the sailor, who was swinging in a hammock in his stall. He climbed down and shook my hand and wished me well and said that he had always wanted to go to Boston, a city of undeniable maritime history and legend, and that if ever he made it there he would look me up and we could go out into Boston Harbor and see what there was to see, maybe even set foot on Old Ironsides, the famous American warship. On my way back upstairs I stopped for a moment to stare at Azad's horse and remember Eugenia the actress who had been in the Broncho Billy movies, and I stood by Mrs Manfredi's stall and inhaled the aroma of thousands of empanadas, and then I went upstairs to say goodbye to Mr Pawlowsky and Edward and Miss Elminides.

I found the three of them together in 4B, Edward making coffee and Miss Elminides and Mr Pawlowsky sitting together by the window. Miss Elminides was wrapped in the Navy blanket because she said she had a slight chill. It was odd to see Miss Elminides in the room, but refreshing to me that she fit so easily, and didn't seem at all out of place. I presented Edward and Mr Pawlowsky with a transistor radio, so that they could listen to Sox games on WMAQ, 670 on your AM dial, and they smiled, and I presented Miss Elminides with a copy of selected poems by the wonderful Greek poet Konstantinos Petrou Kavafis, and she was delighted, and Mr Pawlowsky presented me with an eleventh ham sandwich, in case of sandwich emergencies along the road. Edward presented me with a drawing of an alewife, framed with what appeared to be paint-stirring sticks. I still have the painting, which hangs above me as I write.

I remember still that we all sat there quietly for a while, Edward sitting by Miss Elminides, and Mr Pawlowsky fiddling with the radio; he found a Chicago Bulls basketball game, but he and Edward exchanged looks, and

Mr Pawlowsky announced that in my honor they would wait until the White Sox started spring training to use the radio for anything other than the music Miss Elminides loved, which was generally on WNIB, 97.1 on your FM dial. Miss Elminides laughed at the orotund way he pronounced the call letters, and something about the way she looked at him and he looked at her and Edward looked at them thrilled me and made me sad and I waved goodnight and went downstairs to bed.

★

That next morning, before dawn, Edward put my duffel and my worn shiny basketball in the backseat (I wasn't carrying enough luggage to bother unlocking the trunk), and I arranged the thermos of coffee and ham sandwiches and pears and empanadas on the passenger seat where I could reach them easily while driving. Mrs Manfredi had wrapped the empanadas in such a way that a tiny wriggle of redolent steam emerged from the bag and instantly filled the car. It was a cold morning and I got the engine going to let the car warm up and then I just stood there in front of the apartment building with Edward for a few moments.

When I was a kid I thought that the biggest moments in life would be trumpeted and highlighted and italicized somehow, that you would know when they were coming and could get your feet set to brace for them, and you would know they were upon you, and make a satisfactory effort to memorialize and celebrate them, but it turns out that's not at all how it works, and the biggest moments of your life just amble up behind you and suddenly are just there without fanfare. You fall into and out of love without much drama, you stammer like an idiot as you propose to your girlfriend, your brother just stops breathing quietly without any notice that death has come, your daughter just slides out of your wife suddenly like an otter emerging from a burrow. It turns out that the biggest moments are a lot like the smallest moments, just trundling and shuffling along one after another, each one utterly normal and absolutely the most amazing moment ever. So we just stood there, Edward and me, that morning. We were looking at each other but not staring intently and meaningfully and emotionally like in the movies. I think now that we were maybe drinking in a long last look, each of us making sure we had the other one locked in good in memory, the shape and substance and carriage of body and rumple of hair and ripple of fur in the breeze off the lake. I suppose we stood there for five or six minutes and then I said I better go, and I went. Years later someone asked me why I did not reach out a hand to scratch his ears, and why he didn't sidle up against my legs like dogs do, and I tried to explain that Edward wasn't like that, and I wasn't like that with him, and that you would no sooner scratch his ears than you would rub Mr Pawlowsky's nose, or chuck Miss Elminides under the chin. It wasn't like that with Edward, not at all, which says something important about Edward, it seems to me.

★

I drove down our street. As I turned south the sun slid over the edge of the lake and the whole long line of buildings to my right lit up gently. I slowed down to savor the light splashing against the buildings like surf against cliffs. At Belmont Avenue I saw a bus that looked like the Sound Asleep Bus but the way it was angled I couldn't see the number or the driver. I wanted to honk in case it was Donald B. Morris, but then I thought he would be startled, and I didn't want to startle him, so I drove on, trying not to cry.

Down along the lake, past Diversey Harbor, past Abraham Lincoln Park, past the Navy Pier, past Ulysses Grant Park; past the ragged glories of the South Side, the curved seawall of 31st Street Harbor, past Andrew Jackson Park and Rainbow Beach; and then over the Calumet River, and onto the interstate highway, and then a moment later over the Illinois border into Indiana. I thought about stopping there by the WELCOME TO INDIANA sign, and meditating about exits and exiles and narrative closure and the endings of stories, and things like that, but there was too much hurtling traffic around me to stop safely, and what good would it have done, to weep by the side of the road over some arbitrary and ephemeral line of demarcation and departure?

To me crossing the Calumet River was the moment I left Chicago for good; somehow water was important and defining and crucial to the city, and it is bound and riven and defined by waters, from the lake bigger than many seas, to the pounding rain that fell in fall, to the little dirty rivers long ago imprisoned by concrete and steel. Years later I overheard someone disparage Chicago as a rare American city not built on a serious river, and instantly I saw the lake, cold and vast and wild, stretching so far in every direction that it had no end, water bigger than any river could imagine.

I drove through Indiana, state of the great journalist Ernie Pyle, state of cornfields and copses of oaks. Through Ohio, state of the great journalist Ambrose Bierce, state of soybeans and buckeyes. Through Pennsylvania, state of the great journalist Rachel Carson, state of mushrooms and beech trees. Almost to New York, state of the great journalist E. B. White, state of apples and maples . . .

It was near the east end of Pennsylvania, somewhere near the border with New York, somewhere near dusk, just about the time that even now reminds me of reading Walt Whitman aloud to Edward and Mr Pawlowsky, that I pulled over to stretch for a while by the side of the road. I remember there were beech trees as far as I could see up into a straddle of mountains, and I remember thinking that I had not seen a forest like that for a long time. I riffled through my duffel bag for a pear and a Springsteen cassette that was in there somewhere, and found a small package carefully wrapped in rough brown paper cut from a grocery store bag. For a moment I thought I should wait to open it until I got somewhere with more light, but my curiosity got the best of me, and I tore it open, and found seven pink Abraham Lincoln four-cent stamps, beautifully set between two narrow panes of glass, and framed with wood cut from paint-stirring sticks. There wasn't any note, but it wasn't like a note was necessary.

NOTES AND THANKS

To my amused bemused wise wry dad Jim Doyle, who quietly said to me one sunny Florida morning, "You know, those little stories and drawings you do about your years in Chicago, you ought to walk them out into a novel," which was the proximate spark of the book in your hand; to my friend and former Chicago-journalism colleague Cathy O'Connell-Cahill at *U.S. Catholic* magazine in Chicago, whose appreciation of my stories and silly drawings, and pinning of them on her cubicle wall until the whole place was papered with Edward and Mr Pawlowsky, was an engine of all this; to my friend the masterful Boston businessman Christopher Conkey, for assistance in financial arcana; to the glorious two-volume set *Lincoln: Speeches and Writings 1832–1858* (volume one) and *1859–1865* (volume two), in which I swim all the time, always to my benefit; to the works of Harry Mark Petrakis and Saul Bellow and Robert Casey and Mike Royko, which told me piercing true stories about the city of Chicago; to Carl Sandburg, whose biography of Lincoln remains the best by an American (I think), and to the wonderful Welsh brilliance Jan Morris, whose

Lincoln: A Foreigner's Quest is the best by an un-American (I know); to John Feister, editor of *St. Anthony Messenger* magazine, published by the Franciscan Friars of Ohio, who printed a version of the Muirin chapter of this book as the story "Born of the Sea"; to Leslee Goodman, editor of *Moon* magazine, who published a version of the Het chapter in her absorbing periodical; to my friend Karen Randolph, who found me an apartment in Chicago many years ago, and to my friend Christopher Doherty, who lived there with me for one hilarious summer of basketball and baked potatoes; and to my friend Eric Freeze, now a professor at Wabash College, in Indiana, who, while teaching at Eureka College, in Illinois, brought me to that loamy campus, where I sat, deeply moved, in the chapel where Abraham Lincoln had walked and spoken in 1856, and I felt some electric awe and pride and sadness and thrill for which even now I struggle to find words. I kid you not when I say you could almost *see* Lincoln walking through the crowd, a head taller than everyone else, his face filled with gaunt pride and sadness and humor and pain.

He spoke there in the fall, when he was weary of politicking, and according to legend he spoke his mind without notes or text, so there is no written record, but I like to think that he spoke ringingly of grace and justice and courage and humility, and that when he was finished there was a long silence, as listeners mulled his clear unadorned words and the passionate honesty and humility of the man who had spoken them, and then there was a roar of applause through which Abraham Lincoln walked like Moses walking through the walls of the sea.

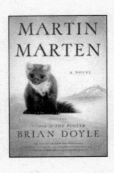
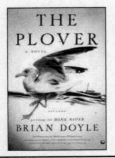